AuthorHouse™
1663 Liberty Drive, Suite 200
Bloomington, IN 47403
www.authorhouse.com
Phone: 1-800-839-8640

First published by AuthorHouse 2/8/2010

ISBN: 978-1-4343-2927-1 (sc)

Printed in the United States of America
Bloomington, Indiana

This book is printed on acid-free paper.

What ever happened to

Rebecca Evans

The life of …

(A Dominatrix)
Improved and Revised Edition

A Possible Memoir

by

Rebecca Evans

authorHOUSE®

A Fictional Representation
based on real life incidents.

INTRODUCTION

AND PREFACE....

Some people are good at keeping "little secrets"...obviously, I'm not. In writing this manuscript, I've made my life an open issue under the assumed name of Rebecca Evans.

This is a book about my own personal journey. I now have a new outlook which conveys a controversial feeling. I learned, or somewhat mastered an understanding of the subtleties of dominance and submission in everyday life, such as husbands and wives, or bosses and subordinates... While entering the world of Domination, I have examined diminutive aspects of religion, psychology and even world politics. I have even looked at the way religious beliefs control mankind's thought processes. Our theological assumptions are what the human spirit runs on...... ticks on.......our own conjuring perceptions of them. Or, of what man indulges you of them...as I will divulge the reality verses the mythical aspects of what I do for a living. While musing, things aren't always as they seem, and I may not be, who you think I am. But I am here, in your oh...so, here and now.

Regarding my past, my life changed in a year. I now do things, I thought I'd never do before, partially because of my own religious background and up-bringing. It wasn't until the age of 30 that I was enlightened to the psychology of dominance and submission, while BEING THRUST INTO CHANGES...I was almost beat into smithereens by people who used me as an emotional punching bag or as a target for all their pent up anger when I wasn't in a position to do anything about it. I wasn't in control when I was young, I had no choice. My mother never stopped my stepfather's aggression towards me. I think my mother was awed by men, their power and control that is. But in my case, (later on in years) it was their abusive power that compelled me with that familiar reason for staying. When I matured, I still let men and women impose upon me not knowing any better, not being taught different reactions... Thinking that, that was the way love was supposed to be in some of the misallocated patterns we shared growing up, with the emotional intensities of high highs and low lows, that make nice boys seem boring. There's not enough excitement of fighting and loving that comes with gangsters or foul men, or just boys who never wanted to grow up at all. I never got the right information out of caring, responsible adults. My mother was way too dependent on men to know any better. You see, my mother took an easy way out, she let her man do all of her thinking for her. My mother hardly ever made one single decision on her own, except to....

"FOLLOW THE VOICES OF MEN"

And as I was taught this pattern of waiting on a man's every beck and call, what I really needed to be taught, was that I couldn't always follow the voices of men, at all, especially the types of men I was used to...But by watching my mother's behavioral pattern, I was taught to never say "no" to men, especially the head of the household who was paying the bills. I was beginning to repeat my mother's pattern, only worse. In thinking I always had to be nice to men, even when I was uncomfortable doing it.

Back at a very young age I could feel their rude comments and even though I didn't know what to do with their disclosures of insult, I went on, enduring this behavior towards me, due to a lack of understanding.

Some people tend to misdirect hurt into anger that abuses others around them, sometimes irrevocably, and with this fury possibly being directed at you, you need to have the psychological tools for identifying causes that can lead to harm. To not self destruct through life with the consequences of your relationships with others.

THE GENERATIONS ARE CHANGING. We are no longer consumed with the old fashioned images of women as helpless creatures compared to the harshness and strength of men. We are not living in the 1950's anymore where husbands take care of women... Some of the movies of that era look so old fashioned in the uneven power exchange between couples, by way of social conditioning and political correctness of the times which sets into motion...

A red headed comedian who stands out in history, could never find her own solution to anything. Personally, I found the insanity of Lucy's incompetence hard to take, the man in her life always kept her down. She always needed him for everything, even while he humiliated her. Lucy's husband bailed her out in almost every single episode, narrowly.... The same thing happened with a Jeannie and a Witch during the 70's on American Network T.V. They could have ruled the world if it were not for their men......

I'm hoping with change, we'll learn how to get along in a different way.

We need a new dawn of thinking...

Just turn the pages of the book, and look at tomorrow's script.

TABLE OF CONTENTS

LOS ANGELES SALUTES ME!!!

"Mistress Madeleine," the "Dominatrix"

Live on the air! With Peter Tilden and Tracy Miller.....

One afternoon in the spring of 1993, a Radio DJ was on the air yelling, "If you're a Dominatrix, call me, right now!!" Peter Tilden hosted many line-ups along with his co-host Tracy Miller. Tilden was a man about 40 years old, a tall figure with a good reputation. He was never known as a shock jock either. One of my friends who knew me at the time and what my occupation had been for the last several seasons called me on the telephone and told me to call Peter Tilden on KABC's afternoon drive. She gave me the telephone number and I phoned in.

I live in the City of Angels, where west coast drivers are dialed into radio to sooth their rush hour commutes. People are inching along freeways, moving a car length every few seconds, needing relief. DJ's can't even have a second of dead air space or a single boring moment if they can help it. Listeners can change stations so programs must involve their audience with interesting chatter. On La Cienega Boulevard sit the studio facilities of KMPC, KABC and 710 TALK Radio......

When I first started talking with Peter on air, the station was owned by another parent company. Anyway, Peter was getting ready to be shifted to the morning line-up on one of the new parent companies other smaller stations to bring up the ratings for KMPC in the Los Angeles Market. My "phone in" that warm afternoon was funny and successful as I ordered Peter Tilden to "Hold on a moment!" and "Wait!" because I was then invited to do Peter's "Morning Kick Off Show" with Goody, Goody Two Shoes John Tesh from Entertainment Tonight fame, and me, a Dominatrix... (what a shift)...... along with Billy Crystal, the Mayor of Los Angeles and many others, who I never met.... (Most of the other entertainers phoned in their interviews and stand-up comedy live on air, via telephone).

Snappy repartee goes on all the time between two very poised, aware, and alert DJ's. Tracy sat adjacent to Peter only a few feet away from him behind Peter's long sleek desk. The studio is dark and sparkling clean with state of the art equipment. Peter was way too rugged to be good looking. Tracy is cute, round and cuddly, a woman around 35 years old, with dark curly hair and a microphone on. Tracy had a nice smile on her face when she wasn't frowning about Mistress Madeleine's profession.

PETER
"ABC and Disney just became the station's new
owners and we want to congratulate them.
It's 7:33 am and we have some very special guests
on today's show, the Mayor, John Tesh, Billy
Crystal and we got our very special guest, our

1

Dominatrix, Mistress Madeleine, who is going to
do a caning for us"

TRACY
"I'm not sure if I'm ready for this one, Peter."

PETER
"Always the voice of reason."

My alter ego, "Mistress Madeleine" sits in a room with Peter and Tracy. As a human being, I never gave myself, "Rebecca Evans" "permission" to purchase expensive clothing. But "Mistress Madeleine" is a woman dressed in expensive vintage black leather, which makes her look as if she walked out of the pages of French Vogue. The hat she's wearing makes her look mysterious, and not like a Dominatrix. Underneath the hat is a ponytail of long auburn hair extending to her waist. She is 33 years old with porcelain skin, five foot four, and a hundred and seven pounds. There is an entire studio full of talent, Peter Tilden, Tracy Miller, "Joe the 300 pound comedian", a man of infectious humor. Joe had big eyes and a boyish face, and was quite professional. Madeleine was wondering if Joe's "eyeing her" was an act or if he was really flirting. Two of the show's producers were also present. They both looked about 30 and preppy. John Tesh sat with a straight spine and Mistress Madeleine sat quietly. Our group is discussing the hot topic of the time. A young American man was sentenced to caning in Singapore for the crime of vandalism. Madeleine our Dominatrix seems even toned and confident when she communicates. LOUD MUSIC FADING UP as we hear the new voice of a booming announcer.

MALE ANNOUNCER
"710, the New Talk station."

PETER
"I find myself getting aroused by this"

JOHN TESH
"Wait a moment, I see a riding crop,
She's also got hand cuffs and chains."

ON AIR PRODUCER
"Chains!!!??!!!!!"

Trying to restore some semblance of order to the show…

TRACY
"Now that we have our resident expert among us, I can only say
that…"If a man came to me and told me that he wanted to get
caned, I would tell him that his stuff was on the front lawn."

300 POUND JOE
"Unless you're rich. Then you can do whatever you want."

PETER TILDEN
"Now Joe, the bitterness always comes out in you in
the worst moments."
(Beat....Peter turns to John Tesh)
"John, do you agree with Tracy? Should there be caning
in America?"

JOHN TESH
"For violent crimes, yes. But not by a Dominatrix."

TRACY
"Really, John?"

JOHN TESH
"It depends on the crime."

PETER TILDEN
"Spray painting a Mercedes?"

JOHN TESH
"No."

PETER
"Spray painting your 62 Mercedes?"

JOHN TESH
"Yes."

PETER TILDEN
"This is our first day of broadcasting from our new home.
We have some very special guests that are going to
call in. But right now we have our very special guest,
Mistress Madeleine who is going to do a demonstration
of caning for us."

JOHN TESH
"Peter and Tracy, all I want to say is good luck! Got to go......."

PETER
"John wants nothing to do with this.
Now wait a moment!"

TRACY
"So all of a sudden John turns into the
"Beaver" on us."

The men working in the control room are hysterically enjoying the breakfast charades and antics of a Los Angeles D.J. and his show of talent through daybreak chatter.

PETER TILDEN
"Welcome to the Morning Kick Off Show!"

Serious and impulsive giggling erupts everywhere right before commercial break.

"MISTRESS MADELEINE"
"I have a fifteen minute coupon for anyone who
wants it."

PRODUCER
"I'll have that!"

Laughter leads to a commercial break.

The show comes back on air after a "Sit & Sleep" Commercial. We catch the end of a conversation that begun during the break…

JOHN TESH
"That's a very expensive project to mount.
(Then looking at Mistress Madeleine)
Oh, I'm sorry, I didn't mean to use the word mount
in front of you."

Mistress Madeleine smiles and says,

MISTRESS MADELEINE
"Oh that's O.K."

PETER TILDEN
"It's very hard for me to focus with her here. John wants
nothing to do with this."

JOE MCDONALD
"I need beating!"

JOHN TESH
"You're my best friend Peter, got to go. It was nice meeting
you Mistress Madeleine."

MISTRESS MADELEINE
"It was nice meeting you."

Peter Tilden stops John Tesh from exiting the room…. John Tesh is polite and stays. Everyone has remained fully clothed.

PETER TILDEN
"I find myself getting aroused, Joe MacDonald is lying back
in his chair. Again it's hard for me to focus here because we
know what's coming up."

LOUD MUSIC, Station break. Talent is still in studio, talking. While I, Mistress Madeleine sit here.

Tracing my elements and wondering......

What ever happened to Rebecca Evans?

And how did she get here?

We are interrupted behind the scenes as Peter and Tracy start to ask Mistress Madeleine questions and we witness a very personal interview. Tracy, trying to reason with Mistress Madeleine but while looking in Peter's direction....

TRACY

"She's such a sweet girl, it's just a shame
she's in such a profession."

"OH.......ABOUT BEING A HOOKER....."

(And you have to be a damn good one not to have sex...)

AND I HAVEN'T HAD SEX FOR A COUPLE OF YEARS, it makes me feel so out of control, because I do not separate sex from love, I still see sex as something special. And you cannot control love and it's consequences, especially when a man is involved with a prostitute, it almost gives him license to go out and see other women, because you are seeing other men. (Using a key psychology note from my "field", YOU CANNOT BE A DOMINATRIX and be the least bit out of control, or even feel that way, your life could depend on it.) So while I've been in this business, I've personally chosen not to see anyone. Because when I do fall in love, if I ever get a chance to, again, I want a very exclusive relationship. I also want a man to be dominant with me, without abusing me in the process. I want someone I can look up to as a human being, a man who can rest easy with himself, who can lay it on the line with out using me as an emotional punching bag for all of his short-comings. And while being a "prostitute", I'm "used goods" which most men don't want. With concern for self, I regularly find that most men dating working girls usually use them for their cash, or think that they can take certain liberties, because there's a pattern... Since I'm a prostitute, most men think I'm easy to begin with.

This process is about therapy on a very personal level for me. While looking into dynamics, I am not recommending this as therapy for anyone else nor am I qualified.

Men and relationships are a lot of work, and in relationships you devote so much time to a man. IT'S BEEN SOCIALLY ACCEPTABLE FOR YEARS, with our cultural beliefs in religion that teach women to sacrifice, and sacrifice.........to find access into the Kingdom of Heaven...(that is, by the traditions of man, anyway...) And in this society, that has been ruled by male dominance for years, and years.....a society that has conditioned some people, like women, across the nation to settle for less wages than men..(in most cases...)

In having a health care system that pays for men's potency pills more easily than birth control. Women even pay more for dry cleaning bills.....Although traditionally, men have usually paid for dates.... After the sexual revolution, I know that women started paying for things. Although in my past, before my submergence into the world of D&S and the middle income bracket, I never could afford the emotional well being of knowing I could take care of paying for specialty things, like expensive dates with men or even expensive items for myself. Most people of middle income never worried about the things that impoverished people did. I took care of my own bills such as food and house payments.

And due to basic instincts, like procreation..... another key to psychology is this.......men like beauty, the way women like security, meaning money.......it has something to do with eggs in the basket, and taking care of the little ones. Males like to deposit eggs, so in primitive

7

nature, they look around, it's only natural for them to want "pretty babies". Thus, living in modern times, men may not want children at all but it's that primitive drive that urges sex on.

While some women stay home, keeping up their youth, their man goes out and earns the dough. In other households, both man and wife may work, especially if the woman is a mother, without a maid, or the lady could even have a career or a job. Most women want their man to say that they love them. They also want that man to take care of them, with security for their young ones, so face it. All I have to say to any woman who denies it, is, "Go marry a bum" and you know what, she won't do it in most cases. But most women will compete for the man making money, or a man with the potential to make money…. And the number one reason for divorce and separation between couples is the lack of capital. Hence the assumption men never pay for things is bull shit, a wife gets half in divorce.

WHEN I GOT INTO THIS BUSINESS, I THOUGHT I KNEW WHAT TO EXPECT OF the manner in which most people would treat me, due to the double standards of man… they would treat me like a prostitute. And I wasn't going to lie to myself the way some exotic dancers have, because we all sell a "packaged" form of sexuality that you wouldn't want to show to a 14 or 16 year old kid, legally.. And you may not want to shatter someone else's sheltered existence of living in denial. As long as you have this prehistoric double standard way of thinking, that women are sluts and men are studs…….. we'll probably have all types of problems with hypocrisy in denying primitive instinct. For many years I had conformed to the traditions of man and had gotten no where doing it. I was used and abused, because I didn't have the right information. And in all of this, I had the approval of men and women though, because I was a quote on quote, "good girl". I was a submissive for many years in the real world of men, and I had been mistreated, deleted into a society with no one else to fall back on to. The good girl traditions of man had cost me and I was sick of conforming to their ideas.

There are good men, however, and women who are lucky enough to find them, the ones who came through in the hard times. Men who really loved women, and not just sleeping with them. But, as women out number men 2 to 1, in most places, I don't live in a fantasy world anymore.

Emotions are not logical.
And even you have emotions, my friend, we humans run on them.
We tick on them.

Way back when……..the Greeks had Agape…..humans thought that love could only be shared among the male species…..and that there was no love of women…..men actually thought that we women didn't know how to feel, being second class to "humans", that we were only good for sex and reproduction. This was man's perception of the era…the out dated distance….

The judges in London who wore wigs... in a form of cross-dress...And then, who also passed laws on women, stating, that, the persuasion of a marriage or even marriage proposal by way of enhancement such as hair pieces and make-up carried great penalties for women.......

The times are changing. These physical bodies that we now live in, will vanish into thoughts someday, into dust. Is my work sacrilege? I do have questions that may never be answered here and I don't want to mislead anyone...

In the history of the Bible...the teller of all tales, it says that prostitution is wrong. I'm not saying what I do is right, I'm just saying that it is not O.K. for man to judge what I do.

There once was a woman in the bible called Mary Magdalene, who knew a forgiver of all sins. This man, Jesus...forgave her and told her to go back into the world and to sin, NO MORE.. And all those "Great Men" who worked along with Jesus, couldn't stand up by his side....in the end...because they were too weak. And Jesus forgave them. But hearing that Mary Magdalene stood close by, on a hillside, along with his mother. (In actuality, there were not a lot of people close by when the nailing on the cross took place, as the apostles, and everyone else were way too afraid.....to even be near him...)

God help me because becoming an abandoned woman is what I did, in participating in a perverted and therapeutic commodity that some people find sexually stimulating. (While I, myself, have never been "turned on" by any of these "acts". I do it for the money.) You must understand that I am not telling anyone to go out there and become a Dominatrix, because there are risks, legal, moral, and the threat of diseases from body contact. Because there is physical touching, it could be on the legs or arms, but there is contact and a scratch is all it takes. Knowing that some people might not accept food from me now because I was now considered "dirty". Thus, pondering a Thanksgiving Day in which I was still an "innocent" handing out turkey to friends as everybody came by so "freely".

But learning this psychology has helped me.

However, I still realize that God is the ultimate dominator.

And we all must bow down to him someday.

In my studies, and in my experience of learning that the whole world operates on this psychology, I have noticed that my examinations have filtered into my everyday life, someway. In my business, men tell me what they want up front, and I supply it to them, at a cost, no lies, no deception. And there is another thing you should know about me, in my business, I ONLY PICK ON PEOPLE WHO ARE BIGGER THAN ME, who want it. And that makes me powerful to them, there is mutual reservation here. People trust me with their secrets,
As we must be discreet to protect their privacy....
Because they have other lives they lead....
FOREIGN TO THESE.......
HERE.
(IN MY DUNGEON.)

I do turn down business because there are some things I will not do. I SELL SPANKINGS, not sex. (And in the state of California at this time, you can beat people for money, you just cannot have sex with people for money. You cannot kiss people for money and you cannot touch people's private parts for money…and hand jobs are considered prostitution in the eyes of the law…although I know some men think that it isn't sex at all.)

So...

In the last few years, I've learned to nip men's and women's actions in the bud real quick, calmly, and effectively. I'm in this for the long run. If you can learn to master your own type of extrinsic endurance to some degree, it helps things. To realize that good psychology books have also been great tools in discovering the truths to hidden, inner emotional patterns.

I hope, I learn things…..

Because something has to make you really angry...

To make you have to change. (As pain and anger are related emotions...)

You have to be hurt so much.....

You're in the narrow, with no place else to run.

I had to do something, someone in my family had to get strong. In 1990 I changed completely. As we go through the passages of my life, or the eras of my existence that culminated in this…

As I lay in this bed that I made...

By following the voices of men....

In those sheets...

I lay...

As.....

Something propelled me into this.

_____

(Author's note...)

"The only thing we can expect in life, is change."

"WHAT EVER HAPPENED TO REBECCA EVANS?"

(The life of a Dominatrix…..)

Choices, choices, choices…we all make decisions in life, we must live with and sometimes forever, as the resolutions can build walls. Funny… as I write these words, I wonder whatever happened to Rebecca Evans….

(.....my life, my soul?)

In ironic gesture, things can change in life at any given moment, and with all the hidden layers of molecules, we dig into our pasts.....So how will I write this great cause in telling you my story? Hopefully, with truth, I'll be able to have the courage to reach right in and tell you of my plight, because I do feel depression at times, a melancholy I have tried to numb for years, and so much so, that I have forgotten some things…

but hopefully..

…In time…

….I will remember…

With an epiphany….

Because we all must die someday…

I hope my words don't hurt anybody, my mom, my innocence, lost forever, in a year... or in days......of so called events. I wished my parents would have protected me more, and given me a better head start in life, like a completed high school education and a safe roof over my head to get one. Some instruction would have been nice.

In my world, in the beginning, I learned that everyone loves with prejudice, whether it be someone they need to "save", or someone they need to be dependent upon. They tend to believe anything and everything that comes out of their "chosen one's" mouths, even the misconceptions, no matter what the consequences to anyone else are. Poverty scared the hell out of me, and unfortunately, for the poor, sex is the only form of recreation affordable, whence, this started my broken family.

I was born into this world an ugly duckling, who's sister was much prettier than she was. And Rebecca who was always being teased by the other children and called names never cried about any of this. Rebecca always knew there were things much deeper….She was never aware of the power that beauty could bring, it never dawned on her back then. The only thing that did cause ill effect was a school teacher Rebecca had in the first grade. She used to shake Rebecca hard in front of all the other children and tell her how stupid she was. The teacher really scared Rebecca and because of this fact, Rebecca missed classes a lot. Rebecca flunked the first grade but made straight A's after she got another teacher.

How could such a sweet little innocent girl grow up to be a woman like me, a Dominatrix? I never even knew that this type of life existed before and that there would be men that would give me a hundred and fifty dollars an hour just to worship my feet.....

And the parallel to that .....being....

I never really knew my real father, either, because he ran off and left my mother and my little sister and me all alone and got rich in the state of Arkansas and never paid a dime of child support. My mother and him had me in puerilely, she was 18, and he was 21. Joe Evans was a bad choice for my mother as the history of caustic complacency in my immediate family is quite wide. My mother, my sister and I had it miserable in times of poverty, growing up. All I ever remember wanting was warm feet in the wintertime, but we were too poor to afford good shoes. . I wish my father would have purchased me a pair of rain boots. Because when it rained, my mother never got up out of bed to drive us to school in the mornings. We had no umbrella and all my clothing got drenched and I looked like a drowned rat. My feet would get soaked and wet in cheap tennis shoes walking a half a mile on dirt roads in storms to the bus stop leading out the highway to Wickenburg… It was where our education was supposed to be starting. I knew I had to go to school, it was my responsibility, part of my work ethic.

My mom never did a thing about my father's dismissal of us. When the state of Arizona ordered him to pay child support, all the adults in the family seemed to have forgotten about this. Joe Evans had a second family with another woman that he spoiled with love. Joe Evans even bought a race car for my cousin to win trophies with. It was for Joe Evans's Family Trucking Business. Joe Evans also owed a lot of money to the I.R.S. I remember once, Joe Evans's mother said, that her son told her that "Rebecca and Edith never sent Christmas cards". Edith and my mother and I didn't have enough money to eat sometimes and Joe Evans expected Saint Nick?

When I think of my childhood and the painful memories of what it was to be powerfully over-ridden and needy, thus reduced, attributing this to cause and effect, being that of my father's ill will and what my mother let him get away with.

Let me go back through my family history. While exposing my ancestors when the America's were first born, a Cherokee Indian united with a European Settler. While fusing together, part of my lineage conjured up to two different cultures. Moreover, the Hebrew word Ezra translates to help and somewhere down the line, an Irishman and an English person merged with augmented elements of very difficult matches, especially for those times. These people were trying to kill each another...

Well, anyway, my grandmother, Anna, was a very beautiful woman, who being brought up in the middle of 9 children lived as a teenager during the depression. She hardly knew her father, as my grandmother's mother was greater than my grandmother's father, at taking care of little ones. My grandmother's mother worked two jobs and screamed a lot.

Anna never thought that she was loved, until she and her sister ran away from home during the 30's while still being quite beautiful to become showgirls. They were making 32 dollars a week and sending money home. On my grandmother's arrival back, her mother embraced her with love for the very first time that she could ever remember..... (But still, they thought that show business was bad, and they were ashamed of their dance girl days because of the perceptions of man.) So while conforming to the perceptions of men, I asked my grandmother, "How could show business be bad, if it helped your family out?" "And how could your family say that you were bad, if you helped them out, too?" And they took that help from you..... As your family did, what they had to do, to feed the little ones...(While musing that women are sluts and men are studs in old fashioned rules....)

My grandmother married a little boy who played in the band. And again, my grandmother was better than my grandfather at taking care of little ones..... My grandfather ran out on my grandmother and mother and convinced another woman to leave her small children, for him.

And in taking on puzzles to be fixed... I hear that my mother used to watch as my Grandmother got beat up by my mom's step dad in the process of defending my mother from being raped.

My mother lost all of her teeth at age22, after having two babies and not enough calcium. My mother was also raped at knife point with my sister and I in the room. My sister and I were too young to remember anything. The intruder came in through an open window..........months after my father had left... My mother never received therapy for her emotional wounds and while raising us infants, we didn't always have enough food to eat. My grandmother told me that my mom never even held my little sister as a baby, because she thought that it was spoiling us. As Edith was named after my father's mother it must have reminded her of failure...of taken away opportunities...And while the rest of the family wanted my mother to put us up for adoption, she thought that she could handle us, although she could barely handle herself yet and was probably too ashamed to admit it. So my mother in her confused state thought that only men needed love, and children didn't.

I think that not having the right tools in life affected her... the shortcomings.....the regrets of never facing one's fears My mother grew up with the fantasy of being the most beautiful woman on earth. Along with this illusion came another-that only good girls who pleased and obeyed their men were pampered. Edith and I always seemed to be in the way of my mother's fantasies.. There were times that we didn't even have clothes to wear as Edith and I ran around in only our underwear until the age of four. I remember by age 5 it began to embarrass me, the vulnerability of being exposed while all the other children wore clothes.

IN SCHOOL....

In the first grade I started getting into fights. It started when I witnessed someone being picked on, I always had a sense of justice.. I went up to the ruffian and stood up to her, told her not to pick on the other kid. The ruffian backed down. The jerk was always a foot taller than myself when I got in the middle of things, in those few inches of space that I would grab as my own, secluded in time, face to face. I couldn't understand other adolescents simply standing there and tolerating this. Maybe it was a show for some of them. It seemed to me that if others stood up to a scalawag as a group, the ASSEMBLAGE would always be stronger. But living in this neighborhood, I had to learn how to fist fight when I was young. And I hated it. But these girls would just jump me and I had to defend myself. I also won most of my unintended struggles with these young women. But the fourth or fifth time I stood up to a bully was for my little sister's sake, and you know what? I got my ass kicked for it by a bigger bully. And even though, I always defended my little sibling with others, Edith and I fought each other like cats and dogs. Edith was never taught properly how to love, but I cherished her more than anything.

When Edith and I were ages 9 and 10, she used to kick our little black dog Puddles around. I would tell her not to kick the dog because it hurt me to watch her do this. She would respond, "I can do whatever I want, it's my dog". To this day, I am pierced when observing other's get razed and eradicated emotionally. I would also learn to stand up for everybody else before I would ever stand up for myself.

I think there was reverse discrimination going on in this one particular neighborhood in the Valley of the Sun. In Phoenix, Arizona, when I was 10, the school I was going to was full of early gang members, I'm positive. A popular Mexican boy once set a white boy on fire in shop class. The white boy was standing in motor fluid while the Spanish guy took a match, lit it and threw it at the other kids feet. The child suffered third degree burns over 30 percent of his body and had to be rushed to the emergency from school after the teacher extinguished the fire. No one was talking, everyone was afraid of the popular kid and retaliation. There was an older girl, named Tammy, who knew the whole story. I hated this learning institution. All the other children used to call me names that I ignored….

As….

There were a lot of pressures out there…..

as I spent a lot of time, alone….

drawing…….

the big escape…..

In my spare time alone, I used to draw horses all summer and was quite good at it. I was an artist. In the first grade at my new school, I had a drawing of Santa put in the Children's Museum. My mother looked so proud of me as my new teacher came to pick my little sister and I up one day so that we could go to the exhibition and see it. Perhaps my mom was satisfied with her child being a third generation virtuoso coming from a "family of artists".

Mom was so beautiful back then, she received whistles while walking down the street with us children to go grocery shopping. . When mom received the rebound of Dan's marriage, she thought that it didn't matter that he had left a wife and six kids for her. Dan was now the head of our household. They wore their tight "boots and bells" together, with him being a cowboy and a Deputy Sheriff. And in a selfish way, because I didn't know any better back then, I used to wish my mom and Dan would have stayed together, it would have been so much better for my mom and my little sister. Dan liked Edith. Dan used to tease us sometimes and (at the time) it was quite funny, but he thought of us children as being his property, telling us, "If we were good, that he would let us live another year." Mother acquired the opinion, "I brought you into this world and I can take you out of it". The only book of scripture that I ever saw in our living room (and for a short time only) was on white lace on a coffee table and it was "The Book of Latter Day Saints". My caregivers with their righteous indignation thought of us children as property. Dan was now in charge of things for a while as we lived in Phoenix, Arizona in rough neighborhoods. I could never consider what a nuclear family was and I only felt part of one for a very brief moment. We had been really poor until Dan moved in, and in the beginning, things seemed to get better.

Mom waited on Dan hand and foot and let him do whatever he wanted to. They drove around in his four-wheel drive pick up truck listening to "Stand by your Man". Dan was a Sharp Shooter who liked to hunt and kill deer while drinking hard liquor. His trophies would soon line the walls of our living room. We'd have venison soaked in beer for dinner. As mom suffered through migraines and I think Daddy Dan, as we used to call him, brought her great comfort and was probably the love of my mom's life. I guess that for some women, men made life easier, while children made life harder..

My parents were always making jokes and talking dirty in front of us kids. My mother's wedding dress that she wore with Dan was up to "The crack of her panties..." as she put it. So these were adults who openly expressed sexual passes, yet they didn't have the insight to realize that it wouldn't rub off on their children in the future was ridiculous.

My little sister was a brat at times, so I wouldn't deal with her. She was so much a part of "them", mom and Dan. Remembering the child hood rivalries that can lead to animosities when a parent would constantly treat one child differently from the other. I remember the time I got busted by Dan for smoking cigarettes and was grounded to my room for a week. As Edith had been smoking with me, I didn't want to spend the entire time with her so I kept my mouth shut and she got off, "Scott free".

One day, in the seventh grade, a popular boy took notice of me. I know it was around the time I started putting make-up on. This guy was a person that all the girls wanted, as I became their wary competition. I watched the other adolescence point fingers at me and gossip loudly about a herd of girls that were out to get me right after the school bell rang for the end of last period, and with god knows what, knives? They were all making a game out of the "hunt" and they were all bigger than I was. I ran out of school, never going to my locker and never going back for the last two months of that school year.

During the following two months of unfinished school, right before summer and all through, we had some neighbors who molested me and took full advantage of a little girl as they manipulated my life.....slowly...Ward and Patty were in their 20's at the time. They had two small boys, ages 4 and 5. They also had Patty's mother living with them in a wheelchair. Patty was a strawberry blond who looked tired all the time. Ward was average looking, clean cut but casual. He had black hair and was slightly overweight. I never saw Ward and Patty fight with one another. They lived in the same apartment complex that my family lived in right before the June simmer that could fry an egg on the hot cement....

In the beginning, Patty ended up in the hospital for female problems. With my parent's permission, I'd go over to help my neighbors by cleaning house for them. Ward and Patty would reward me by taking me to swap meets on weekends, which were giant outdoor, merchandise sales with lots of good, cheap stuff. But soon Ward and Patty recompensed me further by showing me porno movies starring John Holmes as "our little secret". And with my un-experienced presumption, I thought that it was normal for adults to keep secrets in my adolescent way of wanting to grow up. I believed I was being ushered into the world of adulthood by this young caring couple. I thought that shrouding truths were part of the maturing process. My mother and the man who would soon be my stepfather were just a few doors down. They never knew the lies, but they kept their own secrets. I knew things now that they did not know.

And since this was the only attention I was receiving, I was much too inexperienced to know delusion. This life just seemed like normal living, there was no other reflection to compare upon. In my wariness I didn't consider that it was sick and demented that I should find comfort in the arms of a molester. Ward and Patty should have gone to prison for this adventure.

It was 1974 and I was now 11 years old, "Midnight at the Oasis" played on the radio. I quit drawing pictures because I had suddenly become interested in other things.

SEE....

Even back then, men had almost always cost me. Especially, while being taught to communicate sexually.

Surreptitiously…

The John Holmes movies were not the end of the seduction. I couldn't comprehend that Ward was a voyeur as well as a pedophile. He attended his artificial friendship watching as Patty willingly assisted in the exploitation by sucking me, fondling my pre-pubescent pussy in a mirrored room. Ward would be titillated by the perverse charade of pedophilia masquerading as lesbian sex. I was only 11 and a half. And no one knew.

The only thing I knew about the adults around me was that they liked to keep secrets... and oh, how I wanted to be an adult, so that no one could control me. I didn't know that in the future there would be a lot of difficulties.

Soon, Ward's ego started playing head trips on me, telling me things were right, when I knew they were definitely wrong. And during all this strange code of silence, as my hormones were raging in puberty.... I had no one of proper supervision to tell me... things...like the facts of life.. except for these strange adults living on the block. And I, being the babe in the woods, was too dumb to know it. I'm sure my attitude began to change while hanging out with an older generation who turned me on, and then turned me out.....most selfishly....

Dan, my stepdad noticed the change, and in his misunderstanding began his two year interrogation period with me. It seemed like a lifetime that covered my entire childhood. He tried to straighten me out as he drank a case of beer every weekend. Dan was a mean drunk and would start downing alcohol in the morning, slowly, getting more and more inebriated. Right before his composure divided, with him flying off the wall, screaming two inches away from my face at the top of his lungs.. He was a volcano erupting at home in private and my mother never stopped him. She let a drunk raging maniac rage on me for hours and hours on end. I'm not sure what Dan would have done if he had known what had been happening to me at the hands of the other adults in the building and right under his nose and suspicion.

(Thank God I was never raped by Dan, the way some girls have been by stepdads.)

That wasn't in Dan.

Dan was now a truck driver because he had just changed careers, but he still remembered police procedures and would use them on me every single time he was home and getting inebriated. Perhaps it was Dan's shortcomings with his first family. He was now trying to raise 8 children and maybe it was too much for him. Maybe his job positioning transferred his misdirected anger towards me. In a contagious frenzy, in his meager way of trying to communicate to me in his police interrogations that should have been used on grown violent perpetrators and not little ones. Listening to his screaming in the face of an 11 year old baby, kicking the chair I was sitting in, verbally attacking. I was sitting through interludes that made me feel so betrayed by my mother for never helping me while I sat, frozen in fear, not saying a thing.

There came a time when I was sitting on the toilet bleeding during one of my very first cycles as a young woman. I started a couple of months earlier when my mother tried to explain things to me in a nice and caring way. Edith, my sister, was taking a bath as we were in the bathroom together. Dan slammed open the bathroom door violently! The door almost hit me! If I were not sitting on the toilet I would have been hurt. Dan was screaming at the top of his lungs, loudly exclaiming some obscenities about some things Ward Roscoe was telling him about me. He was treating me to another of his tirades as I sat there, once again mortified and frozen in the face of his rage. My mother simply sat in the next room and listened to her chosen man yelling venomously at her eleven year old daughter, kicking at her footing, her chair or wherever she was sitting. This time it was the toilet, trying ineffectively to pry things out. His recourse had the reverse effect entirely, I cocooned instead.

Meanwhile, I was growing up far too quickly with things I didn't dare reveal. I didn't even know that I actually had anything to tell. I didn't know what was going on or what these adults were doing to me was wrong. . I was too immature to even know what the word, "sex", was. And if I told I might lose the adult status I believed those hidden mysteries conferred upon me. Maybe it was just an emotional reserve that I kept some slyly promised secrets clandestine in a little noggin headed for difficulty and hazards... While thinking it dysfunctional, finding comfort while being encroached upon by a deviated man. Ward's idiosyncrasy induced confusion upon one so young. The infection caught a child like myself off guard, while Ward's indulgence took charge.

I was making straight A's until all the difficulties. Pondering back, I realize I must apologize for one thing because I didn't realize what the penalties for smoking pot were...(Especially, while living in the state of Arizona.) Astounding to me, the Federal Law says that an adult can have sex with a minor and only spend three years in prison, (excluding rape). But, while alcohol and tobacco are the number one and number two killers in the nation and they are both perfectly legal.... Certain states in the country will throw you away for just a seed of marijuana. You can spend years in prison for just a joint. Dan never got angry on that point, he could have informed me about the dangers drugs would do to my body, which he never did.

Just like most children, I did not know what I needed. I was in danger from my manipulative neighbors and vexed by the ineffectual efforts of my stepfather to control me. In a contagious frenzy, in his meager way of trying to connect to me… Once, Dan bought a Steppenwolf record with "Born to be Wild" on it, at one of his friend's suggestion. I didn't want to be wild. I wanted to be loved and I couldn't identify with the philosophy of the record. I had just been weaned off the soft music of "The Partridge Family" and Donny Osmond but something changed.

I was living in a building full of child molesters and my

parents didn't know it.

but I did....

little Rebecca Evans,

the kid

knew more than the adults did.

I was drinking alcohol, smoking dope and taking pills and wearing real tight hip hugger-bell bottom pants and crop tops and listening to the music of "Iron Man' by Black Sabbath. These strange adults became my mentors while mom and Deputy Dan played dress-up.

IN THAT VERY SAME APARTMENT COMPLEX THERE WERE 20 SOMETHING YEAR OLD BACHELORS LIVING NEXT DOOR TO US. I had a crush on one. Mark and Randy were brothers and a teen age runaway was living with them by the name of KAREN. She was sleeping with her boyfriend, child molester, Mark...(that is).....she was only 15... (and now she was mad at him...) In lost innocence, she and I planned the move of running away, or "skipping out" for a while. The first thing she taught me was how to get out of state, "safe". The morning we left, I told my parents that I was going to school. I couldn't find
any relief or comfort at home...
Home sweet home....
that is....

After running through an alley and ditching many things Karen said I would never need..... we hitched.....and got lucky and got some real cool rides during the 70's.. Then landed in Joplin, Missouri, her home town, at her mother's house who was happy to see her. The trip to her place took two days, it was snowing and her home was warm and full of love. But Karen betrayed me and gave my phone number to her mom who felt obligated to call someone.

ON THE WAY HOME WHILE RIDING ON A GREYHOUND BUS, I met a black man who was also a pervert. He started to molest me on the bus while it was night time and dim. I didn't know if any of the other passengers could see us or if they were all sleeping on the ride. I got off the bus with him in Dallas, Texas. While going to his apartment, thinking I could stay and not go home, not see my step dad. When I arrived there, it was a real nice place, a high rise with lots of large windows and a panoramic view. I remember him telling me that he was a doctor. (And I never really had any prejudice inside of me, especially when I visited the south). I remembered this picture hanging on the wall over his very clean fireplace, titled "Overpopulation".

Then, in an instant his face went into a maddening frenzy and his eyes got real big and seething as he lunged into me. He went berserk and tore off my pants through this felony. Then, I remembered a radio show back in the 70's that I had listened to regarding a topic on rape and how it said that the attacker fed off of the fight and actually got turned on by overpowering a grappling victim. The show said to almost freeze and remain calm and that this would turn off your assailant because he was after the challenge of the contender in his lurid sense. (Although the information has now changed and the psychological information given by professionals is to fight off your assailant. To never be taken to a second location, although, I was already there.)

So this man ripped off my pants and underware to find a bloody Kotex underneath..... As I remained still and frigid and calm and scared to death....... his face changed, and dropped from his raging fury to an expression of, "Oh my God!" as the blood had frightened him or turned him off, somehow.... or had brought realization into focus...Yes, I thought that it had brought realization into focus........For I remember him changing so quickly...
In half a second...
Handing me back my pants and underwear and telling me to wash up in his shower. And I being the little girl did what I was told by an elder who drove me back to the bus stop. (I had no place else to go and didn't know how to run on my own yet.)

ON TO PHOENIX I SPUN, frightened of what my step dad would do to me. (Many years later, I found out that my mom had to borrow bus fare from my grandmother because my "father" didn't want to pay for my return.)

WHEN THE BUS ARRIVED IN PHOENIX , I WAS HALF A DAY LATE... Mom was crying as she and Dan greeted me and it was some greeting alright. Dan kept yelling for hours and hours that lasted from afternoon into evening, it felt like midnight. He was angry and was screaming that I had gotten off the bus with a "Nigger". This impaired me in mental panic, as he frightened me more that day than what he ever had. I should have known soft things, but instead, all I remember is drunken ranting and raving, a shouting maniac in my face.

I couldn't wait for the right opportunity to get out of there again.

Dan would never know about my initiation into adulthood, and Little Rebecca Evans knew how to keep confidences as Mistress Madeleine does now.

Later on, one of the bachelors, Randy, the one I had a big crush on, tried to break my cherry. He never could, it hurt too much. I did it one day in the shower with my finger.

BACK HOME AGAIN, WARD AND PATTY TOLD MY PARENTS THAT I HAD SMASHED A ROTTEN EGG ON THEIR FRONT DOOR STEP. Dan had thrown me across the dinner table in front of our guests, which just happened to be his six children, my step brothers and step sisters... Being humiliated, I felt I had to cover for a friend...

the little kid, who actually did it....
Some little boy was mad at Ward and Patty too.....
I wonder why I never asked him, why he was mad at them?

Obviously, at the time I didn't know how to communicate. I remember this little kid and I as we were sitting and talking one day. He only lived in the neighborhood for a short while. Musing, he made a statement to me, "Ward told me what he did to you." I just sat there with a blank look on my face. The adults in my life never made sense to begin with. This little boy had some spirit in his retaliation that I should have had. I started to pull away from these two awful human beings but it seemed that Ward would keep acting out his aggressions as I took the punishment.

I kept my mouth shut.

I wish my parents of supervision would have understood and known, that I just wanted peace and the right kind of love communicated to me. But instead, one day it got so detrimental with Dan's vexations, I interrupted him right in the middle of a four hour drama and screamed just to find some remedy....shrieking I had been raped in the alley... This was complete fabrication. I actually made up a rapist to keep Ward and Patty's lies, secret. I never told on Randy the next door neighbor. Afterwards, I remember Dan trying to communicate to me in a real caring manner and asking questions... He also called the police and I filed a false report, which they all found out about…with in hours...And then, he tore into me again, for filing a false report... which he had to clean up... And believe me, even I knew, back then, that that was one, big , pretty outrageous thing I did, to get Dan off my back that day....
It delayed process in the moment I snapped...

Someone had to get Dan off of me because after a couple of years of being tormented and threatened in my own home...badgered and petrified beyond belief...I was beginning to loose my stepping, as it decayed in vivid reality around me, I reinvigorated my exhausted body with a few new found friends ....and escaped in libations afforded by rich kids who turned me on to them....as we had just changed school districts...so that I could go to school. I was beginning to acquire a reputation as a very loose girl....for hanging out with the wrong crowd at the old one..

We moved from the apartment in Phoenix, purchased a trailer and drifted to the middle of somewhere in between Wickenburg and Phoenix... My parents worked hard in their transfer of residence, it was supposed to be an improvement.. Glen Bishop owned the property that we were living on out in the footholds of rattle snakes and scorpions.. It was an opportunity for a fresh start. It was supposed to be a community where people knew each other and looked out for each other's children. And while being taught only selfish needs by adults....in the outskirts….

ONE SUMMER EVENING all of the community that dwelt in this far off location that was new to me, inviting and inspiring to me, had a big get together and barbecue. I was running with the other children, playing and making friends. I wasn't doing anything wrong. Dan called me over to him in the middle of everyone as he told me to sit down on his lap. (Now on a scale of a 1 to a 10, this was probably a 2 compared to most of his 15's on the yelling scale)...But any way, the quandary was about the hippie beads I had on around my neck. I made that wood beaded necklace and was quite proud of it. My mom took me to the store for the pieces but she never said a thing to defend me while Dan and I sat there. He just kept telling me I looked like a hippie and told me to leave and go without my dinner in front of everyone because those people out there were country folk, and I wasn't part of them.

(And I wasn't part of anyone.....

And I didn't belong anywhere....)

I thought we were going to have a good time, just like a family should have. But Dan shifted my perspective into annihilated discomposure and embarrassment and humiliation again. And In my hell, being recognized by everyone in prying intimacy, I could never look at that community the same way, again. I walked out of there... straight out in the middle of the desert all by myself about a half a mile or so, to where I couldn't see anyone, anymore, (I didn't want to see anyone, anymore...) Then, by carving an "R" on my arm with a stick.... I kept scraping the scratchy wooden twig across my arm digging out flesh...and I'm sure it hurt, but I couldn't feel it as I cried that late afternoon while the sun died. Perhaps the "R" was a symbol, so that I wouldn't forget who I was, who my spirit was, or let someone, take her away from me.

...... I was going to get out of there again...

A few nights later, after the barbeque-turned-episode, I went outside after dinner to get some air. There were cows and horses and sheep in pens just fifty yards outside our trailer. Glen and one of his friends were standing out there, under the stars, looking at the animals as Glen called me over to say, that he, Glen, told my step dad that what he did to me that afternoon was wrong...And Glen told him, to "never do it again".

And all I could think of, was ...

WOW!

(wow)

Someone noticed!

I would know Glen in the years to come, but never get that close to him. Dan through an epiphany stopped the torment......

SCHOOLS SHIFTED AGAIN, AND ONCE MORE, I was in a new one in the 8th grade in the violent town of Whittman. The annoyance of destitute and needy children recommended I run. The incessant momentum of me being a hunted primate by gangs of girls trying to beat me up, wasn't an inclination I was fond of. Sometimes, I had to show courage and brawl, which I hated doing.....all..(because it was about my hair...and why the other girls didn't like it...to begin with...)

We were three miles away from Whittman. There were about a thousand people living out on the desert around us, and only a thousand living in Whittman. Except for the new comers in the last couple of years, most of the people who lived out there were related . There were heavy abuse issues and half the town had jail records. There were three bars and no churches and all the community was alcoholic and white and beyond poverty stricken. Men and women mated right out of high school. The paved roads running through the town were all dusty and the houses looked like at one time they could have been nice at the turn of the century. But everything in this whole town was now decrepit.

I never stole anything from my parents. I never picked up a gun.

The night I spent crawling out my window, there was no moon light, or street lamps....as pitch black was all, that was, in front of me. I was getting scratched by bushes and tumble weeds I couldn't even see. I could hear dogs barking in the distance. I walked through the desert all alone, with a small back pack on which I carried a mile out of my way to meet a girl who had chickened out and never showed.... And then, back to the highway through the desert... again... To the road that was alive and led out of there. THEN HITCHED A RIDE AT TWO A.M. I headed back to Phoenix and it wasn't intentional, but I ended up back with my abusers. After staying at Ward and Patty's for a day or two, they called my parents asking to adopt me....so I ran away from them...and I have to remember where I went....but I know where I ended up.....

It was at a half way house where I met this girl who never made it back. Because what we were doing was dangerous. It was the 70's and there was Son of Sam, and little girls getting their arms chopped off, dismembered and tossed like garbage across American Highways. HER NAME WAS MARY ANDERSON, she was blond and very beautiful at 14 years of age. When we first met, we didn't like each other, but we ended up being the best of friends after 180 days together....

We broke out of that half way house through an up stairs window that was half way nailed shut....and then through the second story jumped onto a roof top, then down to a stairwell and on to the ground.... then running through the alley for blocks and blocks until we reached a gas station bathroom knowing we had to leave town. Mary dyed her blond hair, black, and my locks went from dark blond, to chestnut.

It was now the dead of winter as we stood on the side of northern bound interstates and highways, not knowing any better, cold in summer shirts and levi jackets. We ended up at a lot of truck stops, getting rides from truckers. One driver's name was Sam. When Mary and I first got into his truck, Sam who was Southern and about 40 gave me three pills to take. He told me that it was safe. I took the downers and fell asleep immediately. I awoke to find this man trying to take my pants off. I don't remember what happened next. When I finally sprang back into action, Mary was in the front seat of a big rig and I was in the back cabin of it adjusting myself. Mary informed me that I had been sleeping for a day and a half.

Sam gave us a place to stay for 3 months in Tennessee with his brother and their three grown sons who were all in their teens as we all lived in lascivious means. Mary and I both chose one of the sons as our boyfriends, and had sex out of wedlock. We listened to "Fire on the Mountain" by the Marshall Tucker Band and experimented with alcohol, pills and marijuana and were relatively happy until things became demented and the boys wanted orgies. We decided to run again. Musing, I now know, they separated us. Mary never made it back.. They kicked us out, and with myself going back to their house to retrieve some clothes. She waited at a truck stop. When she called, the boys told her I wasn't there. When I returned to the truck stop four hours later, she was gone.

Like many children who grew up in difficult circumstances, I matured in unhealthy ways. As the oldest daughter of a mother who in many ways was much too much a child herself.... my adolescent yearning had me as "Free as a Bird" on "The Stairway to Heaven" while doing drugs and a lot more stuff. (And assuming I didn't get the proper nutrition in that time of adventure and development, I was a little skinny and flat chested due to a lack of nutrients leaving me anemic and starved for oxygen.)

I decided it was time to go home. When I returned, my mother had aged ten years with gray hair covering all her auburn...She looked old and tired. It must have been a strain on her marriage too.

Four months after I returned, Mary's mother would call to ask where her daughter had gone. I didn't know what to tell her. I didn't even know the address where we were staying. We were always in a house behind closed doors and anesthetized by the effects of beer and pills. As I thought of Cat Steven's "Oh Baby, Baby it's a Wild World".....and Diana Ross's "Do you know where your going to?".

I hope Mary made it back. I never saw her again.

There I was back on the Arizona plains, living in the middle of Wickenburg and Phoenix, in the nucleus of Peoria and Whitman. During the few years we had of happiness hidden away in school out there near Glen and Faith... I was attending a great Instructional Institution where finally, finally, all the little children weren't trying to kill each other. The school was in a small city called Wickenburg. The community had more money than the other places we lived in........ Back during the days of high school I didn't realize how selfish I was growing up. And to some degree, I guess it was normal for a teenage girl of 14, who mostly valued herself on good looks, and second on grades. And in those phobias it felt like image was everything. As I lay shallow in insecurities, I waited for change, and started dressing like a lady. But I was still boy crazy. And I never slept with anyone, during this period. It had been a few years since the "Ward and Patty" incident...

It was my freshman year in high school.

The first time I saw him, it was half way down a football field. He was six foot, and a hundred and 90 pounds. He was amazing, as he waved at me.... I waved back... and I saw a spirit in him...and knew it.... and he knew it, too. I was in love with a 17 year old named Jay who astounded me. He took my breath away every time I was around him. He was the most beautiful man I had ever seen, and he was the love of my life, at that time. He was perfect to me. My obsession for him was like a psychosis that left me plundering, hanging on the edge..... Where dreams like that, can only take you so far.... I would have followed that man anywhere ....I would have done anything.....for him. I was under his spell....

23

I learned that as a child Jay had overcame some obstacles, things that I admired in him. He was born a skinny kid with arthritis, who got picked on by all the thugs, but swore to himself that he would bulk up and start bench pressing, and did. So by the time he was 17,

he was lifting 350 pounds....

I saw a lot in him.

I saw my future.

I wanted someone to protect me.....

I dated Jay on and off for a year and a half. From intuition, based on old fashioned logic which were some of the things I learned in the south....I felt the only way to get Jay was to never sleep with him. He would value conquering a hard catch. And in keeping up a good reputation, (I liked moving around a lot because you could always reinvent yourself.) And reinvent myself, I did, using ingenuity and imagination in hard work to keep up with the rich kids in social presentation.

Jay was still trying to get over some other girl named Debbie who left him a year prior to my getting there in Wickenburg. Jay never knew of my torrid past, the molestation and sex. It was hard for me, but I didn't sleep with him....

in forgetting everything else, when I was with him.

He was my life....

And I almost forgot....

everything else...

when I was with him.

In being quite naive as I was...not knowing that Jay was the type of guy who would always leave the doors open for things....like other women... He didn't have much reverence for anything other than himself.

So while living on the outskirts of Peoria, that barren waste had nothing in it for me except for him. After making Jay wait for almost two years before giving into myself to him....As our long soft hair fell around the folds of our bodies on that warm Arizona evening in the back of his station wagon under the stars...As I waited for him to say that "He loved me" first and then I said, "I love you." He entered me.... We planned it so perfectly on that Saturday night date, through the custom of mating rituals and all my moves in between that, I felt like I had landed the big man on campus. Being quite an accomplishment for me as I had day dreamed about having him for almost two years now. I wanted a man like him to love me, I needed security. I knew he was a big man before everyone else noticed this. But still being unaware of the ways of the world with men...and true love...I thought that, that was it, my work was finished. So I started putting every ounce of energy into him, and quit worrying about myself, and in return, I would receive particles of nothing...

The desert had all it's beauty but did have it's draw backs... like getting up at 5:30 am just to catch the school bus by 7:00... In the winter, I had to get up at 5:00 just to turn on the heater which we kept off all night to save energy. My mom never got up with me or my little sister. My mother didn't even have a job. The only time that she ever did get up out of bed was when there was a man in the house....like two days out of ten. It was for this very same reason.... that I had such a hard time trying to get my little sister up for school in the morning.

I felt a lot of pressure in trying to budge her...nudge her...into attending school. But she would yell at me... kick at me...And tell me that I wasn't her mother and that I couldn't tell her what to do. I felt hopeless and would give up after about 1/2 an hour. I never even questioned my mother's ability to act like a responsible human being. My mother didn't care if my sister got an education...or not, but my mother was into promoting boyfriends.

My mother would wake up at about 10:00 am every morning, have coffee smoke cigarettes, watch TV and play with her herd of animals. We had turtles, rabbits, cats and dogs. I remember coming home from school, and doing housework every evening all by myself for at least a couple of hours.....just so that I wouldn't be ashamed when anyone came over...And those summers when the tumble weeds became so bad that our acre was infested with them...... I went out all by myself on the weekends just to have a somewhat pretty yard.....of dirt and smoldering sand storms... and level earth. I worked my ass off in the sun for hours as no one helped me discipline the jungle, and with sun burns I received blisters..

AND TO ELUDE.....I had to go to school to see Jay. It was odd for a child, but Mondays were my favorites because it meant a whole week with him. He lived in Wickenburg and did a lot of drugs and stuff that I felt were fun and exciting. (It is a known factor, that when children are abused....especially little girls, they grow up abusing themselves, with drug addiction and other things like men and relationships.)

One day, in an inebriated stupor, Dan came home yelling at my mom (and questioning her ability as a housewife...) That "There wasn't enough food in the kitchen!!!" And my mom was not cooking for us children....She only cooked when the man in the house was home...(As Dan had abstained from yelling at anyone for two years now). I guess the pressure just got to him in his misapplication of mental confusion. My mother had never been the target of his anger before. But he let loose on her, as she now got a taste of my so-called medicine. He yelled at her for about 15 minutes and then she went running into her bedroom, wailing, crying louder than anything. (He "hit" me a lot harder than he ever hit her with his frustration.... Mom didn't like getting yelled at, but she let a drunk raging maniac rage on me, as she lolly-gagged in the other room, quite happy and content.)

For the first time in my life... I stood up to Dan, for my mom, and

(amazingly, while frightened..) I said to him,

"Don't you hurt my mom." .....(real sternly)

And then all he said was something under his breath ....

And while he sat there looking down on the floor with a cigarette burning in his hand, he didn't come after me, and that was that. I was amazed that Dan didn't come after me...

SOMETIMES... I WOULD GO AND STAY IN ARKANSAS WITH MY AUNT ROMANIA (ON MY FATHER'S SIDE). She was nice to me but seemed to forget that my father was responsible for things. She worked in the beauty business. Romania taught me about hair and make-up and never pushed or instilled a "race" in me... Back then, I was so into beauty, I primped two hours a day and always based my self esteem on looks like most little girls of my generation did, and still do. I stayed with Romania for almost a year, going to high school with 15 students in the room. In the region, I was voted "Most Beautiful" and "Most Popular" in the annual year book. I also got involved in Beauty Pageantry but hated the way it made me feel, an insecurity of needing approval by everyone based on how I presented myself. I always cared too much, and this parading never prepared me for the anxiety that was associated with the beauteous spectrum. (The superficial hues that could make lechers out of men, so young....)

10 months passed, Romania and her husband were getting a divorce and I had to leave. Her husband's sister, Elizabeth, needed "help" with her and Joe's three kids, ages one, four and seven. And when I arrived at the Kents, I never worked so hard in my life, it was a three ring circus, as I toiled night and day....7 days a week with no privacy for a girl of 14. I had to share my bedroom with their eldest boy for one year. (And with all this pressure I escaped into a shell like world...and became shy with other children.) The pressure to be perfect, to say the right words....

Elizabeth and Joe Kent struggled to make ends meat, both worked. It seemed that Rebecca always had to earn her keep, (which didn't make sense, because her father was practically rich) And Rebecca worked way too hard for a 14 year old kid. Joe and Elizabeth had a lot of struggles. One of the only things that made Rebecca embarrassed was the fact that they were very poor. Everyone else had a pretty yard but driving up to the front of the Kent's house looked like a very clean junk-yard in their fixer-up.

The days began at 6:30 am and ended at 10:00 pm. We were living in a college town called Conway where I had never been to a place with educators stuck on a higher scale of disciplined learning in my life. I made "A's and B's". The studious endeavors only took me 15 hours a week, of extra homework. And on top of that, Elizabeth was insistent upon keeping the house in tip-top shape, every second, every day. We cleaned from top to bottom on Saturdays. Including, one day Elizabeth was sick, and her husband woke me up early to do the entire job all by myself... I also had to baby sit and was only allowed to go out one night on the weekends. During all this, I did my hair and make-up like most little girls did. Living in "image land", we all had to look pretty, and pretty I did. Elizabeth and Joe also had their flaws, we all smoked pot together......I know Elizabeth had a nervous breakdown and had spent time in mental institutions...... She told me, keeping busy, was the only thing that saved her life and brought her out of her depression. She also taught me to never call boys and that if they were interested, they would go out of their way for you, and Elizabeth was right.

One day, I saw Joe jump on his eldest son and start scolding him for not that big of a reason. Elizabeth stopped Joe in his tracks, right then and there. She told Joe to "Stop jumping on that boy for no reason." And all I thought of was, "Wow", so that's how it's done. And I wished my very own mother would have done the very same thing for me when I was at home..

There was also a Christmas in which Joe only bought me one record while purchasing lots of other stuff for all the other kids. My real father's other children stole everything that my mother mailed to me. My father let them and I wouldn't know it for many years to come.

I realized I had to see my mother again. I was so afraid that she would die on me and I had forgotten like some resilient kid some of the things that had happened.. I wanted to tell my mother that I loved her ......

Jay never knew what was going on at my house and why I had to leave for months at a time. My freshman year was at Wickenburg, and then on to Arkansas, and then back to Wickenburg... I wondered back and forth between my mom and dad's families for awhile, where ever I felt that I could find peace, because even at a young tender age my spirit knew truth, as most children do. But it made me a basket case sometimes in not having the right communication skills to even comprehend what was happening at the time.

In the summer of my 16th birthday I spent my high school vacation in Las Vegas with my Grandmother. I got a job at a dress shop on Freemont Street named "Anita's" and in the process got a lot of new clothes, things I now wished I would have shared with my sister, Edith. I now look back and realize that I should have taught her some more things.... But being way too much into myself at the time to even notice that my little sister needed me or someone. I didn't know how to give any guidance, I never had any myself.... ..... I remember trying to help her out off and on but it was never ever enough. I just didn't know what I was doing in my youth with limited power. And sometimes she was just so mean to me. Edith would tattle tale on me for everything, so I would just ignore her for years...and sometimes years....In that essence, I felt guilty for not teaching her how to take better care of herself.

And....

All Jay knew was that I was leaving him, but this was the only way that I could work. I couldn't get a job living out in the middle of the desert with no car, now, could I?

After spending a summer in Vegas I went back to school in Arizona for my junior year with an A/B Average.... I was working my tail off, while mom was depressed and wasn't communicating to anyone.

I think Jay expected me to stay all summer on the desert and do nothing but wait on him.... hand and foot. He seemed discontented, like he felt I had abandoned him. In guessing he was just way to young and self-indulgent to even consider or understand what was happening to me with those limited opportunities I had out there, being so poor, with no car. His parent's were going to send him to college and they had already given their son a vehicle to drive..

When Dan left mom, things got really bad. Mom met a man named Rick. It's ironic at the events in our lives...but the man who saved me from Dan is the same man who sent Rick over to meet my mother. Rick and my mother were both going through ugly divorces. My mom was having a quiet nervous breakdown after losing her true love, Dan. He just ran off on her, took the pick up truck as the only means of transportation and as no one had the tools back then to even comprehend what may happen. Rick knocked on our front door and was the most loathsome and hideous sight, standing at six foot three inches and almost 300 pounds. He had moles all over his face, but I was quite polite and never teased him.

I remembered my mother asking me if he could move in.

With a strange sick gulp in my throat...

MY INNER VOICE KEPT SCREAMING

NO!!!!!!!!!!!!!

And as my mom sat kneeling beside me on the dirt in the desert...

I said "Yes" to her.

RICK MOVED IN.....prior to this he lived in a school bus that was now parked on our acre lot. His ride was full of pornographic materials. With the adults being in their 30's, they were old enough to know better about a lot of things. But my sister and I were told by the grown ups to go out and play in the bus. Now we were taught to never go into other people's personal possessions, wallets, purses, etc., But here Edith and I were in Rick's bus and we walked right out, the magazines made us feel uncomfortable, there had to be hundreds of them.

As mom had no job, I'm sure she started to fall behind on the trailer payments...She waited on her new meal ticket, HER GOD... hand and foot. They were now team players, and Rick was playing against us. He wanted to get rid of us kids and he pushed us out.

Two or three months into my junior year...Jay began to act strange. I could sense that something was up. With Jay being the "Big Man on Campus", who was also the Student Body President who made straight A's. Jay was also one of the biggest drug dealers in Wickenburg. No one would tell me anything, and I just didn't get it....but...

One day, one of the girls, a cheerleader came up to me and actually asked me if Jay and I were dating other people. (And I remembered him mentioning something to the effect, but still didn't quite get it.)
But said, "I guess so", as I looked at her astonished and still didn't quite believe it.
Perhaps, as rumors fly around schools... I had known this girl for years, but we were never very close......
But I said, "Why, did he ask you out?"
And she said, "No, he didn't ask me out."
So I took it for face value, not wanting to look any deeper. I was never even taught how to ask questions or how to deal in reality. Reality seemed to be blocked out so much in my existence.... I just couldn't bear it.... Maybe the women before me had so very little self confidence that they couldn't see the truth, that they only saw the pretty in things... So in my fun, my laughter.....my act....of putting on faces......and putting up a front to the quandary and dilemma....

I was going out with Jay and splitting up all at the same time.....

When Rick moved in.

as....

all those mixed emotions........

mixed...

out there on the Arizona plains.

I went to bed early on a Saturday night...Jay and I did not have a date that evening. He was acting mysterious that week and I felt that something was up. I lay there in the god most awful thoughts and nightmares......of losing someone you love.....I was tore up in knots for hours, sick, lying in it, the impairment, that obsessive sickness I carried inside of me for him. I knew something was wrong, it drifted in the air that night and right through the window and landed on the wrong side of the tracks. I felt it pulling my insides out in streams. I lay there in despondency, in grief. I knew I was losing him. Jay was the one I knew, would be hard to hold onto. And oh, how it concerned me, this fierce fight for a man that I might have to provide, as the sheets were tangled up around me, I hated it.

I went to school the following Monday. Jay told me he had a date with that girl, Janet. Janet was beautiful in appearance but Jay must have been a leg man because Janet and I both didn't have any breasts. But Janet was really manipulating the situation and milking it for all it was worth because now in reflection and analyzing the events with the knowledge I have now..... I almost forgot that Janet was a California girl...and as that old Eagles song goes, "City girls just seem to grow up early" ..fast...and sometimes vicious at getting what they want. Janet seemed well trained. She had an older brother with a corvette who would drive her to school in the mornings.. Jay liked flashy women.....I was tired and exhausted and couldn't put my act on anymore.

My "boyfriend" was now driving Janet to campus, because they both lived close together, she was a Wickenburg girl...

I lived out just past Whittman.....the berth between Phoenix and Wickenburg, 30 miles in between.......in "No Where" Land, the land full of drunkards, except for a few good people. (With my intuition that Jay was my only opportunity for happiness out there in that non-outlet, because I always wondered, what could compare to Jay?)

While trying to say "Hi" to Janet, she would walk by me and say nothing. I now know, she was maneuvering. Jay also told me that she, Janet, told him that someone had written something on the bathroom wall about her, and she thought that it was me. AND IT WASN'T. (Jay thought so little of me, to even ask me this, to begin with.)

But I now know who did it because I heard that a lot of people were mad at Jay for the way he treated me... I wasn't even aware that anyone had even noticed things. Even when two really nice people, one a guy, and one a girl told me things, and the games...as Janet was blaming me as she was taking away my boyfriend. Jay was buying into it because he wanted to...... I was so naive at the time looking directly into it. IT HIT ME LIKE A BRICK WALL and I never wanted to feel that pain again, of losing him to her or anyone else like that.

And all at the same time.....
Rick used to make fun of me as I would walk in from school carrying all my school books.. He would look right at me, look at my chest, then up and down my body lustfully, then come right back to my face again, and look me right in the eyes and say, "I can see your boobies".

29

On other occasions Rick would comment, "Na, na, na, na, Rebecca is breaking up with her boyfriend." When I remembered how devastating the truancy of both his and my mom's divorces had been on them, the mental lacerations

I recognized were so lucid in front of me..

Garbed reality...

I thought I was having a nervous breakdown, crying for hours at a time. I had no other outlets as I muse upon the eruption I had on the school yard in Wickenburg at the age of 17.....

The school bell rang for lunch to end and 6th period classes to begin. I lagged around to watch Jay who would sometimes skip studies. Ditching class was something Jay did a lot of. He would leave campus to hang out and do drugs. I saw Janet motion to Jay on the campus lawn, they lingered after the bell rang. She wanted to talk. Their body language screamed across the school yard. Jay was a very passionate young man about everything he did, his body building, grades, women... I could see the signs as they were speaking to each other.... And there was a scene, I exploded.... I started yelling and crying. Jay wouldn't deal with me....or love me. I was making a total fool of myself. As I incoherently descended into ruins ...and while obscuring facts around me impudently brushed against me with an uneasy strain that left me breathless...and dead.

In those difficult passages....

Working in fragmented memory...

In months that scurried through wisdom.....and irreparable causes...I escaped and hung out with Keith, who I never loved like Jay ...but I loved him as a friend. I never even kissed Keith. His family owned most of Whittman. Keith would drive out and picked me up everyday after school to go out and forget about things. He really was a gentlemen and was concerned because he saw the way my step dad treated me......

Keith was over one day, and he asked me as we were walking out my front door,

"Does your mom know what that guy says to you?"

And I said, "No." (Dumbly)

I never even talked to my mother about this. I didn't even know what Keith meant, in all my innocence, all I knew was that I felt nerves on end.

Out on that Arizona desert with Rick in the house, the gate was wide open for rumors to fly by, lecherous tendencies left out to pasture at night, by a step dad who hated me. While my mom was half way watching with her lullaby baby attitude in the same room......... She could never see it when someone was hurting her children, but she sure cared about her men.

I once saw my step dad talking to David, the neighbor boy at the fence line. David was in the same grade as I was and we both rode the school bus together. Rick was always so nice to other children, so admirable and understanding. Rick only did mean things to Edith and I behind closed doors..... (In psychology there is a dynamic noted that one out of every three step parents are very likely to abuse stepchildren. It goes back to primitive nature and the male species only wanting his offspring to survive. You see, when a male lion takes over a new herd, they sometimes kill off the young offspring left by other "kings".) I remember

Rick having two boys, Don and Brian. One little boy was so nice, and the other little boy was the worst little kid that I had ever seen in my entire life. He would go into hysterical fits, screaming in our living room when he was visiting. But Rick was so wonderful in his son's periods of excess..... I remembered watching Rick with his boys, and how compassionate he was to their behavior. He never made rude comments to them and I wondered why he couldn't be the same way with me and my little sister.

MY LOOKS WERE FADING …..FAR FROM HERE.......as Edith and I were fighting, I couldn't stand to be around her or anyone in my family as my hair began to fall out through all the misery.

With Rick's innuendos flying at me, it's scary thinking about the way he looked, and the way he looked at me, too. My mother never did anything about the creep as his infectious gasping injustice colonized my fleeting surroundings.....I really hated Rick, he was debased. I was going through hell but kept my mouth shut, and couldn't relax with him in the house as I was working my way into frenzied exhaustion going 14 straight hours a day just to keep up.

ONE EVENING JAY AND I WENT OUT ON A DATE. We did some LSD and had a designated driver named Dave drive us 60 miles while we were intoxicated. Going home to my family's trailer made me feel so beneath him. We were so much poorer than him and his friends were, although we both made good grades. That night, Jay walked me inside the front door of our small trailer that felt like a tin can ready to unravel in the wind.....as the hallucinogens danced that night the walls closed in around me with all of my good standing...... with my mom and her new man the pervert sleeping in her bedroom. Rick had come a long way up from the bus stop. As no one offered any control to stop this horrible occasion... I guess that Jay and I were very loud as everyone listened to us struggling a little as I gave into his whims on the couch in the trailer in the dark as we went tripping in it... as I stumbled and fell far.....off center...again..... I didn't want to... I said "no!" Everybody heard us... In Jay's selfish need for lust and taking things and in bringing them down to their knees.... He date raped me. I was pulled apart beyond belief but felt, this was the man I loved and that he was going to take me out of there anyway.... I was acting just like my mother, always giving in to assholes.

WHAT WAS WRONG?

The next morning, while looking at my reflection in the bathroom mirror, Edith told me that I had made a total fool of myself the night before, and that everyone was listening. I knew that very moment I couldn't stay in that house much longer. To face love looking away at me, like that...As my whole family were morons and Jay was a jerk but I still wouldn't know it for years, as he controlled my thoughts, my tears. I hated Jay for getting away with his selfish situation. Jay called me the very next day on the telephone with some concern in his voice like he was manipulating me, and through the receiver, said, "That the episode that we were involved in the night before made him love me even more". "Because it proved that I really loved him." A situation that humiliated me, he cherished. Jay loved me most, when I was just like my mother. My step dad the pervert listened too, which leaves a bad taste in my mouth. I didn't convey to Jay that my step dad was looking at my tits....it seemed like no one close had any respect for me and my wishes.. It should have been the responsibility of the strong, to protect the weak. I needed compassion, but everything hit like an explosion in that little head of mine where convulsions swept away my sanity ....And I didn't know how to fill the cup that had tipped over except for leaving him and the mess at home. I was going out with Jay and breaking up all at the same time....

when of course...

Rick moved into range.

And while those around me participated in lost etiquette...

I guess at this point Rick knew that my mother would let her men do anything they wanted to, to her children.

A week later, I lay in bed trying to go to sleep because I had to get up for school the next morning. I heard a big jeep pull up in our dirt driveway... it was a bunch of boys who I didn't know. I never met them. They were all in their early 20's. Rick was in bed and someone persuaded my mother to wake us, me and my little sister....As she entered the bedroom quietly whispering, "There are some boys here who want to see you." We both got up out of bed and walked out to the drive way. As we stood out on the dirt lawn, (me with rollers in my hair and night cream on my face... I endured, even with my vanity, which was now beginning to fade in my emotional state of not moving, not knowing. The young men turned on their head-lights so that they could see my messiness and my little sister.) Something told me just to stay still, even with all the embarrassment on my face. As the boys put on a high-powered beam light, one said, "This one looks better than that one"...meaning me, they didn't like the way I looked that night, but they liked my little sister. Suspecting and for almost certainly knowing that my stepfather knew these kids as they were all friends with David. David was a neighbor who lived next door to us and who was my age. David went to school with me and my sister. Rick was very nice to David..

As all those mixed emotions....

Mixed....

out there on the Arizona plains.....

Revenge never felt good to me... I never knew how to fight for anything back then, so I ran away to Arkansas with the Evans. My father may have been a dead beat dad, but his family was nice...Everyone in the Evans household held up the mustard in those respects....My Uncle T.J. Evans was the greatest, running the back roads of Perry and Morrilton Arkansas where no man had gone before.....

On the last trip to Arkansas, something strange happened. There was this weird family that Rick and mom met, which consisted of a father, a mother and a 19 year old son. They were driving from Arizona to Arkansas... Rick had given my sister and I both a 50 dollar bill for the advent. Rick was enthusiastically ready to get rid of us kids. Rick told us that he had already given this family gas money and that we could keep the money for when we arrived in Arkansas, also known as Evans territory..

In the car, on intermissions and at gas stations and in the middle of driving and at every rest stop we stopped at... This family kept asking my sister and I for more and more money and we kept giving it to them. All the time, I was thinking that this family was taking full advantage of us.

Or someone was......

When we arrived in the state, this family drove my little sister and I over to the Evan's house....for just a little more money. By the time we arrived, we were broke. (Thinking back, my real dad never even gave a dime of child support to us kids during this period....the money that a court of law said he owed to us children. I wish that things would have been different...)

My Aunt Romania was having hard times so we couldn't stay with her..... My sister and I went to stay with Romania's ex-husbands family,

The Kents.

Edith was living with Catherine. Catherine was not a nice person. She was a "me first" kind of gal, and then her kids and then her mansion. At age 30, she had married a gay man and in the process of deceived reality; Catherine was caught up in the fact that her femininity might have been cheated or misplaced, even questioned. She was being thrown into a divorce Catherine didn't want to begin with. Her significant other was a very successful businessman in the town of Morrilton, Arkansas. They had four small children together and had grown up together. Catherine felt short changed in her endeavors to manipulate one so handsome and one who lived a charade ....her effort toward the end had given up with him. As Elizabeth and Catherine were both living in dissolved marriages, both sisters were in their later 20's and both had seven children between them. They both got married right out of high school and Elizabeth, because she had to.....Moreover, Catherine now wanted my sister Edith to help out in her spotless house, which was practically a mansion. Edith ended up working 12 hours a day baby-sitting spoiled rotten brats. Catherine convinced Elizabeth that they had never had any time alone......and they now wanted it.

I remember an episode in which Catherine was driving her big fancy car with her kids jumping over the seats, throwing things as she would turn around, while driving, to smack them with a swing of the fist.......

I also remember being in Arkansas when Fleetwood Mac's Tusk was released.... Miss Nick's was singing Sara on the radio and Jay called and asked me to marry him, (I think he was drunk.) Jay told me he hadn't seen me in school for a couple of weeks....(it took him two whole weeks before he even checked in on me.) I just left at the last minute, not telling anyone about my escape, I desperately needed a last minute ditch adventure....an escape out of there...and I was bad at good-byes...

Since my sister and I were staying with the Kents, they took full advantage (thanks to Catherine's ideas) and used us to baby sit almost full time while we still cleaned house.

(Now, how much would you have paid for this? Seven days a week, with one night off.) And of course, we did the heavy clean up jobs in the house on Saturdays with no bedrooms to ourselves because we had to share our bedrooms with their kids. All we got was room and board. The only good thing I got out of that experience in life, was learning how to work, and I have to tell you something, after living with Elizabeth and Joe Kent and watching their three ring circus, ages 1 through 7, working seven days a week with someone else's responsibilities....and watching my sister with Catherine...I'm surprised that Edith never learned anything...because...

I never wanted to have kids after that.

Maybe for only 10 minutes.

But I never did.

WHILE CHANGING SCHOOLS A LOT, I MAINTAINED STRAIGHT A's, it was amazing. I remember my junior year, having two very heavy math courses, and changing schools every three months with new books and new theories. I would always ask a few questions in class, not being afraid of looking stupid because I needed to understand things. Elizabeth once told me, that she, at one time, had been institutionalized for depression, (which was something I seemed to suffer from). She informed me that the best way to conquer it was to keep busy, and she was right.. I also knew there was some drug dependency and blue moods that ran in my family...

It was in our DNA pattern ...

Elizabeth also made a phone call and made my father Joe Evans buy me a nice coat for Christmas one year. She seemed to really make an effort.

When Catherine was through with Edith......my sister and I were both staying with Elizabeth Kent in Texas in a double wide on a quarter acre lot and something happened that shouldn't have. Elizabeth and Catherine decided to go out and party and chase men one night and left Edith and I all alone with Elizabeth's kids in a brand new neighborhood.... These guys showed up that Catherine and Elizabeth knew. Catherine and Elizabeth were friends with two of the four young men because they were sons of the guys that Elizabeth and Catherine were now out with.... all of us teenagers began drinking beer and smoking pot, and as these guys had these very large bags of pills, I didn't know what they were. I didn't take any. The only problem was...

My little sister did...

and while doing so...

Edith overdosed.......

I'll never forget. I was sitting in the living room and all of Elizabeth's kids were sleeping. I walked into the bedroom to find my little sister Edith with her pants half off and one of the boys with her, they were not moving. I ordered everyone out and off they went! Then for the next two hours I threw my sister in the shower with her clothes on, and then peeled them off of her, wet....then walked over to a neighbor's house at 10:00 PM and called the police because Edith had then went into convulsions on the floor and I felt that she had a hard time breathing.

My sister died three times that night. Her heart stopped.

While she lay there in the hospital, I also found out that two out of the four boys that were over that night were also in the hospital getting their stomachs pumped. Everyone made it out o.k. and we didn't get into any trouble because one of the boys was a Senator's son. The young men were all barely under age and had just committed grand theft from a drug store. My sister had taken 5 heart relaxant pills that a grown 200 pound man would have only taken 1 of, per-day. Edith was 98 pounds.

We had to move again, all of us, to save our reputations.

(And my little sister made it out of there O.K., Thank God....)

I went back to live with Elizabeth and her kids, back to Arkansas. Edith went back to live with Catherine and her four brats, and god what a work-load we had. Catherine had Elizabeth convinced that they were doing us the favor by letting us stay with them. My sister Edith and I were work slave labor .....

Catherine was an alcoholic. When I was staying with Elizabeth and her three children in their home…. One gloomy afternoon Catherine drove over to visit with my sister in tow. My poor little sister was walking around in the back yard in a numb haze. I just watched her... wondering.... I asked Catherine what had happened to Edith and Catherine just snapped at me "To leave her alone." "That Edith needed time to think about things." Edith got raped the night before in Catherine's house by one of Catherine's so called boyfriends. Catherine was even in the house when it happened, asleep in her bedroom and probably passed out from liquor....When my sister told Catherine what had happened, Catherine denied it. I now know that my sister has blocked out some events due to some adult neglect.... Catherine must have had some real fucking problems but she wasn't woman enough to admit it.

When we had finally had enough of this, there was an explosion! Catherine and Elizabeth had us cornered in the kitchen with all the kids. They were going to go out for the evening and they wanted Edith and I to stay and watch the children.

Something happened...

I said "No" to Catherine,

and she slapped me!

(I also hear that she bragged about it.....after being an accomplice in raping my 15 year old sister with her selfish neglect...)

and I didn't hit back.

We didn't baby sit that night, either....

instead.....

The ladies left...as we packed with a lot of little kids watching us. (Who I assumed called the adults)...so...the next thing I remember.... Edith and I were on the road hitch hiking...I remember looking at her, and forestalling, and wondering about her safety and for the very first time that I had ever been on the road, I worried for someone. I said a silent prayer, standing on the side of that highway. I said, "Oh dear God, please God, if anything is going to happen to my little sister on this trip, let a police car pull up... RIGHT NOW...!" And one just did, right that very instant, (in guessing it was a miracle,) the police probably saved my little sister, with her dumb luck there.

Outside the rains of Arkansas... I ran back to Jay on blind faith and on to Phoenix.... I was age 17, trying to go back to high school to a A-B average and I just couldn't make it. I had a job at a hamburger stand for a few days before realizing that it was an utter mess. Living in a one-bed room apartment with newlyweds John and Suzanne, it must have been real hard on them. John was David's brother from our old neighborhood in Whitman. John and Suzanne were just a few years older than we "kids" were.

It was summer as Billy Joel's "The Stranger" played on stereo.... During which time, I met a real nice guy, a cute New Yorker type who had a great family that lived in our apartment complex. And choosing Jay over this guy was really crazy... the patterns had already been set up for me in those misogynistic tendencies I would learn to expect from life, in my old-fashioned martyr complex. We women, who accepted this portrayal of human experience as social validity and conditioning through some religious experiences that might have been misinterpreted for centuries to begin with. Is that what Macho means, holding women down in need, making them weaker than men and why was it supposed to be like that?

In an up-scale apartment complex a few blocks away from me, Jay was now living with a couple of guys with the help of his parent's money. He was also attending the Arizona State University. Jay came over to my apartment complex, we were both sitting out in his truck in the parking lot one afternoon into evening. He and I were discussing why Jay wasn't going to see me for my birthday, reason being, he had to go to a bachelor party instead. And this really nice New York guy waited on me in his apartment. He must have been looking down through his window, on everything, on Jay and me "discussing things". Jay was also feeling up my breast and kissing me through my passive struggling. I would never know boundaries, I would never be taught. After that, things were never the same with that real sweet guy from New York and me again....(And what a loss it was for me because he was the first guy that I had been attracted to in years...other than Jay...But who could blame this East Coast Man for turning his back on me? With Jay and all his selfishness and me just giving into him.)

(Thinking back, I really liked that East Coast man.)

Months later, Jay somehow convinced me to move in to a house in Phoenix with Jay and Dave and Dave, for about six months. I had dated all three in high school, with no lascivious behavior attached, only kissing the other "boys"....But Jay was the only one who ever had me, sexually, so we could all live together at this point in time. (With the egos and feelings and everything else associated with men's territorial gains...when they are really in "love" with a woman.)

I had given up high school again, so that I could get a job, to be with him, while he and his parents paid for his college and he was working construction. I also knew that I wanted to be the "perfect woman"...and make Jay love me and regret what he had done in the past. Jay shone like a beam of light...in the time we shared, I must have been putting a lot of good energy into him, his dreams, his visions, I know my energy helped give him self confidence.... and in return, he gave me, none.

One day Jay came home and asked me to move out. A couple of days later, before I left...

Something.....

Something...told me to look in his top drawer. (My mother taught me to never do this, but I did it anyway...) And there was a picture of Janet. He still had a picture of her right in front of me, on top of everything. That was the only time I snooped in a boyfriend's drawer and I regretted it and haven't done it since, but I needed to know the truth. I just didn't find out the full truth, yet, no one told me about....
The Miss Arizona part.

Jay informed me years later, he had in fact, dated her but she didn't think that Jay was good enough for her. She had married a spiritual man, instead. That was the reason Dave Bean was mad at Jay. In finding out truths from our pasts.... Jay and I lived in an illusion because I was a lie to him. He never knew the full truth of the little girl with a past of molestation and angry step dads. Jay and I both wanted something perfect and when either of us became defective, the other ran away. So maybe we should forget we ever met, forget the smell, the taste, and touch that led us this way. The doors to those pressures just exploded and closed.

But I remember stepping onto a plane. And for many years, hardly ever looking back on that time I spent with Jay, and Dave and Dave.

When I went back to Vegas .....

I knew for sure....

       I never wanted to risk so much on love again.

       or depend on a man for anything......

Some men couldn't see past themselves. I would have been swallowed up inside Jay's shadow. I would have died inside, and he knew it, so he had to let me go.....

I was living and working in Vegas at the casinos as a waitress and the labor was very hard. My first two days on the job, I had blisters on my feet and had to borrow a pair of my grandmother's white slippers which from a distance looked like shoes and I'm sure my manager at work noticed but didn't say anything. They were not regulatory footwear but along with being pretty came certain privileges from upper management... and jealousies from other employees.

Edith phoned me to say that she was living with a high-school friend's family by the name of Joe, a boy I knew from high school who I thought was a very nice guy and with his parents lived in Whitman. (Now you have to realize that Edith and everyone in our household was on me day and night when I was living with her. It was every man for himself. I had so many memories of fights and anxieties which I didn't want to face anymore.) My hair was just now beginning to grow back. Edith called me once to see if she could stay with me, but I put it on the shelf and will have to carry that guilt inside of me for the rest of my life. Edith told me our family doctor related to her that she would never be able to have babies due to a very bad infection that she had. And she wanted a baby. She wanted someone to love her. Edith couldn't handle a baby. It would be a major problem. Babies need someone "To love them." It's hard for babies to be devoted back, because they, themselves, need a lot of attention. Parents who raise their own children hardly ever get any sleep, and that can be laborious. Babies can not fix things, they lack the effort. But my psyche couldn't hear her screaming with those faint little tears inside. I didn't know how to listen as my mother's concerns rubbed off on me in non-comprehension for the welfare for children. Edith asked about mom and Rick and I didn't know where they were or what they did to her. Mom was helping her lost puppy dog, Rick, but she couldn't understand that the children were much weaker than he was. My poor little sister,

Skinny Minnie ...
they left her all alone out there.
She was lost......

In the.....

"ARIZONA WINDS"

Edith was such a little thing.

The compiling circumstances in my life were something I couldn't understand. Psychology was a topic I never studied and mom and Rick and Edith and most every one I knew were so full of it.... and the world taught us that it was O.K. to be left alone with men...

Mom married Rick.......

And no one in the family asked about the children.

UNFORTUNATELY FOR THE POOR, and everyone else....

MONEY EQUATES TO SURVIVAL

here on the material plain.

Edith's resources would be depleted through Rick's lacking hands, guided in arrogance with my mother right beside him. There's an interesting dynamic involved with women who become jealous of their own children, and in ripping their own youngsters apart, psychologically, in passive aggressive behavior, then letting those around them use their offspring in misguided intentions. These women must be so self-absorbed in resenting the possibility of being tied down and growing up. Especially when single mothers start dating, and daughters become competition to men who shouldn't be there in the first place. But because these women loved men too much, the children were probably only a product of them to begin with. What mind game was played on Edith? Just before Rick came into our lives, Edith had her head on straight. She could pick out kinder guys than I ever could. Then everything changed Edith's outlook somehow, things had shifted. Edith told me years later, (when we were both in our 20's), that Rick used to grab and play with my mom's breasts right through my mother's clothing, right in front of Edith. Edith could remember these things, BUT EDITH COULD NOT REMEMBER A YEAR OF HER LIFE DURING THIS PERIOD. Spilling what I recollect, as Edith's "recovering" bits and pieces in the subtle transgressions of getting this story along and the changes that influenced my thinking....

Rick and mom abandoned my little sister Edith at the age of 16 out in the middle of the desert. Mother say's that she wrote down her new address on a piece of paper , which was two states away, and left it with a boy, she said Edith had been staying with. A boy, or a gang, or a tribe that was gang raping my little sister. The same guys who came over that night in their high powered-beamed jeep and the bastards that I have a strong suspicion my step dad knew to begin with. Mom said back then, that, "Edith was old enough to take care of herself." Edith went home one day, simply to find, that they had moved away.

My sister never graduated after Dan left. And as far as looking for things goes...as my mother said she did for my little sister.....my mother would have looked for a lost dog better and harder than she ever looked for my little sister. (My poor little sister, the girl that was hardly held as a little one...) as Rick pushed us away in an effort....he was trying to pawn us off on anyone who would take us, I guess even a rapist. As all the tribulations trickle down to strike out years to come through hypocrisy and lying.

It's almost like they set us up for failure and it upsets me to talk to my mother because she lies for the man who instigated the ruins of my sister's life whose scars would take decades to heal ....if ever.. My mom protects the man who hurt me, she protects the man who hurt my little sister. My mother even let her men re-write history for her, as they lived behind a facade they carried around in public. And my mother's family loved her way too much to know any better. They just wanted to protect her....And this may be way too much work for them to handle in their bombarded lives of trying to make a living. They SUPPORT HER in her quest and desires and I'm afraid that the judgment they set forth will make them bitter. Perhaps the thing that astounds me the most is that my family can't see the evidence in their faces, and they believe a stranger over their own blood and kin. It may shame them, with people's perceptions of public image, that they now twist and manipulate everything with lies that twirl and revolve around an unintelligible mess, as words twisted into non-reality, and as desperation spun like a spindle. My mom and her new husband even hide behind the church, not telling their pastor everything. My sister and I couldn't trust anyone to protect us. With some of the comments coming from my mom, I think that she would have killed me for her man. And it's so hard for me to believe it, to look her in the eyes and know that she thinks I'm dirty and she now, won't touch me.

The subtleties of abuse that are accepted by most of us due to social conditioning can have overwhelming consequences. When a woman manipulates a man into having children, children that he didn't want in the first place........ it tends to build resentments. These women become needy by getting themselves into vulnerable positions through a way of communicating for years and years, through generations of abuse... But...We also have a flip side to this.... Men who lie and manipulate women into having sex and then the shame that women endure for having babies out of love with a sinner of human weakness and how it leaves them....

Again, Edith called me on the telephone while I was staying in Vegas, not knowing what to believe, or who to believe in.. Edith was in Arizona the last I heard, she told me she was out on the streets and that her boyfriend, Owen, who had just tried to kill her and her unborn son. Edith was now seven months pregnant with this bastard's son and he just sat on top of her big pregnant belly and tried to strangle her until she passed out....the father of her unborn.... I was confused.

I called Jay to go over and rescue her. I never asked him for anything else, but I would end up asking for favors along the way for my little sister. I felt such a connection to both of them. Jay said that he knocked on the door of the address that I had given him to the roach infested motel and he couldn't believe it. He told me it was all he could do, to keep from killing this man.
As Owen stood, shaking.
Owen couldn't take it.

So how could my little sister take care of herself?

My Aunt Nancy ended up giving my sister a $50 bill so that she and her new baby, Nathan, could come to Vegas and live with my grandmother. My mother told me years later, "Edith was just following in your foot steps". As my sister and I were moving away, we never escaped the innuendoes and rumors that went around in the family with Rick and mom's improved version of their story. The comments through the years BRANDED US BECAUSE OF IT and blamed us for everything.

Jay was having problems now. He was busted with a pound of cocaine and was only going to spend a month in prison for his ills, while other men were in serving much, much longer terms for just possession of a marijuana cigarette.   He told me that he was very lucky and, "It was because his family had money." And, "It was an illegal search and seizure." And as the chances of probability goes.....he got off light...with a family that could afford a $10,000 retainer....

Jay wanted me there for him , but I wasn't able to bear his inner battle, especially, after my painful experience…. I had no endurance and I wasn't there to help him through, but he probably would have dumped me soon after his ordeal was over, it was the pattern established between us.
I didn't know how to go back to Phoenix…
And moreover, I didn't want to clean up any of his messes.

Yes, as man ripped my mother away from me,

She let him.

In the meantime, my mom and her new husband led us on to believe that they did the best that they could with a mess. Their weapon was prevaricating selfishness. Years later, I asked my mother about these episodes of dialogue delivered under our roof top ... All she said to me was "Rebecca, you shouldn't have been wearing those short shorts around the house." And I wanted to slap her face but didn't. We were living out in the middle of the Arizona Desert at the time and it was 115 degree weather and I was just dressing like my mother to begin with and wore what all the other girls wore. Mom and Rick's handiwork told the family that my sister and I had BIG Pot plants growing in a pitch dark closet that was full of clothing. My mother may have "disassociated" herself at that point with us...Her men were brain washing her. Rick would go through jobs like water....Because it was "Always his boss's fault." As, "The boss had it out for Rick." And it was his first wife Madeleine's fault for his divorce.... And it was our fault that Rick didn't get along with us. My mom said. "That we knew how to push all of Rick's buttons."

In her emotional preferences.....
in those events,
the foundation had been laid,
for me to become a victim in.

This Rick had hidden animosities and jealousies against raising someone else's kids, after losing his two boys in a divorce with ...
(as my mother put it...)

"The Evil Madeleine." with her treacherous accusations...
I hear it was a bitter proceeding...
and we had Mister Bitter...
living with us.

This emotional encounter unfolded and stung with paralyzing exhaustion. It blew me into exile, by being exploited by everyone so dear and close to me. Not even Ward and Patty could compare to this, the way the adults in my family had treated us kids. And in the process, my sister and I went through some desperate times.. with desperate measures...For many years my sister and I were not allowed in my mother's house. If we ever said anything bad about one of my mother's husbands, she snaps. It's amazing, "It's all because we don't get along with him", my mother said. But my stepdad can do or say almost anything he wants to, even making sexual comments to kids. (It's hard finding closure in a parent's denial of never saying they are sorry for anything.)

And I cannot move the wall,
my mom
away from me....

As the veils they hide behind,
the trails they leave
as footprints in the sand
for the little ones.

Years later, Jay would tell me that a neighbor of mine, named David, would tell him how I would throw "ridiculous and hysterical temper tantrums next door to him". "The neighbors could hear me screaming two yards away like a spoiled rotten brat".... David heard me screaming, but no one knew what I was screaming for...but after taking two to three months of Rick constantly riding me...... I just snapped...I broke... into two separate entities that lived far apart from my own very properties of being. David even told Jay about Keith. The 19 year old kid who owned half of Whitman. And the boy I hung out with 5 nights a week to ESCAPE the drama. David totally in his own misunderstanding misrepresented the situation to Jay. David probably told Jay I was sleeping with Keith. And in the process, no one was communicating effectively due to my code of silence and someone else's big lying mouth. Why didn't Jay ask me about the truth? Was he scared?
Or was he just being influenced by people who didn't know the situation?
And ashamed?

Apprehending years later, through Elizabeth, that the house they were living in caught on fire and they thought that we, my little sister and I, did it. I couldn't believe it. It hurt me that they would think that low of us because Catherine victimized us, to begin with, PERIOD. Elizabeth said they barely made it out of the house, alive. And then they found out that it was an electrical problem. And that my sister and I were in Phoenix, or Whitman? just somewhere in Arizona. (A place I never want to go back to again.) So I guess people used and abused us, then said bad things about us behind our backs. Perhaps everyone thought that we were troubled teens and had no parents to watch after us.

I thank my mom. I really do...for my beautiful body. I know she sacrificed all she could... I love her but I'm mad at her.....she loves a pervert more than her own children.... she let her men do, what ever they wanted to do to her little ones. (although, I have actually heard of worse circumstances in which parents actually kill or rape their young and then cover up things.) My mom loved bad boys and married men...

Perhaps....

My mother may have never really wanted us, so with this, I must find acceptance. Please God, have mercy on my family's souls, and forgiveness for us all.

The souls,

We run with, in packs...

(My dear beautiful mommy, who must have been a friend in another life....The one who I wanted to be my mother....the one I begged......to be my mother.....The one I pleaded with...... as she told me it would be a very heavy burden for her...but she did it anyway, loving me in a healthy way for awhile.....and then giving me up as a product of her men.....she carried me.... through...for awhile. And there would be a price, a lie that I must endure in this life.........)

As...

We kept grabbing and grabbing for love.... But no one really knew how to give it.....and just like sand, it kept slipping away from us... I found out that these people didn't really cherish me.... and I was brought into this life....with this pattern being laid down as my foundation. This was the lot that I received from god....and everything happens for a reason.

Furthermore, the only time of the year that my family ever tells one another that we love each another is at Christmas time. And for a while I thought... "I love you mom, but please don't send me anymore Christmas."

And then I couldn't bear it!!!

I can not move the wall,

My mom.

Away from me, .

So with this cast of players, the faces kept changing. While picking away at memories........ and lost illusion... my heart still aches today, as the mirage of Jay still took my breath away for awhile...So in the time that followed....I went to Vegas, worked very hard in the casinos for a couple of years. My first two days of working at Circus, Circus gave way to blisters on my feet. I had to wear white slippers for a week. Then, while having a nervous breakdown, crying for two days straight in Sin City, as the sound of my little sisters voice ignited malady and burning fever..

"Mo", my 30 year old high rolling friend took me to Idaho…. I then crashed my car in Idaho and lost a lot of money while chasing loose lovers on black iced covered highways.

Then I moved to California on a girlfriends charity which I'll never forget, I met Laurie in Vegas while working in the Casinos. And while in Los Angeles, I decided to become an actress and was focused for a couple of years, until things happened, like men.

But looking back, I realize just how far I have come. And I am not the same person that I used to be. I'm the woman who got to discover herself and not identify herself using a man…. I know I must stay in Los Angeles. Where by the way, there are shifts in the sand. We have daily earth quake reports on the news in the Southland that are very small in magnitude.

And at that moment…."I couldn't utter another sentence."…The writer spoke, as he turned off the light and set the keys of the typewriter down…

I was 60 pages away from a nervous breakdown…..

What has the world come to?

To misunderstand so much?

for…

It's not what you do for a living, it's what you do to others

that matters……

AUGUST 31st, 1996

I just got off the phone with a writer and forgot that I had misplaced some things, like true facts. Once you become a hooker, most men and women look at you differently. It's weird, especially with this media thing happening for me. And realizing that Peter Tilden is and was a brave man to give me an opportunity to be funny on the air and to have people enjoy the work that we had created together. He made that happen for me and it made people treat me differently. The musicians and people in Hollywood find out you're a prostitute and they look down on you. Then, you could be a pimp or a prostitute or what ever and they find out you have a weekly spot on the radio, or a T.V. show and they start to look up to you and listen to you.

In one of my favorite shows, titled "Dumb Bells in Prison", we complained about an issue with the California Jail System. In our prisons here, the convicts had use of some very expensive weight equipment, modern gyms were at these men's finger tips. The convicts were pumping themselves up like iron raw men. The rapists and killers and thugs had equipment available to them that the average citizen could not come by without expensive membership to a gym. The cops didn't have access to these facilities and these criminals kept getting stronger and stronger, harder to cuff. They were more able to rape and pillage. We had to put a stop to all that....

Mistress Madeleine
"There are dumb bells in prison!!!!"

Saving a lot of cops......Peter Tilden came up with the perfect solution.....

Peter Tilden
"If they need to exercise, they can aerobicize!"

Indeed, back in the 90's after the airing of this one particular show all the expensive gym equipment was taken out of the prisons in California. No one complained about it.

And the slaps in my face with innuendoes by writers made on the telephone...well, I'm glad to say, I can keep my "cool" during these things most of the time. I try to keep my direction focused and not get caught up in the vanity of insolent configurations. In my intentional commitment of becoming Mistress Madeleine, the radio shows went on.

When I first started doing radio, I changed all the names in my ads, omitting "Mistress Madeleine". I wanted to keep the public guessing...as to whether I was a real Dominatrix or not? I was always afraid that some higher up executive at Disney would be "shopping" and spot my ad in some local underground newspaper and say, "We have to put a stop to this!" I just wanted the spotlight to go on for a while.

At KMPC Radio facilities, the radio interview continues between Peter, Tracy and Madeleine. The Radio Crew in the background, quiet listening..........They are temporarily off the air during a commercial break.

ANNOUNCER
"Kneel and Submit…710, the new TALK Station."

Everyone goes back to work…

John Tesh is popping his head back in and out of the show. Joe the 300 Pound Comedian sits there with all our support players. John Tesh with a microphone then says….

JOHN TESH
"Still going…"

PETER TILDEN
"John stay here, what's happening?"
(Looking at Mistress Madeleine)
"How much money do you make an hour?"

MISTRESS MADELEINE
"$150 dollars an hour."

JOE MACDONALD
"I'm going to start my own business."

PETER TILDEN
"I can't believe they cut us on Channel 5."

TRACY
"I want to go on record and say that I look better
than that in person."

At the same moment, both Peter and Tracy..

PETER AND TRACY
"John, can you help get us on E.T.?"

JOHN TESH
"You have to do something news worthy."

PETER AND TRACY
"Our caning!!"

PETER
(To Madeleine)
"How many people do you see a week?"

MADELEINE
"It depends, I'm going to dress here."

Peter, embarrassed until he sees what is happening:

PETER
"No wait."

Madeleine with one button takes off her expensive black leather coat, dropping it below the chair to expose her dominatrix costume.

PETER
"Oh my god!"

JOE MACDONALD
"I can't take my eyes off this."

PETER TILDEN
"On a scale of 1 to 10, this is a 15."

TRACY
"She's brought in a couple of deviants with her."

PETER
"Bring them in here! Come on, we got to do this by 8:00 A.M.."

Peter motions the two men to move quickly. John Tesh exits the room, quickly!

JOE MACDONALD
"These guys are crawling! And one's got on a dog collar!"

TRACY
"And ones got a prior wound. Plus, he's got on a designer shirt and he looks sad...he must be sad because he's not worthy."

PETER TILDEN
"If you're a listener and you're into this, call Tracy and tell her your not a deviant. You're the guy next door."

MISTRESS MADELEINE
"Always. A lot of my clients are doctors and lawyers."

PETER TILDEN
(To Tracy)
"You're very uncomfortable with this."

JOE MACDONALD
"There is a lot of love involved."

Everyone starts laughing..

PETER TILDEN
"Producer Bill is handling the instruments of pain here.
(Now to Madeleine)
Now tell us about your clients here."

MISTRESS MADELEINE
"One of them has a high pain tolerance and one has a very low
pain tolerance or threshold."

WHACK

WHACK

WHACK

YELP!

YELP!

YELP!

There's laughter in studio…………

TRACY
"One of them is really cute. It's too bad he's a deviant."

"CASUAL PERSUASION".....

(And the wicked ones....)

In 1987, I was living in a very small apartment on Grace Street, in Hollywood, California, just north of Franklin Avenue. I was very, very poor, with an income of about 250 dollars every seven days for about eight years with no help from my family or anyone. My rent was only $300 and I vowed with an astounding resolution that nothing ugly would go into my home. I didn't want to be responsible for junk. The things I did buy were mostly from second hand stores and looked very valuable. I had no furniture in my apartment for the first few years and had ironed my clothing with an iron skillet heated lightly on the stove and covered up with linen....I had been trying to be a "movie star" and had to wait tables in between, thinking that I'd find love in Hollywood if I could only be in the movies.. The only hobby my 107 pound frame enjoyed was singing, which enlightened my spirit when I was alone. I was comfortable in my sustenance, controlling my own space....

Luck brought me work and a few parts, toiling the hard way with a few great directors and minor roles..... With nothing major, except for a National Men's magazine cover from March of 1983 which featured only me and my long cascading locks on it. That particular magazine cover landed on Movie Time Channel (which is now E! Entertainment.....) for a few years running during the 1980's..... I also ran and hid for 5 years after that major display of myself because I was afraid of the lascivious implications associated with the publishing of it. I never realized what an impact the magazine cover had as an art piece and how significant the work was. I never could afford cable, (so I never found out about this until 1993 when a friend told me about it....) But still back in the 1980's.... my boyfriend at the time, Peter once saw my magazine cover televised, hanging in the background of a T.V. Show. Then Peter couldn't remember the station's name or the T.V. Show. I never got to see the "airing" or celebrate. I never once got to recognize any of my victories. (It was like, Little Boy Peter lost his memory on purpose and was startled over the whole thing). I also did a young Julie Christie in "The Big Bet" which I never saw, it went to Europe and was directed by Bert Gordon.....I then played a young Veronica Lake for the Playboy channel. With my training in the field of pretending, I learned to react and not to act, so I couldn't even cry on cue, I didn't know how. I always showed up on time, and with the sets always being so real, and magical, I just got caught up in it...... and so much so, that on three separate occasions.... Directors would see me perform in the background, and pull me to the foreground. They would set up cameras and everything just to get a close up of tears, the real emotions I had on screen ....So with these improvisations.....it was work that required energy...and a lot of struggle with pay being at the bottom of things.... I'm afraid that I loved the glory more than I loved the art of acting.

And being such a slave to the work, in the function of pretending.....here I was, living my hard little life, saving every penny that I earned, and I wasn't going out. I felt that I had no one to fall back on and the waitress work was very tough on my spine. So hard, that I was in pain, sometimes, but I still went to work out of my personal sense of duty. And almost every single day, I traveled the round trip journey of three hours on the RTD Bus.

I had a boyfriend named Peter, but boyfriends are work, no matter who they are. The courtship process is set up so that you can get your love to marry you and take care of you, so that you, in turn, can take care of him. That's what good girls were taught…to never have sex before marriage because if you had sex with too many men, you were then considered a slut. Then the sexual revolution moved into the 1960's and sex got a little fuzzy. People don't know what their social roles are any more....Our baby boom generation has half way, paved the way with the Women's Rights Movement.... But people are still confused and somewhat living in denial. Women still make less money than men do for the same jobs in the average work place. At this point in time, I really wanted someone to take care of me.

I worked at a restaurant named Julie's after it's namesake. A lot was happening in my life back then, things changed for the better and the girls at work hated it, especially Dawn. I was not mean to people, I never policed them. I just wanted to get my work done and move up, so to speak. The girls at Julie's were giving me an awful time with shifts and bad tables to wait on, they were jealous of me with Dawn heading the pack. And since my boyfriend, was actually Dawn's husband's boss to begin with.... I met my boyfriend through Dawn... I always kept my mouth shut out of consideration for Peter's feelings. And Dawn's twisting along the path, in which she wanted to be the center of attention all the time, (which was O.K. with me, as long as she wasn't picking on me or anyone else…)

My boyfriend Peter never stuck up for me. Peter was complacent with me. He liked to do $2,000 worth of cocaine a month while I took a two-hour bus drive into Hollywood from work at 11:30 PM at night from Encino on Ventura Boulevard. Peter was right down the street hanging out with a guy named Jimmy.

I needed flight...

I was 26 years old.

It was something I was used to, not having any support from anyone. I worked all my life, all by myself with no help from my parents and I had bought myself a nice car. I was taking better care of my health and had quit smoking so I was actually looking pretty hot, my skin was milky and soft as a snow flake.......Peter on the other hand was born a third generation royal, of a Middle Eastern father and an English mother. Peter had a lot given to him from his family. His father owned part of the boulevard on which Peter's small recording studio stood.

Peter knew Mark and Dawn longer than he had known me...I didn't know any of Peter's friends that well, just stories told…nor, did they know me, I worked much too hard at the restaurant as a part time waitress to hang out with anyone, then I had my studies as an actress, which seemed to now be going nowhere. Was I already washed up?

Peter told me a story once.......One night, he was over at Dawn and Mark's getting drunk, doing drugs...way before they knew me.... Mark and Dawn were both into the "free love" concept of the 60's.... with Mark being a stand in player for a rock band that was a "huge-mega one hit wonder". My boyfriend Peter seemed to be overly impressed with the fact, that his buddy that he was now hanging out with was a past Hollywood icon who was now living in a one bedroom apartment of medium income. Well anyway, Mark had left the living room party to be with another woman in the bedroom. It hurt Dawn's feelings that her husband was "making love with the other woman" as they called it. At the time, I always wondered how anything could be called free love when it was hurting the people that you loved, like your wife. Peter told me Dawn then made a pass at Peter, (maybe to "fill up" the emptiness..) and Peter did not accept the invitation bestowed upon him. Dawn felt rejected, hurt and upset that my boyfriend at the time didn't want to get emotionally involved with his soon to be manager's wife....I thought they were screwed up equating things like this and I didn't want them anywhere near my relationship, manipulating....playing Peter against me. But I felt, that as a 27 year old woman that I had to stand by my man, to prove my womanly love for him in a far fetched sight of reality...

I MET SONNY after work at Julie's on Ventura Boulevard as I walked up a side street to my car. Across the street from me was a construction site, and I noticed two very good looking guys. The situation was a nice small house that belonged to a 50 year old woman. Well anyway, I did a head toss with all my mane of big outrageous hair flowing through the air for all the world to see... And the boys across the street watched me as I watched them. I lifted the hood of my 1943 Ford to show off, in being the ham that day, flirting with my youth. And maybe thinking the guys would come over and it worked! They did! A blond and Sonny came to my rescue because the Ford had really broken down, mysteriously, somehow. And that lifting of the hood as my subconscious told me to do in the afternoon sunshine... in one of those ironic gestures of life, I know I looked delicious that day. Sonny obviously wanted to know me, when I found out that he owned the construction company, I was awed. And with Sonny giving me a ride home in his sports car, I found the escape I craved with an exciting stranger.

Sonny looked like a Latin movie star who exuded sexuality, the stuff seemed to be oozing out his pores, all over the place. Sonny was mysterious and Peter was boring. The tension got to me... I thought Sonny was a self made man who had gotten somewhere from nowhere. But Sonny was a con, who used a lot of women for fun, games, money and conquest. There were just a few matrons, like myself, who got caught up into his little perilous trip of excitement, which had me headed for a collision course. I was just entertainment that day, but eventually, I'd become a mark to him. Very quickly, he found out where I lived, but of course, I never knew where he lived, just that it was somewhere in Hancock Park, in a house that "He owned", as he told it. He said, "That he lived with a woman who was sleeping on his couch, who was in love with him." "She was an X-Prostitute" and he was "Trying to help her out." And "That was why I couldn't have his home telephone number." "Because it may upset her."
And I didn't see the warning signals, that if a man doesn't give you his home telephone number....

Run! Baby Run!
Because there's a problem.

Accordingly, prince charming showed up on my front door step in the weeks to follow, on what I now call his unexpected and "controlled" visits. While being bedazzled, I let Sonny close in on me. In feeling I needed him for my exhausted vanity and the fact that I craved some romantic illusion after loosing Jay, (it had been a decade..) Sonny knew about my whole existence, while, I knew nothing of his. Six months into my relationship with Peter, I met Sonny, and I liked two men at once. I wasn't married, but I wanted to be, I wanted to be taken care of, I was tired of this boyfriend crap. And with in a month of seeing two men, I told both, of the other. I had to get it off my chest. And because he seemed more needy of the two, the hardest part was telling Peter, because I couldn't live a lie, with either of these guys....or Peter Pans...Because I should have known what they both were. Yes, both of them never, ever really paid for their own way in life....as women paid Sonny's in deception....and Peter's father paid his with love......

Sonny kept me off kilter with unexpected affections and expensive jewelry. He was so much better to me than Peter was and less demanding. I was seeing two men for about a half a year and in my dysfunctional patterns I was putting Peter's needs ahead of Sonny's. Partially because of the woman that Sonny was living with. I sensed there was something more to the picture than what he was telling me. I felt that Peter needed me more than Sonny did. Peter seemed safe, and in my guilt, I couldn't understand why I did this. I think I was repeating my mother's pattern of trying to rescue the lost bird who's wing had been broken. So in culpability I lay with a complacent boyfriend.

As Sonny kept giving me things, he was making my life easier. It's just that sometimes he wouldn't show up as scheduled.

Sonny was a man on the run.

The pain in my neck was like a head ache that pounded day and night....I would have been isolated if it were not for Sonny.

WHY WAS I STILL LOOKING FOR A MAN? As my inconvenient desires were where introspective contemplation evaporated. I learned a very hard lesson, I found out what can happen when you really don't know who you're sleeping with. As men just kept distracting me, I was dreaming about being with them,
especially Sonny.
Who I thought about incessantly...
Who I waited on day and night to call me.....
His thoughts...
his whispers....
were with me.
Although my instincts told me that there was something wrong with this picture, in not having his home address, I was excited in my non-comprehension of things, in living a myth.

My shifts were all screwed up. I had more seniority than other staff, I was also a better waitress, (as the cooks all said.) But I still had some of the worst shifts available to man and it wasn't supposed to be like that. For starters, I didn't have two days off in a row. I worked

Monday lunch, which was the slowest shift of the week, then, they scheduled me for Sunday and Tuesday off. Then, a new waiter arrived, who was now going to get Monday off before I had the chance to, just because Linda the manager knew Dawn. Hearing that the two women were sleeping together as I watched them make intimate eye contact, which seemed quite weird to me as I worked silently. (And I guess it was fun for them to make my life hard.) I never talked about any of these women's affairs or business, nor did I think much about it. Why were they so consumed with mine? Presuming at the time, I didn't want to go out and look for another job, I was kind of lost, not knowing what to do and how to stand up for myself. I had been there a couple of years and Dawn arrived on the scene six months behind me. (Everyone liked me before she showed up, gossiping...) Dawn was now working Wednesday through Saturday evenings with all the best shifts. They still had me working two lunches in which the tips were not as numerous as what they were on dinner.

One day, I had to pick up this very heavy tray. I struggled all on my own and handled it almost expertly, at my frail size of 105 pounds. My back was in distress. I went to Julie the owner and told her. All she said was, "Back injury wasn't covered by worker's comp insurance." Not being educated at the time, I stood there and let her tell me that nonsense. I also heard that Dawn hurt her back on the job, too. She and I both had the very same shoulder injury due to the big heavy trays we had to carry on one side of our bodies. Julie told her the very same thing... (The one thing I learned there was, normally, the way people treat you is the way they treat others most of the time.) Julie and Dawn were supposedly friends..... they hung out together and seemed to be very close in irrational lesbian contact. A few women who worked there were gay. Dawn and Julie were both married. Dawn was married to Mark, the manager of my boyfriend, Peter's Recording Studio. And Julie was married to Sol, a man 30 years her senior who drove around in a red mustang. But Julie and Sol had separate apartments.... I heard that Julie was much more into girls, using Sol, musing the women really did deserve one another...after all...

Dawn and Mark went to a huge amusement park and claimed Dawn had been dragged by one of the park's transportation vehicles and had injured her shoulder in the process. They were suing the amusement park, my boyfriend told me. I remember everybody at work and especially my boyfriend thinking that their claim was bogus and a crock of bullshit.....

One evening, Dawn and I had a big verbal fight. She was saying a lot of rotten things behind my back... I informed her, "That if she didn't have anything better to do with her life, than to talk about me, that her life probably wasn't worth living to begin with..." and a bunch of other stuff...because the girls were so ridiculous ever since I got my new car and a couple of boyfriends. I was getting tired of quietly accepting their witch hunt, the way in which these women treated me. So I just exploded on the target of all my anguish, and she had it coming to her. I didn't think I was all that hard on her, considering........

Sunday night came around and Hank called me and asked if I would cover his shift. I said "Yes", and took the bus into work to make the extra money. Working dinner that night was Mike, (the other waiter,) Dawn, and John, Sol's son, who was a cook in the kitchen, along with myself.

There was a lot of tension in the air. I had a closing station, which meant I would be going home late. It was slow. Dawn the hostess was supposed to be giving all of us equal amounts of tables to wait on. There were four waiters on the floor, one of us should have gone home, which was standard practice. But she kept skipping my section and not giving me tables. I was getting practically no one to wait on. Everyone else had three four tops which were good tables, they would leave at least $10 tips. I had one two top, I was making no cash. Mike the other waiter noticed this too. Mike and I decided we should say something to the boss about it, in all fairness to the boss........

Julie was scheduled to arrive by 9:00 PM. She was having a bottle of wine and this evening was no exception that she and Dawn should be together, sitting at a table, talking.

As Mike and I stood there explaining things to Julie, all this woman told me was to "Go punch out on the time clock." As she and Dawn both sat there laughing, I thought they were joking. Julie then stood up and while pulling me along by my wrist. I was in a state of shock..... Both women were bigger than I. They walked me to the hallway time clock machine that calculated the employee's hours. The time clock "checked us in" and "checked us out". Julie removed my apron by grabbing me around my waist. She and Dawn both handed me my time card. While this 26 year old "Actress", Restaurant Owner, due to her older husband's money, manipulated me over the edge, I should have known better. In this senseless and incoherent state, I didn't see the path of minor destruction I was in. I didn't know the signs because I had been taught to always look up to authority figures who I couldn't believe were perpetuating this incident, which I thought was antic in proportion but I still was not getting it. In being instructed by a superior... I was taught that they were individuals that had worked their way up.. And at the time, it seemed so ridiculous. My instincts were screaming and I didn't want to listen.

"We" punched me off the time clock with tables and handed over tickets... Julie told everyone, "That she and Dawn alone would take me to the side of the building", as they both hovered around me, gently pushing.. Julie had her hands around my wrist.. All of the employees were watching us from inside the restaurant as someone was cheering for this one and someone was cheering for that one. (But I think that most of the cooks were supporting me because I was nice to them and the other girls were not.)

As my spirit was abashed and insulted, I just let them drag me along in a fear-ridden path out the front door in the bow of everyone. In that scene that Julie and Dawn created for their amusement.. Julie walked us to the side of the building and let go of my wrist in the place or spot where the fight was to be on a grassy lawn against the brick wall of Julie's restaurant. I was being bullied into a fight that I didn't want….I even told them so, twice. But in my suspended animation I forgot that they were mean and who I had been dealing with.

Julie grabbed, kissed and told Dawn, "Good luck." (It was like, "I love you, have fun." Dawn was four inches taller and 30 pounds heavier than I was...) There I was standing face to face with in 11 inches of her dare… I was looking at Dawn, eye to eye in an insane way of trying to communicate...Dawn was British and thought that I was just plain dirt. She thought that you could never change social classes, that you were born what you were, forever. What ever the legacy in your family's blood was, you would remain until the day you died.. (But I was taught in America, that a poor man could work his way up in a land full of opportunity...) And Dawn's family was worth half a million British Pounds, I was born into a dirt poor family, and she knew it.

Unknown to us, John the cook climbed up on top of the building to watch us. Isn't it ironic? Dawn started to tattle tale on a portion of material regarding John as he was sitting on the roof.... I'm sure she was mean to a lot of people. Dawn said to me, "You shut up." "I'm going to talk, and then maybe you can say something." "But don't you say anything right now." And then she said, "As a matter of fact, you can't say anything because you're nothing but gutter trash." I thought to myself that it must be a real low life like her to do nothing but gossip and make things miserable for people like me.....the underprivileged...

I EXPLODED!

And said, "I may come from the gutter of poverty but at least it's better than being born rich, and then leading a life headed towards the gutter like you". Then she hit me hard across the face which left a scratch mark on my cheek, and said, "You can't talk to me like that." "But I can talk to you anyway I want to"...Then I said, "No you can't!" As I started swinging, she hit me again. She next went to push me down. I grabbed the nape of the neck of her shirt and in the process of learning how to roll into a fall.... I spiraled and coiled back as the wall caught me safely after I revolved backward into soft grass... I got lucky with this grace because it gave me the opportunity to slam Dawn's head directly into brick and cement.

BAM!

I grabbed and rammed her head real hard and she deserved it. She attacked me first and was much bigger than I was. In musing I told them that, "I thought this was crazy." When I began to kick my foot six inches past her face in an effort to get her invading and almost laying on top of me presence off of me! She was striking in rage and anger. I had to remove her and I gave Dawn a black eye in the process.

After a couple of minutes she got up and I could tell that she was disoriented, so I gave her a few seconds space in my mercy and compassion. I could tell that she had been jolted hard and I didn't attack her when I could have done or inflicted a lot of damage on one so large. Because who knows? Maybe, I could have really hurt her, but with such resentment and animosity, I showed restrain. Then, that bitch said, because she was losing, obviously ...which she wasn't expecting..., she informed me, "I think that we have had enough fighting for tonight." Like she thought she was the high authority and I was stigmatized as nothing. And as we were grown women, I couldn't believe this was happening. I thought that adults were civilized in a modern society.

With a marred and scratched countenance, I walked back into the restaurant. My surface was falling apart.... How could "I lose it" at age 27?

Neither one of us should have been there. Some people perpetuate mannerisms that costs them things, to this day, I now know, I had the personality traits of a victim. Not knowing back then, I wouldn't learn for many years, how to be treated right. I settled for people like this around me. I was so beat down in self esteem...in taking the blame for everything, my body began to take on it's shape. Dawn attacked me, she wanted to, with the consequences making me use force to stop her, an unknown ability I did not want to use. She and Julie planned it, having fun in the process until that moment of realization that Dawn could be the one who got hurt with her manipulation of situations for lurid reactions.

Observing, I was the odd woman out. These dames obviously didn't have much going on in their lives. I wish they would have found something to fill themselves up with. I witnessed that people could be easily manipulated if they were charmed by you, or awed by you. Human beings followed different causes every six months, depending on the political climate of the moment. An interesting lesson was, that you could get away with almost anything, even murder, if you were cunning enough to. I lacked the communication skills that Dawn definitely had. For the big contending, Dawn taught me something else, she taught me about temper tantrums thrown at the right moment and how to get something out of them by playing little games with people... For these episodes would normally lead to some form of occurrence.....

I punched back in on the time clock (out of my needless sense of duty...) The cooks were all cheering, "Rebecca won!" I didn't say anything but went back to my tables with no mirthful expression, there was nothing ecstatic in that moment as I was saturated in humiliation.

(I should have called the police and sued Julie, big time..)

I closed out from work that night, fragmented in agitated emotion that tied me into the wind on the drive home that evening. When I arrived, I called Peter, my boyfriend. He picked up the phone. I could tell that he had been sleeping, (for the first time in months he went to bed before midnight.) But just like the pansy I was, I said, "Peter, did I wake you?" He whispered, "Yes." (And I under my breath, crying...) while Peter couldn't hear me, or the tone... I said, "Oh, I'm sorry, I'll let you go back to bed.", and he did. He didn't call me for two whole days after that. Rebecca needed love and protection, while Peter provided none. After that moment with Peter, it was too late for anything else, the closeness had subsided in us and sank beneath ruins.

Rebecca, being the idiot that I was back then, actually went back in to work to do my lunch shift after that. It was Monday, and Julie and Dawn were drinking cappuccinos in the office with the door closed. I apprehended that annihilation had not changed and something in that moment made me wake up. All the cooks were telling me that Dawn got a big old black eye while I was kicking her. They all said that she looked worse than I did that day. I wouldn't have even known it. I couldn't look at her. But while I was all alone with SOL, (Julie's husband, the actual owner and financier...) who made a gesture at the cash register implying that the fight was all my delinquency and misconduct......(Now for a sixty-five year old man who drove a 1965 red Mustang convertible and chased women a third of his age...) I almost lost it as he was trying to intimidate me, so, for the very first time, I spoke up. And while looking directly into his eyes, I think I said, "You can take your fucking tables." Sol's jaw dropped in the process of saying, "Oh." Because I think at that moment, he began to see things differently. I handed Sol back all of my tickets, went over and punched out. Then, dropping money in the pay phone, I called the police. I was looking for clarity, for guidance

I drove to the police station, walked in and walked over to the desk officer trying to escape imposed aggravation...In a quiet, faint voice, I told him of my plight and all he said with a big old laugh and a smile on his face, was "CATFIGHT!" (This was back in 1990 before all the new laws had passed on threats and violence.)   This officer must have not been trained in psychology, especially with this very loud insult coming from an authority figure ....again... while he sat there laughing........   my face dropped in the silence of utter pain with this man's comment. There was no amusement on my face. I stood there in that millisecond of necessity, the torment inside me was raging.

(Only Sonny seemed to understand things...)

But no one else around, did, not even the policeman, until that moment he saw my face, my eyes.. lit up his in understanding, I think. Another officer from behind the desk saw our conversation and walked over to me and tried to extend a helping hand... and told me that we could now take a photograph of the scratch......But at that point, I walked out of there with no picture because I could not think straight and couldn't understand the way that people had treated me after an incident like that.

Standing there alone, all exposed emotionally, watching the crowd go by me..... I didn't have anyone, not even Sonny... Truly, my body and soul were screaming for human companionship and closeness and understanding or just someone to talk to, about being attacked and defending myself.

Two days later, when I finally did get to talk to Peter, all he told me was...while laughing on the other end of the telephone receiver....was that his manager told him, (Dawn's husband that is...) was...."Boy! Did you hear about the fight last night?!" They had made a big joke out of it, and I let him. Peter wasn't going to be there for me, especially with this crowd. And while finding out that people "without means" got violent, I realized I didn't want to be like them. I still accepted Peter's behavior by keeping my mouth shut. Hurt, and humiliated, and uncomfortable, I should have left him on the spot, right there and then and finished it..

I never went back to Julie's after that, hearing that Julie got rid of that time card, the one I probably should have taken home, as evidence.. So in those personal, painful days, I had no one but Sonny. Sonny would come in and out of my life bringing exhilaration. I felt my own life was boring in correlation to the existence of others, there was nothing directed towards me, but caustic complacency.

Linda, the manager at Julie's called me at home to tell me she was really sorry for Dawn and Julie's coercing, as she put it. She was appalled, she said. Maybe she was extending her hand in a good faith gesture for a kind of good-bye... (I found out years later...that I could have sued big time with a good attorney.)

Mike called me to tell me what Dawn and Julie's new alibi was. He really liked me, explaining the new fable.

In the days that followed, attorneys from the amusement park that Dawn and her husband had visited would receive anonymous phone tips with information regarding Dawn's worker's comp situation. Dawn never did receive that much money for her law suit. Hearing that she wanted to purchase a house off all the profits, she never got the chance to, because of a previous condition assaulted on her due to lifting heavy trays in the work field. And I would file a law suit for only the back injury in the nick of time.

I heard through the grapevine that Julie had Sol, her husband, sign papers out of trust, and he lost his half of the business in the process, (the man who financed her to begin with.) I also heard that Julie lost her restaurant due to high worker's comp insurance costs... The lady couldn't make it on her own.

Another astonishing fact was that only two weeks after John was on top of the roof, staring down, looking at the fight. The next day telling me, that I was the righteous one and that Dawn was the bitch, the one asking for it..... That he was glad that I won, (with me acting numb and uninterested in a defense for my sanity in disbelief).... Again, only two weeks after this fight was over John was swayed into believing that I am the villain. Astounding, while being there, the impressions I received trounced the self confidence out of me. As some could get away with fabricating so called truths, especially when you knew that they were not promised in authenticity to begin with.. In recognizing that people could be so easily swayed and managed....

Especially the weak sheep of the earth....

Dawn's distinct character traits had this game plan down to a fine art......

of...

Casual Persuasion...

Perhaps at that time, Peter and Sonny felt a little weird, sharing me. I wanted to be compassionate to both their needs and feelings. But with life being tough, I also wanted someone to take care of me. I now know my relationship with Sonny brought distance between me and Peter. I was still seeing both guys and driving my 1943 Ford around town, as men and women pulled up to me in their big fancy cars inquisitive to a trade. The car that Peter wanted me to sell, he said I was living beyond my means. But he and Jimmy were still spending two thousand dollars a month on drugs and partying it up. As I would take the bus ride home late at night when the Ford broke down, which sometimes was a lot.

(Thank God, I wasn't using expensive drugs...)

Through difficult passages I got a new job at the Roosevelt Hotel in Hollywood because I needed it. There I was working hard at cocktails. At least I didn't have to wear high heels, like in the past.... I was getting the slowest shifts, with the longest hours because I was the new girl. The only other two waitresses in the whole bar area had been there for many, many years. And the manager, Chris was OK, but he could also be a pain in the ass and everyone knew it. I was having back spasms but thought I had to keep up this schedule because I wanted to be an actress, it was all I knew. I didn't comprehend that all these things I was doing in my inebriated state were killing me... All I knew was that I had to pay my bills someway, and daddy wasn't doing it. I had a severe headache which was an annoyance for three months straight. I was popping over the counter medication like candy and still going to work. I was having a hard time making ends meat.

But I kept going to work, in pain...Popping Advil like candy.....

Pop.. pop....

Popping...

This position was a lot better than the old one. Chris headed only the food and beverage department. Frank was over Chris's head as General Manager of the entire Roosevelt. Perhaps Frank and I got along because we had both worked in Vegas, and Frank knew that the unions taught us how to toil.

Recalling those temper tantrums of Dawn's.... One night Chris the manager hired a new girl. I guess she was a friend of his happy butt and his happy gay lover... Anyway, that night all four of us girls were scheduled. One waitress was supposed to wait on people in the lobby, which was the slowest station of all. Perhaps in those long eight hour shifts of working, you were lucky enough to bring home 40 dollars....we all hated it. The "Grill" was having a hot jazz show, it was known you could make 300 dollars in only a few hours..... My back was killing me and I had already worked there for a year. Chris wanted to break in the new girl, and he wanted me to work the lobby so that he could teach her the ropes in the "Grill". The girls with prior standing to mine thought that it was wrong. I exploded calmly in front of Frank and everyone in the lobby right before work. I was looking right at Chris and you could see my face, raging with out even saying a word. Chris asked me to go into the backroom office with him, alone, and I CHARGED! After he closed the door shut behind us. I'm sure everyone could hear my screams which intimidated some, as I decided right there and then that I wasn't going to put up with this bullshit again. And you know what? I GOT MY WAY because I knew I had grounds. I wish I would have been able to do that at Julie's. After that minor incident, Frank had nicknamed me "Rocky", which I loved.

But I still pervaded and stretched with insecurities.....

Still seeing both Sonny and Peter at the same time. Peter in his nice sweet naive world, because his father had helped pave his way off a large inheritance of Los Angeles Real estate and cash. So in essence, Peter's lectures to get me "To go out there and earn it, the way he had". He wanted me to have the incentive to get things. As I sat in angry silence because he looked like such an idiot saying this. He may have worked hard for four years to put together a studio with his "investors" which in actuality ended up being his dad. Peter didn't understand that if he had to go out there and earn it on his own, it would have taken him many more years. His father owned the property he was sitting on. But the ironic thing was, was that Peter was much closer to his mother. As he drove a four hour journey almost every other weekend to see her. Peter was telling me how to get my life together......

Sonny seemed quiet and strong. In smelling danger I went against all my better instincts with this one. Sonny was fulfilling all my preferences, being the most obliging and agreeable guy that I had ever known...(or at least I thought so at the time....)

Un-expectedly, one day, Sonny gave me three hundred dollars cash out of his pocket to pay the rent with, because I was crying, explaining, why I needed it so desperately. I wasn't expecting his generosity, as he handed the cash to me. Another time Sonny took me into a dress shop after we ate lunch together, picked out two outfits for me... walked out to his sports car and pulled 300 dollars out of a briefcase that had a load of massive cash in it... I was awestruck......But, was also ashamed and felt guilty that my public image had me wearing one of those very same outfits that Sonny purchased me out on a date with Peter. Sometimes, Sonny stopped by, unannounced. He did one day while I was waiting for Peter to pick me up.......as I ran out to the drive way in a quiet frenzy.

Peter was still a part of Mark and Dawn, and the incapacitating crowd of Julie. Dawn the Bitch had given Peter a message condescendingly to give me, which was..."Tell Rebecca that I'm sorry for what I did, but we could never be friends." Dawn had to assert her ego one more time in my direction through Peter's mouth.

During the last year of my relationship with Peter, he started giving me nice things, like a delicate gold necklace with pearls on it, and a matching bracelet. He had really splurged on me this time, and I appreciated it. (While musing upon an issue he mentioned once, that he wanted to make sure that I wasn't after his family's fortune.)

At my apartment, my dysfunctional neighbors in Hollywood also enjoyed waking me up and loved gunning the engine of their THUNDERING LOUD JEEP PARKED RIGHT OUTSIDE MY BEDROOM WINDOW. When I had the late shift I would be lucky if I got to bed before 1:00 A.M. These guys started their engines at 7:00 AM.

There were six young men living in a one bedroom. They were all going to college on student loans or working part time, or not working. The "Scam" I heard was to never graduate, to keep changing majors, with only a few months to go to get your degree. That way the government kept giving you money. I heard that people were working the system for decades like this. (While we stopped welfare for hungry kids after five years.) These guys kept saying that they were Italian when in fact they were really Middle Eastern....... (In wondering with this type of identity crisis, if these individuals feel that they are getting glamour by taking on a fake character instead of being themselves?) For all these conflicting pressures and expectations that society puts onto us.... For all I could see, the neighbors loved hanging together. The landlord's atmosphere always somehow took on a party attitude, hardly anyone paid their rent on time, including myself. Maybe the neighbors think I snubbed them...... but in actuality, I was laboring so hard just to make ends meet. My 14 hour days were pretty long. In Hollywood, almost everyone wanted to be someone, including me. Most of us were angry at ourselves because we weren't sure if we were going to find the adoration of stardom... There were so many subliminal hues, tones and voice mannerisms that gave warnings that people really were not happy with themselves. As the land lord seemed to pick up dysfunctional people, almost everybody in the building was some sort of struggling artist, everyone seemed to be subservient to the land lord. As the land lord was usually a very busy man running a night club. He "seemed" to forget that he was giving away the same parking space every two months as incentive for new tenants to move in.

Sonny started staying with me, the neighbors quit making loud noises. You see, these boys were big enough to harass me, but let a 190 pound muscle man stay with you sometimes and all of a sudden they learn how to be quiet and nice...No one but Sonny was there for me, and I loved him for it, really I did. The love making was great and passionate beyond belief.

One day Sonny brought over this well polished black man. Sonny said Art was a good friend of his and a very important man. Art wore 400 dollar suits which he carried well. As the boys visited one afternoon, I remember feeling a little uncomfortable when my shirt fell aside and the sunshine exposed me through linen...It was just the way Sonny and Art glared at me, like I was fresh meat (or something) But I couldn't put my finger on it...so I let it slide. Sonny was so impressed with Art and said that he had known him for seven years. To me, Art just looked like any guy I had recently met who had risen in the entertainment industry, he also smelt like mafia. Sonny and Art were hit and miss.... things were beginning to get strange for them....I was numb to perception...

Once, Sonny was making love to me, I could feel him on the floor...encasing my flesh... dripping sweat as I got the tactile sensation that he could kill me if he wanted to with one snap. I didn't move but felt safe for the moment as I felt his "love" around me, this strange love with him...kept transforming unnaturally....

Sonny came in like a beam of light. (Like Lucifer the Devil, the most beautiful angel in Heaven's firmament until the time of his departure into sin. So as the devil seduced Eve, she was eased, lured and captivated...just like I was.)

And Sonny knew something about ensnaring.....and...

At the time, he was actually living with a "widow"...
THE ONE HE SAID WAS A "PROSTITUTE", but in actuality, it was the other way, around. I didn't know it at the time, that....
Sonny lied....
And lied....
and lied.....
Embellishing Sonny called, needing money. I couldn't believe how frightened of him I was, in the susceptibility of inducing danger, pushing him away in suspicion and panic. He started to materialize in strange clothing that looked like it had come off of the street. While Sonny remained quiet and calm, his voice so gentle and little boy like in his one hundred and ninety pound shell.... my soul felt demoralized and ashamed, I made him leave. I fell short in his eyes, the first man who was ever this nice and generous to me. I abandoned in selfish confusion and felt I had sold him out in lies and hiding. I thought he was mixed up in something I didn't want to be part of. I couldn't believe the man who helped me out so much in the past was tangled up in things that were way over my head. Reality was already hard enough and I didn't want to be mixed up in anything worse. I was way too alarmed to respond to anything. As I was losing my mystery man, I somewhat regretted it… the apprehension was overwhelming...

Two days later, Sonny called me on the telephone and asked me to marry him.….He said that he was running and that he had a half a million dollars…. All I could say was "No" in confusion…… (thinking that he had stole the funds from the mafia….remembering his suitcase full of money…) I never saw Sonny after that.....

I was still seeing Peter though, through all of his moods and boyishness. It was always his needs that came first and I resented it. He wanted to spend more time with me, because, as he and his friends said, "I was the perfect girlfriend." "Because I never complained about anything." Hell. I sit here and remember the time Peter invited me out on a vacation with him to Club Med for a whole week. I never had a real vacation in my whole life. I wanted to go with him. I was working at Julie's at the time, right before the big fight as they called it. I had to get off on Monday, which was the hardest thing to do, so that I could go on this rendezvous of love and caring. And then, finally with Linda's help, and three months of worry…my little note was on the wall near the time clock for all the other employees to see. I finally got the Monday off just three days before my vacation. Then, Peter decided to take his father instead, and told me so one evening, two nights before our vacation. I'm sure that Dawn and Mark had some input and wallowed in it. After Peter got back from his great vacation with his father, it took him a whole week before he even phoned me. He told me that he thought I would be angry at him, but I was so sweet, again.

Musing, that Peter was going to marry me and take care of me for the rest of my life. But with that type of treatment, I guess I'm better off we never did get attached.

My back pain was really bad. Ibuprofen just wasn't enough anymore. Peter introduced me to Doctor Vanyeck, who worked, amazingly. But I would always go back to work in pain, not ready to take on 9 to 5 yet, I wasn't ready to conform. I still thought I'd find love in Hollywood if I were only a star. I was no longer going on auditions, I had not grown up and taken responsibility for things. I was still looking for daddy or a man to do everything for me, wishing and hoping…. Emotions are not logical…. I was in "love" with an illusion and Sonny was gone…..

During one of my visits with Doctor Vanyeck, he informed me that I had arthritis in my spine…. I dealt with that issue right then and there on the spot, I remember crying on his table as he told me the news.   I QUIT MY JOB RIGHT AWAY, taking such an upset to get me off of my butt and moving into another direction. And Peter was there. I had a week off to think and loved to sleep. It always made me look so much better when the alarm clock was off. But a few of those nights, that week, were spent with big baby Peter, he wanted it that way. I was beginning to get sick and tired of him. Recollecting, waking up with him in those mornings at his apartment. The alarm would go off full blast and I hated it. I would lay there for an hour. Peter never stirred, snoring loudly. I never turned off the alarm either, (I never wanted to be responsible for him not showing up at the studio and work on time…) With myself, not being able to go back to dreamland, so that "hung over Peter" could sleep through the entire hour with all those loud noises. That should have been just the excuse I needed….. I wanted to sleep for hours. It was one of my only pride and joys in life, especially for relief and comfort at night….. And I would soon have to go 9 TO 5. And I had a headache for the last three months straight. Every single day that I woke up there was quiet misery. With only one month left on the statue of limitations, I finally filed a law suit on Julie's place of business. By now, she must have been served.

SOMETIMES IT RAINS… SOMETIMES IT POURS…through difficult passages, temp work was all I could do, I still didn't have all the right "tools" to "stroke it"….(Musing, upon Dawn and how she got things.) I thought I'd try her behavior for a while to see where it took me in life. Things like kissing up to the boss and telling everyone else off, who I didn't like, in a very dashing way with a great Drama Queen Personality of sorts. The only thing is, is that I didn't like myself doing it, it felt like empty behavior with no soul. And acting at that time was a lot of work, especially with a headache. I just wanted to make my life easier.

Getting jobs at many different places, I was taking the RTD bus by getting up three hours early. If I was lucky, my car would be running and I could sleep in a little later. This new schedule of getting up early in the morning was killing me and bringing havoc to my spine. I desperately needed rest and assurance. I still had headaches that wouldn't go away..... anywhere...in sight.

Having a commitment on a film called the "Doors", I was taking off days in between at a film company called Hemdale. Martin, my boss, had given 2 weeks notice and was leaving. I decided to quit too. And while working on the Doors in transportation...I got lucky and got to write some dialogue in the film for a bitch, for a condescending reporter, which happened to be me. At that time, I was acting like Dawn and beginning to feel like an utter mess. But it was getting me results in this dysfunctional town. And with the transgressions for these episodes I hope to get over...

Before I quit working at the Big Film Corporation, the boss asked several subordinates out to view one of his movies on a Friday evening. He was quite generous to his in house employees, like me. But the Thursday evening before, I stayed the night with Peter because he wanted me to. He got up in the morning to take me to work and bitched and screamed at cars and everything else the whole way over there. Now after a poor nights sleep, on top of everything, I felt nauseated at his bearing, because here I was, managing my social graces, but with this behavior in my personal life, in receiving another's misdirected anger, musing, I could control my manners with him, but he in return couldn't be polite in driving me to work. I was giving this guy love and sex, and it was wearing on me. It was hard keeping up paying my bills when I was still, so poor. Although I didn't look it as I scrimped and saved... And Peter was going out every weekend with Jimmy and spending hundreds of dollars and having fun, freely.....And Peter was telling me that I should start paying for things too, like some of our dates. And I couldn't afford to pay for any and I never did. But in the meantime, I let Peter be more selfish with me, then what he already was. Peter was having fun and I was taking the bus, I didn't say a thing. It was even getting to the point to where I would go over to Peter's on a Saturday night and sleep on his couch as he and the boys went out. I needed relief as my body was screaming for it. And Peter wanted to see more of me with the same old bland hang-ups and attachments. He wanted me to drive over to his apartment three nights a week and then he insisted that I park my 1943 Ford out on the street, even though his landlady told me to park in the drive-way. But on the other hand, Peter insisted on parking his nice new car in my driveway which upset my neighbors, especially, when I thought his car looked average. Peter thought that he was being nice by cooking me dinner, but dinner just wasn't enough when I had to drive an hour just to get it, it was easier for me to stay home and save gas money. I knew I couldn't take this treatment much longer.... I knew that I was going to have to leave soon.

One day I was over visiting Peter at his apartment with his nephew Ray. Peter exploded over a broken glass in the bathroom that I think Ray had dropped. Peter was screaming at me, scolding me in front of a 12 year old boy. Ray just looked at me like there was something wrong with Peter and the kid was right, it was no one's fault. But Peter debased and vanquished me from his house. (At the time, I think Peter might have been having an affair with a bleached blond, big breasted singer who looked really cheap on film. Peter was actually "producing" her on the off times at his studio in the middle of the night. This awful looking blond with inch long black roots was the lead singer in an all girl band. Peter was putting money into her, that is... for her one and only demo song. As Peter said, "She didn't have a very large library, like she said she did".)

I broke up with Peter, walked out his door one night because he ordered me to, and boy, what a relief..... I heard from a friend of Peter's that he had a hard time when I finally did leave. He never called, (probably because Dawn and Mark told him not to.) I wanted to leave Peter and his lack of understanding for a whole year. It was way too much for me to handle in my busy work load. It was 20 hours more each week of driving and spending time with Peter, "visiting", and as Peter's needs were no longer above my own, I needed freedom from anyone's demands, like all my precious time and energy needed to make it. I was tired and cranky and my back hurt in it's condition.

Time went by and I had a couple of jerk boyfriends in between...They really didn't matter, emotionally ...But one did hurt my back while trying to make love to me...He called it "slamming"...and I just hated him for it. My neck had been slammed like an accordion by him, squished, and it hurt for days. I got rid of that jerk in one second, flat. His family had a real bad history of abuse. His father had once poured a pan of hot oil all over his mother's head because he didn't like the dinner that she had cooked one evening.

I was beginning to see the warning signals with men.

I was working and working and getting up early in the morning...One day I was driving and wondering..."What ever happened to that really nice man who helped me?" "Sonny." Musing, how he always sat there so innocently in my living room....

"INTERLUDES IN 1989..."

I'll never forget the day Sonny came back...with a knock on my door at about 10:00P.M.
I said, "Who is it?"
He said, "Sonny."
I said, "As in Sonny Estado ?"
He said "Yes."
And was surprised that I remembered his last name, because a lot of people couldn't.

Concluding Sonny's big come back included his two friends, Art and "Tiny". Tiny was three hundred pounds with curly red hair and freckles. He was also from the south and as Sonny said, "He dodged bullets for Art and he was dumb as a door nail." While still living with illusions, I thought that he was joking. I wanted to believe in fairy tales, but then mused upon those instincts from before. Sonny told me that he "had just gotten out of jail for tax evasion." And I believed him, never thinking to question anything in having a short memory span. But I recalled the last time I spoke to him and he told me that he was running that he had half a million bucks tucked away.... I remembered thinking that he was running from the "mob" and I wanted nothing to do with him or anyone who would be dumb enough to steal from those guys....

Sonny was now telling me that he had paid his time back to society and was trying to make a come back into the world. He also said that he had been framed. Perhaps with this emotional intensity nothing was logical. My life was mundane and I felt obligated to help him, he looked un-tidy and somewhat needy. He had helped me in the past with no questions asked, and there he was, needing my help.

He told me that he had a hundred thousand stashed, and that if anything ever "happened to him", that he "wanted to make sure that I would receive all the proceeds." "And to do this, he needed to have my sister's children's social security numbers so that he could set up a trust fund with his attorney."

Buddy Boys were up to "something". I didn't know what it was and didn't want to. I thought it was better that way. Sonny was staying a mile away from me in a hotel on the Cahuenga Pass. The guys said they worked in Entertainment and I had my own struggles to deal with, like working for a living in pain and anticipating the arrival of my law suit money. My first "big break" that had given me a large enough sum to start a savings account with, so that I could finally get some things done in which I wanted to do for some time now... Operating on a premise in which I still had dreams of grandeur locked away in the glassy mirage of Hollywood's image factory. I was told by several people that in order to be, what I wanted to be, I would need plastic surgery. And I wanted it. I practically broke my back for it.

I started spending time with Sonny at THE PASS HOTEL on Cahuenga near the Hollywood Bowl and it was so tranquil, except for the vibe in Sonny's room, it was like a gray cloud that left a dull residue.... Big old Tiny was in the extending room next door as Sonny and I slept together in a bed with no boundaries, no extending door to close at night which left the way wide open.

Sonny knew I had been waiting on a settlement for a long time. Comprehending that I should have received more than just the 10,000 dollars, offered. He also knew what I wanted the money for. I told him of all my hopes, of becoming "someone", (for all the wrong reasons.....) Sonny got on the phone one day and called my attorney who was handling my case and told my legal representation that he, Sonny, was going to go to the bar association and report my attorney for misconduct. My attorney promptly handled things after that and informed me that my file had been lost or shoved in the back of a file cabinet. Sonny got results that I never could. In a way, I thought he was a miracle worker. Well anyway, I received my $10,000 dollars and Sonny was there....almost everyday, now.

I'll never forget as I cashed that check from the insurance company, I had to pay about 700 dollars worth of bills. Sonny had not yet blown his confidence with me... In a naive fashion I handed Sonny $6,000 dollars cash and told him to go out and get money orders to pay my responsibilities...Persuading me, he told me about a business plan he had. And I guess as my greed crept in....he went on to say, that he knew a Plastic Surgeon in Orange County who owed Art a favor. I can't even remember the doctor's name, but Sonny said that the doctor "fixed" faces for the mob.... I also remember wondering if this story was just an imagined effect on his behalf...He told me that Art had some special connections with the boys. Art and his wife sang in Casino Night Clubs....(And Art's wife did indeed, have a nose job…)

Hollywood distorted my sensibility. I was living in chagrin with him and didn't know it yet. I didn't know that con men set you up with "gifts" as bait to get favors Sonny told me that since Art was owed this favor as they called it.. that I could double my money for nothing, if I just gave the cash to Sonny up front, not to the doctor, that they, Art and Sonny were handling "that". While musing, going to my bank to get cashier's checks as I divorced my money, with matters of revenues I showed imprudence. Perhaps in always following the voices of men....I let him lead me. While looking at him, he also signed his personage nonchalantly, right underneath my name and it was all my money! So legally, he didn't have the right to misrepresent his intentions. (I remember my subconscious screaming, and the bank teller giving me a funny look.... I wish that the bank's employee would have just said something. Like, "Are you the owner of that account, too, Sir?") Where as, I thought this was part of the "deal"... and the way he did things....as feelings of slight embarrassment floated to the surface.... I was overwhelmed with dreams of Prince Charming as Sonny was taking my money.

He arranged a meeting with the plastic surgeon and myself... I remember driving to Orange County with Tiny and Sonny in a delusional state. Letting the man take care of everything, I wasn't even paying attention to the street posts. The Doctor's office was in a real nice high rise. Half of his assistants had his breast implants and were even willing to even show them in a "professional manner". When we first walked into his office, Sonny said, "Michael from Vegas sent us." The doctor looked down and away, out to drift.... and on to me. It was as if he and Sonny quietly understood, that they had some little secret, that I wasn't fully in on. There was something about the doctor though that hit me as rather strange. When I looked into his face, his eyes, feeling the intensity of his emotions, it was the way the doctor was handling me.. I remember the doctor discussing the pain I would go through with a smile on his face. And innocently, as I thought no pain, no gain...(I also deliberated subconsciously that the doctor was really into or liked afflicting lacerations.) In my imperfect state, I took the bait of evil. As the doctor was touching my breast, he held a nipple for Sonny to see. In not trying to escape the depravity of this web...I didn't discriminate like I should have......these people were really sick. I thought I could remain impeccable, if I were not inquisitive.

The plastic surgery was going to take place. (It felt strange, and I didn't know it back then, but a patient is supposed to be on antibiotics for four days prior to the procedure, in not speaking to the doctor...) The actual date and morning came that the surgery was scheduled. I stayed the evening before with Sonny because he and Tiny were going to drive me. The boys got a mysterious phone call in the morning that "precluded" our visit to Orange County. They had to take care of some business for Art. So instead of surgery, I sat in a dirty motel room on the pass with my nice clean apartment just a five minute drive away....I decided while crying to have the maid clean up the place while I watched television. While impaired in a critical condition of penetrating mutilated nonresistance, I sat there and did nothing all day, conditioned to, waiting for my man.

I went home at about 5:00 PM. And by 7:00, Sonny had dropped in, he said,
"He knew I really loved him."
And I let him make love to me.

IN THE NEXT FEW DAYS, SONNY GOT A NEW SUIT AND GOLD CHAIN. (It's like you give a con an inch, and they take a mile.) He said they were gifts from Art for his release from prison and that the suit was from a dress shop owned by a friend that he had helped finance in his big hay day, big shot days, "Right before he met me." As much as Sonny and Art liked playing good guy/bad guy with the other, using themselves as escape goats....they were always dealing with the "boys" or the "Mafia's got it". They wore expensive clothes which were "gifts given to do business properly in". In not looking for any warning signals, I just listened. There was always some new story that railroaded me into compromise and deflowering.

THEN, AS THE WEEK WENT ON, SONNY WAS ACTING ODDLY REMOTE with icy planning....Sonny would go out with Art in his new suits and gold chain... Telling me he and Art needed money. "That they had their eyes on this hotel that belonged to a widow." "Her husband just died and left her to run things." As Art and Sonny smelled opportunity..... I thought they were going to buy it. I didn't want to believe that they were actually trying to steal it. But their deal "fell through", because the owner had good sons that stepped in, just in the nick of time. Accordingly, I never knew if Sonny's stories were real or not but I JUST SNAPPED. I couldn't imagine such deceit.

THAT SAME WEEK, on a Saturday....The shop owner that had given Sonny his new suit "Because it was a pay off on some money that she still owed him.".....was throwing a party. I never felt more uncomfortable in my life. There were eight girls at this place with Sonny being the only man. I couldn't believe the reaction women gave Sonny. They just swarmed around him as I sat there quietly, casually holding my composure, with insulting innuendoes thrown towards me. I didn't know how to deal with it at the time, these women were just plain vicious as everyone kept talking about money as Sonny stood by. One woman made a comment to me as Sonny and I were walking out the door. She made a toast "To the only blond in the room." As I smiled... The Shop Owner Lady that was giving the party said to Sonny, under her breath, escorting us out, walking directly behind me, "She really is naïve, isn't she?". With my presence not knowing why the girls had been so rude to me... Sonny said it was due to the fact that he had helped the one woman out. Perhaps all the other girls were looking at Sonny as a meal ticket and me as the competition. So in essence Sonny in his charming way took me to a den full of bitches in an average house in the valley…. as these cunts sported diamond rings given to them from "daddy", and eyed my car, guessing, they must have thought it was Sonny's….

Sonny said Art didn't believe I really loved him and "Art" wanted me tested...the surgery would still come, if I could prove my love….(while trying to aspire in the man who saved me…. comprehending that Art was scum because Sonny set me up to believe that Art was a thief , and I really didn't care what Art's opinion was …) Sonny told me that to prove my love, "A woman's place was to never get out of line." "And I had to learn how to be a good wife, and never talk back or disagree at any cost", because Art was the "boss". "I had to learn how to keep my mouth shut, so that Art would give Sonny permission to marry me". Sonny said that "We couldn't show them any weaknesses in our union, because they are against us to begin with." And just because Art was nice and polite to me didn't mean he really liked me." "And besides, Art wanted to fix Sonny up with someone else. A woman with a "better family" and a lot of money. " I also had to learn to control my emotions in public.. "Everyone spied for Art." I hated all of Sonny's friends.

In intimate discussions, Sonny told me "HE WAS STERILE and that he had never gotten a woman pregnant before." We had a lot of unprotected sex….. He had my naïve assumptions dangling and believing that things would change immeasurably as he mentally and physically invaded my presence, while overtaking it...

The surgery was now off for a while "Because the doctor was having problems with some Federal Investigation"... The boys were doing tricks and throwing bones... .In the meantime, Sonny fed off my guilt in administering mutated compositions of thought and lunacy....

Sonny took me into a jewelry shop way out on Ventura Boulevard. He said that it was a business that he helped finance. In, we walked to find the very same woman who just happened to own the house that Sonny had been working on when I first met him. The purpose of the visit was "To get me a diamond ring so that Sonny and I could get married." Sonny said that this proprietor owed it to him. Sonny knew a lot more about diamonds than I did. He picked out a perfect 1.67 CARAT diamond ring that was worth about $10,000….(he said) It was his diamond from a business deal and this lady knew it. Sonny told the woman to mount it in a setting and that we would pick it up in a week. She told us the setting would be 400 dollars and that we would need the money to fetch it.

I went to work five days later, then drove over to the Pass to meet Sonny. When I walked into the room, he motioned me to be quiet. He was on the telephone with a woman, he was giggling. I got upset and walked out to the parking lot. He followed me and said, "That was just a dumb model that he and Art had hired for some show." And that "The model was a slut and a whore." Then he yelled at me while asking "Do you want to be a slut or a whore?!!!" Shocked, as I stood there, still. He then went on to say "That her boyfriend was on another extension, and that they were "both" laughing about eating ice cream after working out." (So if her boyfriend was on the other line, why couldn't I speak to them?) Something rang loud! The facts never amounted to the evidence. I still didn't say anything, trained to.

Into night, Sonny and I sat there on his bed in his motel room with Tiny practically in the same room. As Tiny fell asleep, Sonny and I were in the dark. Sonny started to tell me a seemingly contrived story, he started to tear up with…. no emotion. He just started shaking to pull off this achievement. It felt like he was using a sympathy ploy, like an actor crying on cue the way he made two small tears come out of his eyes mechanically, like a special effect. It was amazing. Because I did feel compassion for people in a lesser valued situation than myself, like an ex-con "trying to make it". But with Sonny's call, I had not been taken, he didn't seem real to me.

In the next seven days I DECIDED TO PICK UP THE RING WITHOUT HIM. Sonny had all my cash, which he kept telling me Art was holding…..Musing, I had been informed the diamond ring was worth $10,000 dollars…. In taking the gold bracelet my grandmother had given me so long ago… I went to the pawn shop.. I wasn't going to lose the bracelet, I just took a loan out on it, to raise the 400 dollar mounting fee… which brought me 250 dollars cash hawked, and a 150 dollars that I worked for.

I walked in with the 400 dollars cash and said "Sonny sent me in for the ring." This lady just handed me the gem, and smiled. Never forgetting this woman's face as I picked up the jewelry. Now you would have to imagine a 50 year old woman who always kept poker written all over her, who was now giving me a slight smile just like the Mona Lisa….(I think that she too enjoyed giving me this item, without him, like they two, had some unfinished business… to keep…In later finding, the jeweler switched the stone to one of a lesser value…say 3,500 dollars…..And I didn't know the quality of stones and how to look at them….The diamond was the same size but had a slight white color to it with one major flaw…. I could even see the "lined crack" with my naked eye) But this was Sonny's "friend" and I trusted her…I didn't know that Sonny's friends were all thieves and always out to get someone, even possibly, him.

I took the ring back to the pawn shop and got back my grandmother's gold bracelet which had a lot of sentimental value. I hid the gold. The ring just represented a bunch of lies and part of him. I'll never forget, it was about three or four in the afternoon. I left Sonny a message on his telephone answering machine, which said…."This is Rebecca and I picked up the ring." "As far as my cash goes…""I'll just file small claims papers in court and get back the $5,000." (Because at the time, I had spoken to a friend who told me I could get up to 5 Grand this way…) I REALLY NEEDED HELP, I was living in pain….And grabbing that ring made me feel good…it gave me collateral.. I had a little more control of things…(like equity for remuneration…) He had something of mine, and now, I had something of his. I wasn't married to him so I was going to give him his ring back, for cash…

That night at 7:00pm, Sonny was knocking on my door, telling me that he loved me. "That he and Art had a big fight over me." "Because Art said that I wasn't good enough for him." Sonny said "Art was going to keep my money, now." "And that Sonny was going to try to get it back for me." (As I mused upon the fact that "Art had purchased Sonny a new suit") Here I was, perplexed and angry, still scraping by and feeling obligated as Sonny was telling me that "Art didn't like me" . "Art wanted Sonny with a richer girl that came from a good family". Thus, attributing the manipulation of inadequacy ....that I felt every moment. Sonny said that "Art was mad about the message." "And that Art was a very important man. Now Art wanted my ring." "And he also wanted my grandmother's bracelet", which I wasn't going to give him. I was a very private person keeping my nose clean, working, minding my own business before Sonny came into the picture.

Throughout, Sonny began keeping company with my neighbors in Hollywood, then managed meeting my bosses. There were some girls staying in the building who had been rude to me from time to time. It was strange watching the way women behaved around Sonny as they giggled and squirmed. I noticed his behavior. He had a quiet, calm way about him. His body language read conservative as he would sit there still, sometimes with his arms folded together and his legs apart, watching with privileged information ...he studied psychology and could have discussions on many assorted topics.

Moreover, Sonny decided one day, with his "friendly way of handling people", to take my neighbor, Tina, to the jewelry mart in down town Los Angeles in my car.... Tina was friends with a girl named Susan who lived next door to me. Sonny suggested this right in front of me, in front of her. Perhaps, knowing psychology and my "make-up", he knew, when I had been put on the spot like that right in front of her.... I would be too polite to tell her there was hardly enough gas money, plus, I didn't want to belittle Sonny. I liked Tina but felt she was naive. She was a voluptuous woman of color and she was telling Sonny that afternoon, her father owned two bars and paid for a lot of Tina's bills. Sonny and Tina flirted in front of me as I drove them around on hills with a clutch, feeling uncomfortable intensities. I endured, as they made chit chat in rush hour traffic which was stop...and go. I hated him for it...

Art and Sonny drove around in Art's fancy cars and "worked" all day, as I knew it. They made comments, rude statements like, "The $5,000 thousand wasn't really that much." (Now to a starving man in Africa, a bowl of rice is a lot.) We had hard times considering Sonny wasn't bringing home any money for awhile..... Sonny said, "Art, the boss, was making him, meaning Sonny, pay for it, for being with me, Rebecca Evans. And it was a matter of life and death, with all of this bull shit conspiracy..."

Jealousy links love and hate.

While working on my 1943 ford on the side of the road one afternoon....Sonny started yelling at me, exclaiming "that I was standing there, looking way too sexy with my full body covering work out outfit on", with "My hip cocked!", as he put it, and when your young, and in those days of my early 20's.... I didn't know what to think. I was the target of his misdirected anger.
His animosity. His jealousy.
His stink.

Sonny was beginning to control everything, my paperwork, my so called friends and business associates. He was taking messages for me on the telephone as the disease of codependency progressed, obviously, I wasn't getting all the signals....

SONNY DESCRIBED A SAGA ONCE..(Now knowing it was a manipulation, after checking in with some of his other victims..) About the time he knew me before, when he, "Was rich and helping me out." (As he insinuated quietly) How he, as his "STORY GOES" "sat up on a hillside, with a pair of binoculars.....just to watch me out my back door". With his epic being totally fabricated...... in blind trust I believed that he really needed me. At the time, I didn't have the evidence to show otherwise. And Sonny never gave me his driver's license number or anything on purpose but a telephone beeper number to track him down with....

My instincts were screaming, loudly! And I should have learned how to trust them. But instead I lived with my impaired pledges with men.

Anytime I got out of line with him, when I started asking questions, he would throw me off with some emotionalism.....like slapping my face...and not very hard the first and only time. It was, as if, he did it for some kind of special effect....as he sat there calmly watching my expression, my face, my eyes, like an experiment he was trying to contemplate my reaction, as I calculated his. It was right after I got dependent on him for my safety with his fiction and my sense of oblique binding. He kept telling me, "To let the man of the house, handle everything." In watching my mom, I did carry on this tradition, especially regarding the handling of important matters, but in other personal matters.........it was like, he was setting me up, so that I, would get rid of him. So that he could have an excuse to leave me "Scott Free", and put me off on the money he owed. He wanted me to take responsibility for the break up, so in essence, it would be his fault and he would be blaming me, my instincts were screaming this...

Sonny said that he was proud of me, the way I handled myself at the pawn shop. He said, "Rebecca, you really do know how to take care of yourself".......And I remember thinking, "Fuck You". (If only I had known what his real jail record was.) So as usual, Sonny went with me and met the pawn shop owner....The redemption slip on my jewelry became due. And there Sonny was with the pawn shop owner, telling me I could let it slide a day or two past the notice that said, the pawn shop owner could legally redeem it, as my internal inherent screaming told me not to let them do it. I paid the ticket's interest and got a written receipt anyway, against the guy and Sonny's advice...While walking out, Sonny told me the pawn shop owner had taken that as an insult, but I got my bracelet back. (And I really didn't care what they were thinking.) But Sonny sure made me feel a little low in the process and beneath the "game" of "mankind", he insinuated. (I thought that Sonny and the pawn shop owner were both trying to steal from me. Or that Sonny might have told the pawn shop owner that "Sonny wanted to pay for it, as a birthday present for me...and that Sonny would pick up the gold later, man to man, face to face").

I was working a lot of temp jobs and Sonny used to call me three times a day on average, just to "Check in", (and because of my preconditioning, I wanted to share my life with a man.) But this guy was actually keeping close tabs on me. And right before my very eyes, it was hard for me to watch it. I didn't want to see the truth, the ugliness in another human being, my illusion could not be spurious…. Sonny told me that if I hung in there with him, that things would get better. "The surgery would still come…. and come". And of course, thinking that was what love was all about, sacrificing ….. He let that carrot dangle right before my very eyes, the very one I paid for.

Embellishing Sonny said Art wanted Sonny to go on the road for "family business"…(as he put it..) for about six months and that I wouldn't know where he was…but when he got back, he would have all the money "Art stole"…..I didn't believe Sonny. I was needy and crying, a nervous wreck and bitching all the time because I thought Sonny fabricated. Sonny told me that Art had taken from me because Art was mad at me on the grounds that I had stopped Sonny from doing well…BIG LIE AGAIN…Sonny and Art wanted to have time to con other people…LIKE A CORNELLIA GUESS, who's father had left her a big fortune..(and the boys didn't think that she could handle it..) But instead, I was to find out…..they had to baby sit me, so that I wouldn't go and file small claims court papers and ruin Mr. Con Man's parole job..(If I would have been alone, long enough to think, I might have just done that.) But I screamed a lot, because nothing registered. I SAID "NO" TO THIS REQUEST because I didn't want to be left.. And Sonny didn't want to jeopardize his freedom in my rattling hysteria that he had created to begin with in his illusory double cross. Sonny had to stay with me a whole year so that I wouldn't file legal documents. He didn't go to jail for tax evasion, it wasn't the big guy picking on him after all. Sonny had always picked on people so much smaller than himself and he couldn't get caught doing it, again. Sonny was on probation a whole year and I never knew much about legal terms and criminology…. I was still working, paying the bills for a while. And there con man was, spending all his nights with me, not dispensing time with Art, and he wanted to. He wanted to be with his true love and partner…. emotionally…. and physically… the man he wasn't carousing with anymore…….Sonny started lying around my studio apartment almost whining about missing Art.

Sonny worked as a bouncer in these underground clubs. He had two friends who worked with him, their names were Eddie and Phoenix, who were also ex-felons. Phoenix was also a Playgirl Model who was quite nice to me, and quite a bit flirty. (I wonder if Art put Phoenix up to it?)

Accordingly, Sonny "filled me in on the fact that he had been molested as a child, at age seven, violently by a stepfather's intoxication". Hearing that his mom was around the authority figure and took an interest in direction during the exchange, not the defilement, just supporting the man who did it through the entire after process and psychological ordeal. Sonny told me the name of the brand of beer his step father used to drink and the way it made him feel, RAGE! Towards the smell on someone's breath. Sonny even asked me once if I wanted some of that particular brand one night… as he was working a bouncing job with Eddie and Phoenix…. He told me it made him go crazy, as these people thought of violence as a normal way of life, and it still didn't register in my brain yet. I didn't want to believe that someone would want to hurt me like that. Sonny could have made up this story for sympathy…about holding his puppy when he was young, the one his step dad put to sleep as punishment. But out of all the outrageous stories that Sonny told, this is the one story that makes sense, because it could explain a lot…..But in no way, should this be used as an excuse. Because Sonny's now a man and could have been helped…and…

One night Art came into a club glaring from fifty feet away with an insane look in his eyes that frightened me. He looked vicious, like he was raging on cocaine in a $300 dollar leisure business suit...and 300 pound Tiny by his side, with bright red curly hair, who was pale as a ghost. But I, like Art, was mad at Sonny. I guess we both felt that it was a design on Sonny's part. . So in all those mixed up emotions of insincerity, I felt pretty fused….and messed up, as my instincts were losing...their grip...as I was being played into his scheme of things.

Christmas time came, Sonny acknowledged that Art invited us over to the "bosses" home. Sonny announced that Art had given him, or us, some money for Christmas. It was about five to six hundred bucks. Equally I remember Sonny pulling the money out of his pocket in front of me like I should appreciate the "luck" and "love" of Art...I wasn't buying it, I wanted expulsion from these 2 malefactors....

We drove to the clothing mart in downtown Los Angeles and went shopping. I had been upset for many weeks and I'm sure I was acting like a bitch. And looking back, I'm glad Sonny had to put up with those months of it....and living poor... he deserved it. I thought all the money in his pocket was mine, the way he handled it, with his control about it, HIS LOOKING DOWN ON ME like I didn't know anything.

Sitting in Art's family mansion in Hancock Park, realizing they were living much better than most...... THERE WERE BOXES AND BOXES OF GIFTS ALL AROUND...And I recollect thinking that I had financed this family's Christmas with the help of Sonny, their friend… I bit my tongue. The house was large, two stories with a "stage" in the living room. The outside was brick and looked in good standing with a manicured lawn and round driveway. But when you entered there was no furniture. The dining room table looked sick and the white paint on the walls looked dirty. Sonny informed me it was hard for Art to keep up the mortgage payments. And I thought especially with all these consumer goods sitting around here.

Intentionally hiding their ethnicity, Sonny said that Sonny was Italian, and Art was half Italian.. When in fact, Sonny was really Mexican and Art looked African. I felt sorry for the guys for a moment. I felt every human being should be proud of what their true heritage was. Sonny and his friends didn't like what they were to begin with. Pondering, that their conduct bestowed conflict upon themselves.... and others…

Sam, Art's wife, who had been a big model and was quite beautiful had been wrapping gifts for their spoiled little girl's Christmas. A cute little thing of about 4 who had a castle to live in and lots of things other little kids didn't. Sam asked if I would wrap another gift, as I blurted out "No" in a snappy tone, it just happened. Maybe she felt I was prejudiced because I really didn't know if she was in on the take or not. But the mother fucking truth was, was that I felt that I was being ripped off, white, black or brown, I didn't care who it would have been, I would have been mad at them. I was mad at my real family and I was mad at all of these people too. And in not keeping my cool....as Sonny "instructed" me to....I'm sure it gave someone just the excuse....to trick me...and manipulate me with words...again, and again, and again...Excuses, excuses, excuses....The only problem was, was that I was the only one taking them, time and time again. I should have learned how to stand up for myself at age 29. And not cave into peer pressure... It was as if, I had no value to anyone, but conceivably, one day I would learn to stand up for myself. Finally.

"INTERLOPES AND TURNING POINTS"

Sonny's parole officer came over to my apartment one day as a joint of grass lay on the coffee table right in front of him as Sonny lived off of me those first few months. I was considerably upset that the parole officer of Sonny's couldn't tell me anything to begin with…..especially with privacy issues. But when a felon on probation is staying with someone vulnerable maybe the rules should bend, considerably. Sonny was a good "shrink", with acted gestures of calm, the officer was duped. This particular official had ridiculed a "Big Hippy Movie" I had been in. And "I was the only one Sonny had to stay with. So please don't take away Sonny's freedom because of Rebecca's pot". Unexpectedly, Sonny's parole officer would show up and on one occasion had stopped by when Sonny was driving me and my car out to a location. (I wonder if the parole officer thought the car was a gift from Sonny? I don't think so. I worked two jobs for that thing). And to this day, I don't understand in God's name, with this man knowing Sonny's real history….I don't know what the deal was but this parole officer must have been in on the take or just infatuated with Sonny. Or even as the saying goes, "One of those do-gooders who are conned by con-men". (Believing these men have changed or found God or something). So who knows what this parole officer was, (stupid?) Or was Sonny lying? I wasn't the one with the jail record. No one taught me to think, to ask the right questions or to contemplate hiring a private detective. I felt I was living in non-reality with him. In "Un-Comfortable Fairy Tale Land". As wife beaters come in all shapes and colors, perhaps society is not in a position of protecting.

One early evening when it was still light out, Sonny drove me out to meet one of his sentinel friends for dinner. The prison guard from the penitentiary was clean cut and nice and he definitely liked Sonny. Sonny was a trustee in the year that he spent inside of the reformatory. While we three took a spin with the officer in tow after dinner, Sonny was mentioning a counterfeit ring and busting them.

Inaugurating my car as "his", Sonny was driving my 1943 Ford all over town, (God only knows where), always undermining my good intentions. Sonny told me that he watched as "all the swinging dicks in town were yelling, hey Rebecca!" He told me that "he never saw a woman have such power over men, the way he had over women". There were lots of times Sonny just "snagged Betsy", when I needed "her" for work, in turn, causing tardiness. Sonny was also hanging out with some rude guys, who, after seeing my magazine covers, were asking, "What my tits looked like?"

Sonny was driving my old antique, when he "informed" me that a very important Judge from San Francisco stopped him to make an offer on "Betsy" for 11,000 cash…The man had given Sonny his business card, it looked prominent. I called the number once, Sonny dared me to. Then out of my hand Sonny grabbed and put down the telephone receiver as the man said, "Hello" on the other end in his Judge's Chamber's…

Sonny picked me up from work, two weeks later on a sunny afternoon. He and Eddie were riding shot-gun at 4:40 P.M. Sonny knew I didn't like him having others in the car because it was not insured for passengers. Here Sonny was yelling and screaming at me in front of Eddie... just like before... (in the Arizona winds..) I sat there like a "good" little girl while we dropped Eddie off. Then I had to listen to Sonny tell me how inconsiderate I was for not wanting a felon driving around in my uninsured car for passengers. Later, my insurance agent Jim with State Aim informed me in writing that Sonny's driver's license had been suspended on 11-21-88. My insurance would no longer cover him, so he was now excluded from driving "Old Betsy". He got my mail and casually put it on a shelf, where it was hard to see and away from me. Then took my car anyway. Until I found the letter on a book. Which made him upset that he had to go out and get his own second hand vehicle that didn't look pretty to begin with.

With happy invites, Sonny took me and two of my neighbors, Susan and Steve out to dinner with our "rent money". He invited them loudly, in front of me ... He told Susan at the dinner table, in front of everyone, that he, Sonny, USED SEX APPEAL TO PERSUADE WOMEN into things.... (So I guess in him telling her that, he knew that with his quiet calm expression in "confession", that she would believe that she was special enough for him to tell her the "truth", and that he would never use those tricks on her.... too). As I watched her body language as she pushed her chest out and giggled, and told me, loudly, in front of everyone, "You need more meat up here", then pointed to her breasts...Steve and I just sat there, quietly. After dinner, Sonny invited them into our apartment, into my private territory, expanding it's horizons with women who would walk on me. With Susan getting down on all fours, while raising her voice in a high pitched tone, to get Sonny's attention so that she could show him some back exercises. She was doing dog tricks for Sonny in front of me in my living room, and I didn't like it. As he was contemplating the space and controlling it's occupants. As some of the environ women acted like vultures surrounding meat.

Art and Sonny wanted me to think, and almost had me thinking at the time that Sonny was a prize catch. As Sonny said, "That he'd be back on top of things." (The "honest way", for a "mafia man", like him...) Oh YEA, Oh RIGHT. (I personally thought Sonny was an asshole and I was drowning in ambivalence. If that was what women wanted, then they could have "it"),

---

Sonny and I had been living in my studio apartment until we moved up stairs into a one bedroom. The landlord insisted that the apartment be put in my name. Both Sonny and the land lord knew a lot about business, and unlike Sonny, the landlord was a real man and not a fake one. And you would have to have been born dirt poor to understand this one, to make something out of nothing, that is.... on your own backbone without a lot of support. Sonny would flutter around the landlord, like a kid trying to impress. The landlord saw right through it...

Sonny moved Tiny in downstairs right into my old studio apartment. The place was right in front of the building with windows watching everything. I was angry all the time but felt no way out.

Sonny frightened me one afternoon, with his fists. He came at me violently as I WENT OUT A WINDOW. I was only a hundred and five pounds. The tiny skinny neighbor guy, Joie, next door, heard me and witnessed almost everything. Joie was the type of guy who could never stand up to Sonny.

Prevarication generated in the many folds of the day when Sonny told me he was sterile and that he had never gotten a woman pregnant before. I never longed for children, especially with this man. (As some men fabricate when wanting sex, Sonny was way beyond that....) HE GOT ME WITH CHILD to trap me "into taking the blame", in knowing I wanted other things.. and unfortunately, a child would have made things impossible. I was malnourished and anemic, starving. I never graduated from high school. I didn't have a decent man and would soon learn that he had an extensive jail record. He didn't even want to take care of "me", let alone a bunch of kids. (Musing upon the way my step-dads treated me, knowing that Sonny was 10 times worse! To understand that I would have to live with a man, like him, forever.) I didn't want him reigning over me and this baby, through me. . I didn't want to have any part of this man lingering, eating away at my very soul, all I wanted to do was to get this man out of me! Forever. The only bad thing is, is that I had to make a choice, and an innocent one was the one who had to pay the price for my sins. The abortion was performed quickly, in the first four or five weeks, I hoped that it was only tiny molecules and that the embryo didn't feel any pain...(oh please Lord!)

I felt that I was going down, and down, to hell, with him.

In their shame embedded rendezvous, Sonny went to "visit" and "manipulate" the girl downstairs. The one who was supposed to be my neighbor for a few years now and she still couldn't be polite to me. She sure liked men though. So Sonny and Susan, with the complicated web that we weave....A grown woman who couldn't keep a car, slept until three p.m. everyday and who by way of student loans, had gone to college for ten years going on 15. And she still wasn't qualified to get a decent job in her chosen field with her attention deficient disorder ..She didn't have children, wasn't married, yet she thought she had the right to judge me...and she didn't like me, it was obvious. So perhaps Susan thought that she was helping council Sonny with their "big secret". The one that everybody knew about, the one regarding mine and his problems. As he raped me into getting pregnant in the first place, when he told me that he was sterile..... He probably told Susan that, "Since I, Rebecca, was such a "drug addict", that I aborted to be mean to him", then he probably "watered up". "His unexpected miracle, that could never happen again." (When in fact, I was told later on that Sonny did indeed already have 3 kids that he didn't take care of or even care for.)
(In pondering if Sonny gave Susan gifts too?)
The way he played people..
MANIPULATED specimens
and shaped them..

Sonny didn't have a conscience. Especially with Susan protecting her private excitement, validating his need for approval, her bad boy, who wouldn't be bad to her, too.... The emotions he must have proclaimed in her, speaking of her roots and her African injustice from the past...

Sonny had positioned his support team around me, while all the time telling me Susan, "Really was my friend". Oh, YEA, oh SURE...The one who kept secrets with my lover behind my back... What a girl, what a friend. As I hated trickery and had no one around me I thought I could trust.
I stood on a floor that was crumbling.....

With people judging me so quickly with their preconceived prejudice in this physical world of lust, greed and needed attention... Some women, I'm sure go through the unnecessary consumptions bestowed upon us by our surrounding circumstances. I never thrashed Susan, we had been neighbors for three years. She had a great mom who she didn't appreciate. Her mom was a psychotherapist, and a real good one, as Susan expressed to me her mother's opinion about me being afraid of Sonny.

With life comes an assumption of risks. Mercury collided with Mars and in carrying on with the sons of Satan, I didn't have the power to save him. Comprehending, I was living on a Ball & Chain. Like a dog on a leash that had been uncared for, and the snake, I guess in his gentleness was much more persuasive than I was. Life offers all types of animals and serpents you don't want to meet, or live with….. Sonny must have studied my submissiveness all through this.. I had slept with deception not knowing any better. I was young, dumb, and acting on emotions. And I was just beginning to see what could happen, when you became dependent on a man of immorality. I had been in the wrong hands for too many years. Someone once told me that if you were in an uncomfortable situation...GET OUT OF IT! And they were right. With Sonny, there were so many people coming into my house that didn't seem honorable.

Mentally, I had to sum up the events of the past few months.....Around September, 1989, I received $10,000 dollars for a settlement (that I should have received more on). And there Sonny was, he got my money for me alright, and then, he took it right back again, and "invested it", he said.

Crashing my car was a new situation as Sonny and I argued while I was driving. I was in complete shock and let Sonny take over. We had one of my friend's help drive the car away from the scene, slowly. SONNY HANDLED ALL OF THE PAPER WORK. The other driver was at fault so the damages were to be paid for by their insurance company. I told Sonny to call the police because, again, I was letting the man take care of everything, still. It seemed to take months for Great Franklin Claims Management to come through. My car had a very big dent in it. We were not traveling that fast because I was getting ready to make a right hand turn on to Ventura Boulevard when the other car came up and hit me from my driver's back side, with me in the driver's seat. I got more of the impact than Sonny did. I was going off course, I couldn't see straight. Sonny was getting meaner every second jeopardizing my personal psychology....

Confiding to my established insurance company about the accident. The claim representative for State Aim, Steven, (who was also an X Preacher who had left the faith because he had questions...about things..) helped me out sincerely and took over the paper work from Sonny. He wrote Great Franklin Claims a letter. While I told Sonny to go out and start getting price estimates on the car since everything seemed to be taking so long. The vehicle wasn't going anyplace. So here we were with this cause of getting this little silly car fixed, with these photographic images of dents.

It was April of that year, the month of my birthday.... Sonny informed me one day that the car had been towed into Antonio's Custom Auto Body Shop. Sonny said he knew the owner, Antonio, and that the car would be around $4,000 to $5,000 dollars to fix. I never talked to Antonio up to that point, I only spoke with Sonny. Sonny told me the auto work had already been started and not to worry about it because he and Antonio had "worked out a deal". I said, "Are you sure, because I can not afford it?" Sonny said, "yes, that he and the insurance company would pay for it". Sonny signed all of the repair orders. I didn't know it, but Sonny represented himself as being the owner of my motor- vehicle. Along with the repair work, some restoration work would also be included, all at Sonny's request.

Amid the mess, I was taken to the shop and shown "Betsy". I still hadn't signed any repair order. I saw the car with a $7,000 dollar price tag and got mad at Sonny and left Sonny at Antonio's shop. Walking to the bank with such adrenaline and fury, I walked a mile in 10 minutes. I was standing in the bank, in front of the line, when Sonny walked right up behind me. With in seconds of my arrival he wrapped his arms around me, like a serpent, he engulfed me, as I stood there shaking... others must have mistakenly perceived that, this was what love was all about, (in this "non-threatening" way...of his.) He said, "Don't you ever do that to me again."

The bill kept going up on the car and Sonny kept signing. The last I heard, the auto bill was up to $8,000 dollars. I freaked out and called Antonio half way through the work order and told him to please stop, I can not afford it. Antonio told me that he could not stop the work because Sonny told him to do it. I told Antonio that the car belonged to me, and he still didn't believe me.

"Paramour Sonny" was acting very ugly and remote. One night, he came home to clean up as he threw a big wad of money, it must have been thousands, into the closet right in front of me. I watched him shower and change and run out of my apartment...all in 20 minutes... It was almost as if, it were a test, and I was a dog on a leash with a bone on a shelf in front of me, as he listened in the shower that was only a few feet away ...testing and attending, the starving hound...to see if it would make a move for the food, before it's master went out on the prowl...

Antonio started calling my home for Sonny asking where his money was. Sonny was never available, anymore. I panicked internally but was still keeping some of my composure.... I was still working my temp jobs. Sonny was now working for Art in Vegas on occasion. One time, I went with them.

Steve from State Aim came through for me and gave me a check for $5,000 dollars. I signed it over to Antonio with a memo on the back of the check saying, "cashing this check avoids any lien against 1943 Ford". You see, I learned how to make a contract out of a check a long time ago....

With Sonny not returning calls to Antonio, I had my attorney call the mechanic but he would still not stop work. I was suspicious…..…..My car was still in the shop. I promptly went down to look at it. I discovered another estimate in the glove box with Sonny's name on it, as Antonio told me, that "that was nothing" and just to "put it back into the glove box". In not going any further because I smelt danger all over this place, I did exactly what Antonio told me.

But in the meanwhile I would talk to Antonio on the phone, as Sonny would dodge him. I was stuck in the middle of my car with this Italian Shop Owner and Sonny. Great Franklin claims was not coming through. I started calling Antonio's, demanding my car like a lunatic… Antonio told me that he was putting the pressure on Sonny to pay the remainder of the tab. I then decided, while I was "out of my mind"….and I'm sure that's what Sonny "Fake Tortellini" told Antonio I was, and everyone else for that matter. That I would call Jeffery Knowl, who ended up working for a law firm that specialized in laws relating to cars and the manufacturers of cars. His firm represented the big boys. I didn't know the law before, but I'm glad I found out that under California Civil Code #3068 sub.c, that in order for an auto repair shop to perform over $750 dollars worth of work to a motor vehicle, the shop owner must have the written consent of the owner of that motor vehicle. I could file a complaint with the Bureau of Automotive Repair…and I had the paperwork in my hands. This was now the month of October. Sonny was staying with me on and off…or as the story goes, in Vegas, instead.

Antonio and Sonny worked out a "payment" plan of $500 dollars a week. Antonio told me that I was "stand up" because I had come up with almost $5,000. I THOUGHT, YEA, RIGHT, (give me some more sing along). Antonio told me that he, Antonio was going to make Sonny come up with the rest of the money. I was ready to go to court to stop the "sale", due to the series of events in which Sonny physically started forcing me to let him handle my business.. Second, one of my attorney's was witness to a telephone conversation in which he, the attorney myself and Antonio were discussing the car. In which I told Antonio to stop work, now! Antonio had also mentioned in front of the witness, the attorney that is, (who might have been afraid, himself, as the attorney was also a Judge…and knew the "In Crowd in Law" and who could break laws and "things" "scott free" through corruption), that when Sonny brought in the car, to begin with, Sonny said that the car belonged to him, Sonny, that is. So Sonny lied to Antonio…… PLUS, I HAD MEMOED THE CHECK, the one for $5,000.. MAKING IT A LEGAL CONTRACT, meaning that when Antonio cashed it, he was abiding to the terms on that check, in signing it…. And I didn't want to go to court…(I didn't know if Antonio kept doing work after I told him not to.) But, I told Sonny that if I didn't get my car back in so many days, that "I was going to kill myself and leave a big note and mess for the cops to find out"….as maybe this would get someone's attention, and you know what? It did. I wasn't really going to kill myself, I finally learned how to push his buttons…and he and Art really wanted freedom….And I had threatened their sovereignty. …and was willing to pay the "Ultimate Price for it." (Yea, right…) Like bullshit…There was a big storm ticking. I had pretty much kept my cool during all the panic. Although I was now sick…

Presuming that week, I was actually going to get my car back, and you know what, I did.....in the sweep of an eye...in an inch of a wink.....Antonio called to tell me that on a Friday, Sonny came down and paid the $3,000 in cash, (I later found out that this was actually a woman named Emma's funds who Sonny was now taking out, or "helping out" or whatever.... The money that she had given him, as a gift for me... Emma would tell me this story later on. That she had over heard Sonny and Art talking about my car and the situation with Antonio. Emma didn't think that it was right, she thought she was being compassionate towards me because she thought she had stolen my man.) Poor Emma. This was when she still had $180,000 grand saved from years of hard work... She also shared with me years later, as I suspected, that Sonny was actually planning on having the Judge from San Francisco purchase my car from Antonio for $25,000 bucks..... So the boys would have made a profit, and I had ruined their deal.

Tough luck.

There once was a wishbone in the house that Sonny and
I shared on Grace Street, and one day we broke the wishbone in
two......

AND IT SPLIT RIGHT UP THE MIDDLE..........

And I still have it in luck.........

The day my car came back.... Antonio wanted to "finish" it and keep it over the weekend. I wouldn't let him. I was afraid that he or Sonny would change their minds on Monday.. Or the bill would run up another $3,000 over the weekend. .....So I had the tow man load it...on the spot...with a personal check for $100 dollars paying off the balance in full. The "Boys" also made me sign a piece of paper, (that wasn't legal, due to auto regulation codes.) But the paper said that I wouldn't sue anyone if the engine fell out, half way down the road... The money the Ford was worth gave me power and I wanted that over Sonny. Antonio commented to me, "I had nothing to do with this." As I LAUGHED WICKEDLY out LOUD in front of all of his employees, as everyone just stared at me in the Auto shop's front office...astonishingly, jaws dropped at my outburst..... Then, Antonio helped me up in to the big tow truck with my little, white hat on......me at one hundred pounds.

For $100 dollars out of my own pocket, and a "whole lot of collision"...Jimmy, (another one of my old x-boyfriends) told me that I actually got about $5,000 dollars worth of work done with a $8,000 dollar price tag on it..........

Sonny called me to tell me that "he was proud of me, that now I, Rebecca, really did know how to take care of myself". And that was one of his last insults....as he tried to nuzzle up to me... I just felt that I was way beyond anything normal at that point. There were all the memories fading into the walls...

Steve from State Aim called me on the telephone to inform me that my file was laying out on his desk, when another adjuster walked by and noticed Antonio's name on the file and conveyed a little story, which was...that many years earlier, that same unmentioned adjuster was on another case for a business man... Well story has it that the adjuster went out to talk to Antonio at Antonio's house, because the business man that State Aim represented kept crying that his bill was going up and up...and the business man wasn't signing, and Antonio was threatening a lien sale.... Antonio was always threatening lien sales, maybe even hundreds a year. (The adjusters didn't know if Antonio had someone paid off at the Automotive Bureau...) but anyway, when this adjuster was out at Antonio's house, there were about six men sitting around a coffee table with guns. Antonio told the adjuster that they were all in the olive oil business and many other things....and that the adjuster had better keep his nose out of other people's affairs. So the adjuster did, and I guess the guy lost his auto...

Like so many other grown up people....

Except for me....

The 30 year old kid.

(The one who looked old and tormented by now.)

"TURNING POINT PART ONE"

Discerning there must be some type of compromise going on with Sonny's situation. There con man was, acting like the hot shot, bargaining with all sorts of people, I never met, nor did I want to. He now had his own telephone line, as he spoke to a lot of new friends. There once was a girl who called him, she sounded calm and unrelated in her approach on the telephone with me. She asked if Sonny was home, and as usual, I told her that he wasn't. When Sonny arrived at my apartment later I asked who the woman was, who called. He told me that she was a Dominatrix and what it "exactly was" that this girl's occupation was. I said, "That was sick." He said that this woman and her boyfriend wanted to start a business with Sonny. They wanted Sonny to be their boss. (He always had a story for everything and this one was probably true.) He now had expensive suits, lots of guns and $20,000 dollars worth of jewelry on and it was classy stuff. He was treating me like shit (all the more so, I felt like he was sleeping around, but I hated his treachery even more than that, the way he could sway people so easily with his transport away from the truth.)

Although a couple of men saw right through Sonny, they wouldn't tell me so for years. I wish someone would have explained to me, straight out. (Although most people in my position probably wouldn't have listened, to begin with..) But I would have, being the fact that I never liked liars in the first place with their burdensome particles of baggage. My life had always been an open book, no CAMOUFLAGE. I didn't have kids and I didn't have to put on a "front." While others kept secrets, most people were just trying to protect themselves, (because of the statistics in most situations. With battered women attacking outside rescuers in intense situations that can get people hurt. More police officers are killed in the middle of domestic cases than in the middle of bank robberies. 90 percent of the women in jail are serving time due to retaliation crimes against their abusers. But some of these women will become so dependent on their social myths with these men for survival, and it's hard pretending everyhing is O.K. These women "snap", don't have any decent job skills and they'll do almost anything they can to cover up the façade they live in. (It's like the "good-little-16-year old religious girl who goes to church but doesn't want to confess she's sleeping with the 24 year old neighbor boy who could go to jail for rape). The layers of deceit keep piling up with subconscious denial in the process, sometimes, concluding that women will kill to protect their man, their families meal ticket as a policeman is taking scum bag of in hand-cuffs.) But as a neighbor once said, "I don't think he's on the up and up." To a naive girl like me, what the hell is that supposed to mean? I wished the people around me wouldn't have been so apprehensive in telling me things...
like the Nitty Gritty Gospel.

When Sonny wasn't terrorizing me on Grace Street, he was hanging out with all of his new found friends that I didn't want any part of. He had Eddie, and some other guys, who all hung out at an apartment building as Sonny had a set of keys to the building's weight room. He seemed to know his way around so many things...the things he wanted to, anyway. He even carried guns, now. His other friends were some guy and his girlfriend, named Emma. I never met Emma or her boyfriend, through Sonny's clever manipulation, I'm sure. I was hardly ever around him anymore, he was always "working". I heard Emma was an actress who had a small part in a major movie and who kept herself up at age 40. She was five foot three, a hundred pounds with straight hair down her back. (She looked just like Sonny's mother). AND AS THE STORY GOES OUT OF SONNY'S LYING MOUTH....That "Emma lived with her boyfriend who beat her up all the time and stole her white Firebird". Sonny had this way of giving you the ground work for a con in one of his little Italian fables that he told, in really wanting to be Italian.. As poor Emma needed advise, and Sonny was going to help her, as his imaginative goes...and goes...and goes.

Sonny brought over what looked like this big formidable "Professional" pharmaceutical vile of some liquid drug, (that my instincts told me Sonny or someone else had stole.....) It looked like it had come from a lab or a government facility. I never saw anything like it anywhere. Sonny told me that he and Art were distributing the stuff for some "big guys" that they had met out at the airport. He asked me if I wanted some, and "No", was all I said. I told him to "try some first" and he faked sniffing the fumes.....then he left right away, looking shaky... like he must have gotten a partial whiff and couldn't do "much" after that....(Maybe he was trying to kill me, and make things look like an overdose....with no bruise....) For there are some names I should not have and some facts I choose to forget. Sonny was a pawn for many, many things. He also used others as covers... a masquerade ...and he probably just blew my cash from before on new suits and indecency.

He was setting up some show programming ideas with this woman producer from "Sharp Copy" and flirting with her in front of me on the telephone, degrading me constantly, he was driving me crazy with all of his innuendos and insights...

Nothing was registering...

With emotional insanity creeping in...

Fading into the walls around me....

Buddy Boys were having a good time. They started working for a very rich lavish Hollywood widow. She was a black slender woman, age 45, who at formal dinner parties chew food with her mouth wide open, as the boys made fun of her. I was so sick of his business, I didn't want to know anything about his affairs anymore. They were all going to Vegas for shows. Sonny was driving a fancy car now, that Sonny said belonged to the widow. She let him drive it. Sonny offered me a well paying job to work with them and I turned it down because it was corrupt. He told me that another girl had taken the position and I was glad. I wanted my life back... my innocent heart...and not this bitterness. I thought he was scum. I knew this job had to be similar to the one Sonny told me about. He informed me about a receptionist that he and Art had placed in some mobster's porno place.....so that Art and Sonny could "collect messages"....(it sounded pretty scary and dangerous...especially if some naive young girl got caught, unexpectedly.)

Lying Sonny was now "going to work in Vegas for the weekends" for "Family" business. (Which was a big lie again, he was spending his weekends with Emma, the stripper, who he ended up with for awhile…. then he ended setting her up. And I wouldn't find out about it until two years later.) To think, when Sonny took me over to their place on occasion, I was probably visiting her building at the very same time Emma was in it. All of Sonny's friends knew what was going on, except for me. They all thought that I was the one, holding Sonny down…with the "honorable bull shit mafia men stories" he told them. And with myself enduring comments made from everyone of them.

I didn't know the Widow but I did know her name. She left her number on my telephone answering machine, very late one evening. Sonny hated it, the 4 times I called there. All I had was a beeper number on Sonny

Sonny was bringing home all kinds of expensive stuff, "GIFTS", as they were called. Things I didn't want any part of. Something just didn't feel right about it. He told me the items were from the widow. Sonny had taken everything pure, that I had worked for, the hard way, the things that I was proud of, out of my life, and had given me shit instead. I hated it, I wanted it out, I wanted him out. He had threatened me in private, behind closed doors and had held loaded guns to my head. And since he wasn't living with me full time, anymore, I told him, I wanted the stuff out of my apartment.

Sonny brought home some porno movies, (I thought), one day, because I didn't have a VCR, and there was no way for me to see them. And they were of no interest to me, I wasn't into "men's stuff"…. my self esteem was so low, with everyone believing in him, and not in the truth, or myself even believing in myself, anymore. I was beginning to question my own ability, I didn't feel sexy, I didn't feel alive. Sonny was just beginning to use and abuse me in bed, I'm sure I looked 40 at age 30.

Sonny loaned, as he called them, "these little Bondage and Discipline movies" that he wanted to "Share, man to man with Joie", the next door neighbor who was girl crazy and girlfriendless. As we all met out on our front porch that we all shared in the apartment complex…….Joie had returned the movies with in two days, though, telling Sonny he couldn't watch them. And that was all I knew….Sonny had his own way of communicating with people behind my back. (The boys had something in common to the effect that they had both been in jail or prison…)

Before Sonny left, he had to give me a reminder of his depravity.. He lost his keys and I couldn't open the door because I was in the shower, so…. One Tuesday morning Sonny crawled in through the window as I stood there yelling and screaming, frozen in terror that drifted into sensory deprivation. He crawled in, in seconds and wrapped his arms around me, right in the middle of broad daylight. He grabbed me and pulled me through our dwelling and slug me hard into the bedroom wall, then he twisted and held me down…and then with all of his strength and all of his might, he raped me from behind as he held me still on all fours as I cried loudly for someone to help. (The landlord wasn't home, or he would have heard. .. Sonny always had a way of planning his attacks so ingeniously..) As he was raping me, he laughed the whole time, I cried.

I wondered if the neighbor girl Susan heard any of this?

Now take it, this was back in the days before some of the laws had changed and judicial procedures gave criminals more protective rights, than what were given to victims in domestic violence cases. Men could do things to their wives, that they couldn't do to complete strangers with out facing the issue of serious consequence…and I was living in hysteria being attached to a man like him, a man who found pleasure in watching his loved ones suffer through destroying the things they loved and treasured, by breaking one's spirit, the way he did mine, that day. Having any child of his would have been insanity for everyone involved…. The two children I would have shared with him, in my opinion at the time, unfortunately, had to be stomped out. Unfortunately, just like they didn't mean anything….the guilt….the transgression….But everyone who really comprehended Sonny , said what I did, was best, no matter what their religion was. Sonny thought that child abuse was normal living because of his mother's treatment of his case. (And what were the probabilities of my children being molested in his hands before they were 7? How would they have suffered here? Would they have turned out just like him?)

I've become a recluse with my own obsessive indiscretion for years. Trying to examine this aspect of my life. Being afraid of repeating the same mistake, again and again. At the time of my second abortion I wanted my baby to go to a better place, I wanted God to take it back! I understand I don't have the right to judge. I AM NOT TRYING TO JUSTIFY THIS…….. in feeling so inadequate as a woman. Wondering, how will I ever get over this? In comatose thought, Sonny frightened me, and petrified me for the little one…the one who couldn't escape "us". The electrons had been damaged. In my isolation with no one to help me, but him. My foothold had shattered and I thought that I was losing my own bearings, thinking I couldn't trust my own instincts because I had followed the voices of men…… After laying there, crying a couple of minutes, I had a thought, and it was just like he knew it…. I went into the bathroom after the attack, while he just lay there in bed. I wanted to collect evidence in a bathroom tissue… I was bleeding from behind as he came up like a viper. I was about to sit down on the toilet, but he moved right into the lavatory and kept an eye on me throwing the tissue down the bowl. He was breathing on me, standing 6 feet tall in front of me, and three inches near me… Before he left…he grabbed all the sheets off the bed and put them in a plastic bag. He said, "If I didn't watch it, that he'd fuck the neighbor girl, Susan, in there, to get back at me for being a bitch." (I hated him…)

Later on, indeed I did find out, Susan was listening and thought that everything was "O.K". Susan had such a screwed up perception and focus on all of this.

Sonny last volunteered, "That if I ever went to the police, that one of my nephews wouldn't make it home from school one day", in a calm even tone. While screaming, this scared me. He knew where they lived. He had gotten their social security numbers from me. It was my fault. I had to take responsibility. In the beginning of our relationship, he told me when I was still trusting and naïve, before the "investment". "That he was setting up a trust fund for the kids…and he wanted to make sure that they would get all the proceeds…..."and not the mean, evil widow who set him up"………And me, in all my self made greediness, convinced my poor little sister to give up the numbers to him on the telephone. I think that Sonny gave this information to an attorney named Harley and I still have his number and some of the attorney's contacts, so I'm sure I could track him down. Looking through Sonny's history by way of county records and expert opinion that I finally trusted. Being so angry at myself for playing God with unborn children and being stupid!

Sonny and Art were also, so bad at keeping up with paperwork and bill payments...They kept losing what they made because the "High Rollers" kept rolling it away...and were too lazy to play secretary. There I was, around all my new found "Family" and friends. Sonny told me I could never go to the police with the "Mafia" around. (And God, we all know how afraid of the "Mafia" we are..... I wouldn't even go out with a guy with a half a million bucks on the run from them, who wanted to marry me.) And probably just for cover... in using my name for hotel registers........

Sonny would have many problems to score.

My legs and stomach would be black and blue for weeks after this. The back of my thighs would have large hand prints embedded in hues of darkness over my pale frame. God help me, I have stayed here in the very same apartment for years. People know where to find me, no one ever has to go looking for me, through my family.. And because of this mistake....I haven't participated in the real world for awhile. I've sat here in my own guilt and humility. Other people have sacrificed so much more than I have and in the many folds of the hours of the day...I am no greater than the men who hurt me..

I hope to God that I will never have to go to battle with Sonny. Praying nothing comes my way, or to my house.

No contentions I may have to conquer.....

And I swear to god I will fucking have to win them...or kill him. Then I will probably go to jail...or I'll pay someone to kill Sonny, and now I know people... Now I have Sonny's driver's license number and his social security numbers which I got from another one of Sonny's victims. And child molesters and the killers of innocent ones, are not looked up to in prison. And everyone will know what he did and what he is responsible for. So how could he be his "fabulous, mafia self" a "man of honor".......and so on..... and so on...and so on......and we can all go to hell.......together...on earth....

And God, forgive me.....and hold the little ones....safe..

so that we don't have to....

Sonny still had the keys to the apartment we shared..

I changed the locks.

Sonny never got my keys from me again.

That was the danger of living with someone else, who lives in other "frenzies" or inside "sphinxes" or "spheres" as you would or might call them....for the Bible said there would be men born into this world with no conscience.

And I had one living with me, for awhile..

Equally, the demons had been released into society and we were subsisting among them.

As no wind blew through this house for years.

The day after Sonny raped me, Susan was waiting in the courtyard of the apartment building, watching my doorway. In retrospect, she was stalking me from downstairs on her front porch. She ran up to "meet" me on my staircase, (the one she had no business being on in the first place.) She got right in my face, and told me "Not to go to the police." (That was the first thing that came out of her mouth without me saying a word.) Her next statement hurt me the most), "I'd believe him, before I'd believe you." (She was seizing upon me, as I sat alone in my unit after the attack from Sonny. My identity as a human being was beginning to diminish, humanity left me with a lack of regard in a hostile environment.) Susan then said "Don't play the victim." I never said a thing about the attack to Susan. Musing, Sonny's last words, his last breaths upon me. I didn't know how to handle people like Susan or Sonny. I stood there incoherently muttering something under my breath, I couldn't speak straight. Then Susan said, after a few minutes of staring me down as I stood there, fearful, "You're on drugs, you'll never know what your talking about." This really had me off kilter. I never even talked to Susan about the rape. Sonny must have gone downstairs right after. I couldn't even call my mother and talk to her. (I tried to call her two years earlier, but she had hung up on me telling me not to call her because it bothered her husband. Rick didn't like me). I was walking around dazed, and couldn't say anything. I couldn't think! I had no one around. This neighbor, I now know was a bitch. She never should have stuck her nose into the middle of a domestic problem in the first place. Anyone with a better up-bringing would have almost slapped her face or called the police on her.... Sonny's particles had parted me in many directions...and... in the days to come, I would have to listen to Susan's remarks. My neighbor, I would soon find, reminded me of my past. This Karmic familiar connection hurt me, still. I was in shock and was barely waking up to the fact and disbelief of having women and others believe in con men over me. Being too emotional, in my lack of logic and good communication skills, I now know this had me off balance before I knew any better.

Susan had studied psychology and she must have hated me. But I also know that Susan used alcohol on a daily basis...and received many "handouts" from the government. But, as she would say.... (in the months to come...)"You should thank God, for what he's given you." "He gave you your car and everything else." (No he didn't!) So what a sense of power she must have felt, hurting someone like me, (her "competition" for Sonny). As, there are women like this and I wonder if she would have cared to have seen him with others...in the process of his ENTANGLED DUPLICITY. Maybe, both she and I had given away our notions....And I wonder if she was the type, who thought that she was going to win Sonny "back again", and that I was the evil one, keeping them apart, (the real bitch that she was, that is). In being convinced this is where the "Split" in my sanity was beginning to take place...in explaining some key psychology here......

There is a romantic illusion of staying with someone who has had a very rough life, and then has become a self made man. Which Sonny wasn't, I just didn't know it at the time. And the fantasy of saving him...giving him a "softer" side to life...There is some information I should give you right now. I read it in a book just a month after Sonny left me. I still can't remember the title, but the topic was, "Inmates, and the women who love them".

Absorbing, most women in this position, are normally the type of people who would pick up a lost hurt bird to rescue it. Now, there is nothing wrong with this, but these women are not fully educated to the facts of the personality traits contained in these types of men and their abuse of power. Some of these women's backgrounds as children, show, they probably had fathers who showed no kind of decent love for them. So they, as women, were brought up in patterns, which they repeat again and again and again, until they overcome thinking that this is normal behavior with men. Delusional in their assumptions that they can change the broken winged "boy" and redeem his soul in some way, thus, giving her a fake sense of power in a mythical sense. Most of these men have no conscience to begin with and are fully aware of their manipulations and use these women as conveniences.....with charm, manners, and muscle.... people are swayed.

Sometimes these men have many women they are stringing along...And if you really feel sorry for little boy "lost", because of the fable he tells you....... he can manipulate you. BECAUSE EMOTIONS ARE NOT LOGICAL. . These women think they feel needed by these men, thus, giving them power in the fact that they are necessary. And as managed deviation goes........She helps him out in some way, say like, "Can I borrow you car?", (to use in a crime.) She just doesn't know about it at the time, because no one told her that part. And again, if she helps this poor guy out, it may redeem her soul...she thinks...You should try to meet some of the other women these casanovas hang out with, and see what's really going on, in reality land....that is… not his words....

Lonely women express subtle mannerisms that these con-men mentally "Hone in" to... And when a person becomes vulnerable, they become gullible to these con's tactics. The swindler usually presents the story about something that's supposed to be too good to be true. Notice that when you have a handsome killer in the media, some women come out of the woodwork writing love letters.....As the cheater always has an excuse for his bad deeds. Almost every inmate in jail has found "God" (as an "act" for his parole officer,) but no one makes their child support payments before buying alcohol and drugs... With controlling communications with all his stories, he was framed, or taking the fall for someone else, and that it's an honor and a respect thing (but it's a lie). In this unbalanced world with innuendoes and scare tactics which bring heightened emotional intensities, leaving a very dysfunctional relationship going on in the fact that he is trying to control a disturbed woman and she thinks she has the power to save a con.

It is said that the devil is, or was the most beautiful angel in Heaven, who had fallen from grace....he was so beautiful, that he had seduced Eve in the Garden of Eden with charm and it wasn't an apple that she ate.

Again, every situation is different...some women are excited by evil. Or they are into bad boys, and you cannot be a good girl, if you like bad boys, because bad boys make you do bad things, like lie for them.

There are a few women who write to, and fall in love with inmates. Some women are attracted to a sick kind of power and live vicariously through these men. Other women think that if they can control a killer, that that is the ultimate deposition because these men have taken life. Maybe she has the ability to always sooth him through her being there for him, her beauty, her ego, her charm as a woman can save him. (Because she is the most exceptional lady on this planet and will always be.) Forever and forever, till death do us ... part? Right? Wrong.. (I don't think so.......) Because...

CON MEN ARE OPPORTUNISTS AND MANIPULATORS. And sometimes you get master manipulators. Some of these men are so good, they will have your friends and neighbors believing that you're on drugs, or crazy, or that everything was your fault and he was just trying to save you. This is a way of life for these men. And as long as you have emotionally naive women, you will have dames flocking to these pathological liars with great performances. These women enable these men to do things, they otherwise would not have been able to do............

So in those naive fucked up psychological assumptions,

ALL A CON MAN DID WAS COST ME

a lot.

Perhaps there was a reason why all of these things were piling up and I was getting mixed up in them....so help me walk into this, as these are the people that lay in bed at night, thinking about how good they are and how far they have come, to have swayed the world so far.....the way they have, the way they made it work....

I never wanted to be attached to someone like Sonny. I felt he was possibly a child molester and I would have had no way to protect my children down here on earth with him... I know that when a victim, say a child is raped....and he or she knows in god's name what has happened. But, let's say, what you have, is a mother or a father figure who steps in...and because the perpetrator is say, a family member, a provider, or a "trusted one", the dominant one with the power of responsibility over the child, the one the child looks up to, the child's guiding life force, it's "god"... tells the child that what the child saw, was actually wrong...."your reality does not exist!" Is what the child is told in essence.....

Since the reactions of victims are different than the reactions of well balanced individuals, especially strong men, or women who have never been victimized before. Victims mannerisms lack confidence, so the shaky pattern that I resembled was considered condemned error. Since I was so used to taking the blame to begin with, this mental monologue created, "What you think, you are." … I was… an emotional wreck, and just because someone is emotionally, "out of their mind" does not mean, they're not telling you the truth.

It's not until you lose your ego completely.....

Completely.......

That you can learn, not to hide behind it.

And as...love fails sometimes, for seven years after that event, I didn't try to look pretty anymore.

So I quit doing my hair and make-up.

Sonny had the best mind ripping techniques to "Rip anyone a new asshole", as he would say, and then delight with a laugh in the process. He had twisted my shape, my innocence, and had an orgasm in it.

Vaguely...

In my subdued mode of suppression, I never once complained or said one bad word about the babies that were never to be born. And if Sonny never wanted me to get the abortions in the first place, (as he controlled my every move...) He never would have driven me down to the abortion clinic...twice...

———————————————————

"TURNING POINT PART TWO"

By this time I could see that Sonny and Art were playing games...in my secluded place of watching departed spirits run rapid through things, I called the widow and told her what they were up to, and what they were doing to me, and how she should watch them too. She laughed. I guess Sonny and Art had already "told" her about me, that I was crazy, and I was on drugs. (but actually, Art and Sonny experimented with heavy libations..) . So anyway, in the boy's tales to the widow, they had manipulated me into the felon...and "they were helping me out. Rebecca was Sonny's jealous x-lover." "The one who he lived with for a year." "The "one" he aided". "That I, Rebecca would say anything, because he wanted....away from me".

The inflections in her voice tone conveyed that she wasn't going to believe me..... I gave up, trying to tell her things in that one telephone conversation that afternoon, perceiving the complexity of the situation. I then, "Thanked her for all the nice gifts that she had given me and Sonny". Hearing her "GASP" was all I needed to detect and recognize she finally believed me. We hung up.

I screamed and yelled and called mother fucker 30 times in one fucking week!!! I had no one around to support me, and I was beginning to lose it. I kept telling him on his pager, time and time again...."to get all this fucking crap out of my apartment" and to "give her shit back!!!" In still being "voiceless" enough to believe that he would. I didn't know where the stuff went, but he moved it out.. I tried to call the widow once again, and someone else picked up the phone, who wouldn't put me through to her. (It must have been the new girl hired by Sonny..)

After leaving those 30 something phone calls, I finally got through to Sonny. On my break at 10:00 AM, he told me that he played my messages for his probation officer. I stood there on an employee telephone at some X-Pop Star's Production Company's facilities that I was getting up for at 5:00 A.M. and taking two buses to the beach in the mornings. It was for a job way out there in the middle of distance and a two hour bus ride…trying to make a big come back ….still living in my old ways.. in disbelief... after Sonny.

In a light happy tone, Sonny informed me on the telephone that he and his probation officer decided that if I kept calling, that he, Sonny was going to file harassment charges on me and I just had it. All rules had changed and he had changed them. This contradiction of his gave me justice in going to the police myself. He was calm, and cool, he really meant it. I could feel him smiling through the receiver, as I had enough. I said, "Go ahead, that will be real interesting coming from someone like you." Something in me just snapped, and in that one instant I wasn't afraid anymore, until I found out more information. ..later on…..(But in that second, I was beginning to get as mean as he was.)
He just went silent.

Lurking Sonny still dropped in sometimes on his surprise visits before we got the gates up and the screen doors on.... On this "visit" Sonny was mad. He and Art wanted to know what I told the lady........(As I thought "Big fucking deal")...Now this widow was beginning to catch on, too, but she, like I, was still too afraid to do anything.

While checking into matters, I found out by calling my bank that the money orders I had given to Sonny for the "transaction" with the "doctor" were actually cashed by Tiny, the 300 pound slug who lived downstairs.

Sonny told me that when he got through with me, "That I would never want to get close to another human being again." While musing, when he was still with me, in my conditioned clinging I even begged him to stay once. Being so ashamed of myself for some of the things I did with him, in being so incoherent, I had believed completely in the power of man.

In a flash,

I realize...

I got clarity and knowledge.

and grew up.

One of Sonny and Art's attorneys made the headlines of the local news. Their legal council was going to prison for fraud. One of their attorneys many businesses was going into blind senior citizen's homes, befriending them for months, and while doing so, would get one of "his associates construction companies" (like Sonny's) "working on a roof or whatever needed fixing…" Then, get the old timer who was blind and totally unaware of the situation, sign documents regarding deeds, trust and payment…..

I needed money. I had to make a living for myself again in a much higher priced apartment. On a Sunday I once played clean-up lady for Tiny's abominable place. The landlord remunerated me with $50 dollars…(lowering to my self esteem) Right in the middle of the scum and everything, Sonny called me six times that Sunday, I guess he was in a panic.....and I missed the calls, being elsewhere in the complex...Sonny came bashing in through the courtyard, demanding that I let him into the apartment to pick up some things… Within seconds he went straight up-stairs to my residence to where he had hidden or put his "porno movies". The ones I had forgotten all about...all eight of them.

As Sonny ran out the door, he said that he was going to make a profit off the sale of "these little films"... I didn't get what he meant at the time, because I never saw any footage or anything.

Furthermore, two months later when I was talking to Joie, long distance on the telephone, who used to be my next door neighbor and who had finally moved out of state.... Joie said to me, that it was devastating...and..."Didn't you know what was on those videos?" I said, "no." He then told me that it was snuff and that those girls were really dying... Joie said that in the films they would tie girls up to stairwells, suspended, all arms and legs extended. These girls were real young, possibly runaways. Men would walk in frame with hoods on and start punching victims to the point where teeth were flying out, these girls were screaming and it was real! In hearing this story from Joie's lips…plus more...I was shaking as my tremors paralyzed me, I couldn't stand up..... Joie described images that made my flesh creep....and tear...it kept me awake nights... for weeks...months...When I finally dozed, for the first time in years, since childhood, I had nightmares. I would fall to sleep, beginning to dream and start flailing my arms in the air...to get men off me. Realizing, probably the reason Joie didn't tell me when I had the evidence in hand and could have done something about it was the fact he didn't want to get involved with a psychopath and a co-dependent. The antagonists and saboteurs were impairing me....

When I did talk to Sonny about "My conversation with Joie" a couple of weeks down the road, (we kept in contact for six months...until I changed my number to wean the serial psychopath of me, slowly, that is in my invented psychological "Bore out" that kept me talking in mono-tones, killing my emotional responses.....so that he wouldn't know... that I knew anything. I wasn't expecting the truth from him, I just wanted to see what he would "give me"). The only response that Sonny had to this comment I made about my talk with Joe was, "Joie's on drugs." And I knew well enough alone, to let sleeping dogs sleep, alone. I was now very sick... he had gotten inside of me, and I had gotten inside his mess....

I was startled.......
and on another tail spin........
In all this mixed up Karma ....

And….

As I sit here I feel the rushing through my veins to my heart…

Running…

Yes, I still must be afraid of him, somehow…

And…

As I sit here, I feel the rushing through my veins to my heart running through me…

Pounding…..

There was a noise which sounded strange outside my apartment one evening, with voices whispering, then, an apartment door closing. Susan, my neighbor was home, in addition to that, there was also an empty apartment unit right underneath mine and right next door to hers. Susan's lights and music were going…..softly….. I stood out on my front porch balcony where I could see everything below me, observing Sonny as he moved five feet beneath me, off her front porch after he exited, and as he "ducked" into tall hedges, thinking maybe, I didn't see him. He had on his tight, muscle man T shirt ..and something told me not to look any further… to shut up. (Not to make a scene the way I did with Jay so long ago, in the schoolyard..)

As an emotional nervous breakdown propelled me into this. Lunacy arranged the day. Watching the cycles of duplicated or repackaged relationships....as people floated into our lives that remind us of our pasts... The players have just changed "lots"...or....faces and ...Susan reminded me of my mom....and in some way, with some of the comments that she made, I reminded her, of hers, the mom she didn't appreciate. With Susan's inaccurate assessment, why was she so ashamed to admit that bad boy had been in her apartment? Because his comments kept coming from her....She actually accused me of stealing from her... the salt and pepper shakers he brought home for me from one of his "trips"..... were actually hers.... I never got mad because they were meeting behind closed doors, it was just the behavior associated with it. I tried to ignore Susan and her friends, (she seemed to have so much time on her hands to hang out with the other tenants and everyone...)

Smiling at me, on occasion, Susan informed me that "I was the one...who was jealous of her". (Like this brought her pleasure to have someone hate her). I just sat there on the step as she stood prancing. All I said was, "You have nothing that I want, so why should I be jealous of You?" Then I went on to say that if "Sonny was ever going to get back at me, that he would use her, to do it," (as I looked her up and down.) Her jaw just dropped and her expression got real sad. Maybe Sonny appealed to Susan with a "Black Power Statement" that he used when he was around her. Because behind her back, Sonny was always using the word "Nigger". And with all of those bad things going on, it definitely hurt me and everyone around us......

As the neighbors got in the way of my doorsteps, Susan instigated trouble and hearsay with her violent pride that she felt she was entitled to... So in the years that followed I would not only be accused of stealing from other tenants but also be blamed for calling the police on everyone. (It would take me along time to realize that the woman on my front door step was a perpetrator and a chronic liar.) And I could never have true happiness in this building but it would contain me like a prison. As her rumors spread, the viciousness began a cycle, which I hid from in work. (I had no idea, that what this woman was doing to me, was wrong.) I didn't have time or even know how to analyze it, it felt so familiar to me. Susan and most of the other people here had someone to fall back on financially while everyone that I knew leaned on me. Perhaps Susan thought that the only way she could save her virtue was to make me out the "liar". As she reminded me of one of those hypocritical Christian Fundamentalist who should have read St. Matthew...

Emboldened Susan was bragging to the landlord that she had once helped the Middle Eastern guys, (who lived here) steal and hide a motorcycle from some woman in our backyard. She was laughing about it. This bitch really got off watching women get hurt. I was very numb when OJ Simpson got off on his murder trial, I almost expected it with the legal council presented. But it was more shocking for me to see Susan and her friends and the landlord all cheering and applauding the verdict. The situation made me feel like a spectacle. Johnny Cochran in the Trial of 1995 in Los Angeles fed off the Political Climate of the jurors at the time, right after the Rodney King beating. And with evangelistic causes that appealed to people in an infatuation of the moment, in justifying what they really wanted, by living in denial. In falling for things.....people just seemed to feed off the excitement of violence and drama, mine, his.....and with short memory spans of forgiveness of sins gone past.......people just needed something to entertain them, an idol called man for dramas of inspiration and escapism. And as some human beings were really shallow this way..... In all the harshness, these people were not at a level I wanted to be at. But, when that was all I surrounded myself with, (by paying low rent so that I could be, somewhat independent). It would have startling consequences in the years to come. With myself not realizing that I was appeasing my enemies, and that these people, (like my family) were actually violent towards me and other women. They might have been jealous of me because I was the poor girl who had bucked their system....in making something out of nothing. But I still couldn't understand why I didn't feel secure enough to leave this place...I had gotten so used to living like this....and change is a scary thing.

As some dogs pick, when you are down...as they wish big, and

play small, digging ...around....

...Perhaps.....

We women let ourselves go... by...

Following the voices of men.

As I sit here, I feel the rushing through my veins to my heart...

Running...

(Yes, I still must be afraid of him somehow.)

And...

As I sit here I feel the rushing through my veins to my heart

Running....... .

Because I had to live here and I didn't want to run away from things again.... with...

THE SHIFTING OF MIND MOLECULES.....

I was standing ten minutes away from a nervous breakdown...

Sonny and Tiny moved out of the building. But I still felt under surveillance, with Sonny making so many new friends in the neighborhood.

Ten weeks after Sonny moved out, he drove right by me and stopped in a driveway 25 feet in front of me. He was in Emma's white Firebird and I did not recognize him, not even for a moment.... (In a glimpse of mental confusion..... I had forgotten so much of the past and had ...tried to move on.) He stared right back at me, with a key card in his hand extending out the driver's window. It was a gate opener to a huge apartment building .....like he lived four blocks away from me on Yucca and Wilcox... I gazed in disbelief... not really knowing him... ....in serious shock... I couldn't recognize faces... For...

Some mysterious power put these men into my life for a reason, to make me learn. Maybe I had been manipulated for egotistical reasons. Sometimes, I had these handsome men, and sometimes, I lost them, but this one was good riddance. Still being confused back then.... I thought I loved Sonny, I must have..... And it was much too dangerous for me to get involved with him, ever again, in this life.

It was the third month of the year
And I had been born in the year of the cat.

─────────────────────────────────

(Also years later, Susan would touch me in a dare with her fingertip on the sidewalk, quietly. Within a week she had lost every hair on her head by way of cancer in the form of a tumor which had her belly exploding and looking pregnant.)

"ROMAN NUMERAL III"

Turning Point

I had been swindled and shamed....

I should have joined another faith...

It might have given me a whole new outlook, on life...

Because I had based myself...... on a lie.

On the preconceived idea's of man, and the traditions of them.......

So where were the one verse Charlies? The ones who could never give you the Chapter or the Book to which the Verse was found in......The verse, that they repeat again and again....... and, who apply that one, singular verse to every given situation instead of looking at that particular situation in which the verse is given ...

Existing throughout with the compelling circumstances that I still followed the traditions of man and the ones I had around me, cost me.   I tried to go out for another modeling audition. Apprehending the building that I was walking into, a structure that also housed a recording studio that once "belonged to Sonny", the muscle man told me, in his "earlier days of glory"

While waiting out in the hallway and waiting for this photographer to show...because I was early.... in walked these two guys......one named Phil and one named Dave who worked for Phil... Phil said, "if I wanted to, that I could wait in his recording studio until my appointment showed." I took him up on his invitation, and you know what? it's a small, small world... as I walk into my past..... I sat down on a high stool...and it was hard for me to keep my balance...(.... knowing)... for when I sat down there, I said, "Oh, this is the recording studio that Sonny used to own." Phil sat down beside me and said, "How do you know Sonny?" I said, "I was married to him"... (I lied, because Sonny and I always told everyone in business that we were married.... it was programmed in me.... Sonny said it made things look better for us, and it kept women off of him. Concluding, that Sonny had taken me into his world, and I was beginning to be like him...a little bit....) Phil sat down next to me, his face dropped in shock and sadness. He said, "Are you O.K.?" And I still didn't quite get it, that I was in the middle of a nervous breakdown............(they push you to the breaking point and then they push you again, and again...it's like...they enjoy...seeing you gash and splinter......)

After I met with the photographer.... I was walking out of the facility. Phil met me in the hallway and said, "I want you to meet someone".   I walked into his office, and there was a woman of about 44 years old... Kim was her name......she was the Kim Sonny told me about... the "evil widow", the "prostitute he lived with" the onc "that was sleeping on HIS couch". The lies that he had spread with that smooth forked tongue....of his....about her...were all fables.... she was the one of sincerity.... It was her home in Hancock Park that her late husband left her. Learning the real reason Sonny went to jail in the first place, it was for grand theft by deception, Kim had been the victim. In giving me the truth she helped save my sanity that day...a wee bit...but it hit like an earthquake...and it shook me and in shattering a layer that was part of me... through "him".....by proving to me, that all my instincts were correct.... Decisively.... knowing that.. clarity was now in my perception, my grasp.... were the very same things that she had bore witness to, too. And in some understanding ......the layers were muffled up, again and again... Nevertheless, my mental images were not a myth...…...my perceptions of reality were truth...(equally as frightening is when you first find out that you based yourself on a lie.) For it's better to find precision, instead of losing reason. I had been manipulated by my emotions and I was losing control of them. (In the next two months, I was going to be a basket case, and I still couldn't speak straight...) So in the meantime, I just looked at the liars and wondered why they exaggerated ...and distorted things.....as everybody had always wanted something from me...and I had nothing left to give them...

and in those moments....

It's not until you lose your ego completely...

Completely...

That you can learn, not to hide behind it.....

In the days that followed….

Kim informed me there was a friend she wanted me to meet. The gentleman was a Fed who knew Sonny's past history. Sonny was involved in much bigger things, that I, wasn't formally aware of. Myself being so diminutive in Sonny's world now, which I had been for some time, now ... I wanted to know the truth....to see how badly I had been manipulated in the illusion that corrupted me. As the glass menagerie got muddy, it clouded up in lies..... I had gotten inside his head, to hammer him...watched him for a year, closely...on the inside....and it had ripped me apart and given me a nervous breakdown....because in the past, I never fared well in relationships. I think I saw what it did to my mom and how it frightened me.....

the way a man could engulf your soul..

like that...

And sometimes deceive you, as Sonny pitted so many people against me in defamation. And the ones who were supportive, he kept at bay......So...(as I slipped....) into oblivion with him, into dreams or misconceptions about reality....all kept in memory boxes hidden beneath the many layers.….

How wet the glass menagerie,

She almost fell into the sea...drowning.....

And there Kim was, trying to recover from being angry...And I was so needy and had no one around me who understood, except her. Kim would sometimes get short tempered, because I guess, that this, was way too much for almost anyone to handle, to be ripped apart like that....a second time around....

Going through all the things Sonny gave me with Kim, asking if anything belonged to her. Some of the jewelry did, so I gave it back. Part of which being an old antique watch that had been given to her on the day of her son's birthday by her husband. But Kim still couldn't trust anyone......For Sonny could leave you on edge, looking down......and I was coming from his direction.....apart...So along with Kim's visit....came my checking the lock on the front door 10 times in 10 minutes....I wasn't even awareuntil she told me I was doing it. Kim and I both knew that after he went through you, Sonny would leave you in ruins with his stories of your credibility with anonymous phone calls with numbers that he would get out of your books when you were not looking.....As he'd play an act, maybe, say, your manager.....or you "recommended him highly"....or he would just get an address and bump into somebody, casually, without you knowing it.

As malicious hearsay and defamation became gospel....

Sonny's comments gave me the excuse to go to the police myself. I talked to this Fed and it scared me. Information is a valuable thing, I learned from Sonny.....when your coming, when your going, when someone could meet you out in a parking lot without a lot of witnesses getting wet in the rain. Rainy weather and parked vans scared me for a few years after that. The Federal Officer informed me Sonny's record was for pornography, pimping of underage girls, drugs, extortion, scamming the vulnerable and so much, much more. And he had just gotten off probation so when was enough ever going to be enough with me? And with this agent knowing so much and me not saying much of anything, things were pretty scary.

But, who was covering for who, anyway? Years later, Emma told me that the Fed actually worked with Art and Sonny. I didn't know what to believe, for Emma too, had been brain washed... I just thought the Fed didn't want to see anyone get hurt with no evidence. The Feds had their own way of working with secret information, and I still didn't know that much about Sonny's other crimes, personally.....just that he had raped me. And I was "out of my mind".

The Fed said that Art and Sonny were very dangerous men. I felt the necessity to hide some things, some letters, to protect my sisters children. Extremely, I went to an old boyfriend in the Entertainment Industry, who also worked with "certain unions", and found out that he had a friend who owned a Bondage and Discipline club called the Leash & Chain. It was my idea, FLIPPING SONNY'S BRIDGE AROUND, right on top of ASSHOLE, , with two very mean men helping me.... The guys didn't know everything... and I didn't know anything about the one guy who owned the Leash and Chain. A year earlier though, in ironic gesture...Sonny had mentioned knowing this Bondage and Discipline owner...Sonny even knew where the man's club was....I never even met the owner of the "S&M Establishment", or even knew what bondage and discipline was all about, nor did I ask, it never came up. At that second my complete focus was on getting away from Sonny with all my possessions and my families protection. All I knew was that the owner of the Leash & Chain was best friends with my old boyfriend and Tony had a temper and I wasn't going to ask any questions.. He had just been generous and given me someone to lean on...

In Sonny's duplicity, he informed me so boldly that he was going to get back at Art someday, for "Sonny going to prison for him". (Whether he did it or not, I really don't know. Maybe he was just telling me this as a story....an effect....to keep me wandering around on "his" team for awhile.) He informed me he was going to take Art's house away from him, and "watch" his face....lose it.

Indeed......

Art and his family lost their house in Hancock Park, their "Christmas Palace", in some "business deal"... After hearing this, within days, I was walking to the post office in Hollywood in a deprived state....a daze. I thought I saw Art's wife, walking by. She wasn't in her big fancy car, either.... She looked just like me in old clothes....a white T Shirt and old blue jeans....her face's expression looked hurt, distant and hollow...

By contemplating poached souls.. I learned a lot by watching things....day in and day out. Sonny didn't realize it, but he taught me how to keep things...and in the process...I began learning how to fight. So in the voice tones that matter...the flowery words that mean, I'm telling you the truth........(my truth that is...) I would abandon my relationships with humans for about 10 years.... And would be totally absorbed in my work....

Finally, crying a few months later, sitting on my rocking chair in my apartment on Grace Street, just north of Franklin, thinking of my babies, as the molecules dispersed away... realizing I had repeated the pattern of my mother ....only worse...my children paid the price for my sin. (Musing about my own identity crisis, concerning compassion towards other human beings... I had to ponder to some degree, if it was all for my own vanity?) And in my visions, about the abortions.......the metaphors of my daily life that I didn't have any identification with these mortals... these babies… that is.......(his)..... and how I understood this disregard...and how it hurt me......that I too, could be this inconsiderate. Realizing ..it was just a dream....and that it will all go away.....into particles....and space.

As I get up very early these mornings...sometimes at 5:30 A.M. (An odd habit I got into naturally, with no alarm clock ...when I started doing radio with Peter Tilden..) And as I blend into the streets and fade away...into glass...I have to live with these facts. And as Susan and John Daly both told me that I should write, I feel like I need to venture out again..........

8 years in the same place might be way too long.

"ROMAN NUMERAL IV"

(And Sub-Divisions)

Reducing to my old ways didn't work anymore. I wandered the streets and the job market of Hollywood, (at $8 bucks an hour) and the tangibility wasn't right in any event. I was living in a tunnel and nothing fit.. I had outgrown my past and my illusion of the bubble had been busted into pieces forever, and they were all now little jagged compositions and crooked orchestrations.....

I went back to work on a movie again, for Edward James filming the "Z" Suit Riots on Universal lot. It's where I met Gino Greco and we started dating. Gino was a mystery man who took care of his two boys, who were quite well behaved. Gino seemed to know a lot about a lot of things.

Before Sonny left, we had painted and refinished the floors upstairs in the "new residence" using Sonny's construction company. The apartment was a mess with big holes in the carpets and I couldn't comprehend living in it, as is. The landlord liked living next door to me because he said that I was such a great neighbor because I always minded my own business.... which I tried to do for years. I was six months behind on the rent and the landlord must have really liked me because he never even knocked on my door. He knew something bad had happened.... I was grateful, but no one, not even myself comprehended for many years that one of the landlord's employees had also been an accessory to my violation. Susan did the landlord's books.....

The depression was so overwhelming for one so small. I would get up in the mornings and not move off a chair for three hours, thinking that it had only been ten minutes......and as time slipped by, I was hungry and didn't know meat. I don't know what I would have done, without my real friends around me.

(Contemplating, Sonny told me, "We would have to fix my ugly face...")

"SUB-DIVISION I"

Standing in line at a casting call, I met an actress named Elizabeth. She conveyed to me, in a whispering tone, that she was a Dominatrix. My jaw dropped. I was interested in her, immediately. All I heard out of her mouth was,

"Beat men, make money, and no sex!"

Announcing...

I would have to be a submissive before becoming a Dominant. "In order to be a good Master, you must be a good servant first", (as the old saying goes...) She told me that she didn't like discussing her business.... she just liked doing it. Elizabeth and I exchanged numbers on a warm afternoon, where she once got a little "Snappy" with me, but I still just listened, intensely, because I wanted information from her, but I could tell that she was a little crazy, and indeed she was on medication... and in fact.... she did have a condition and she did have a shrink...

The very first time I ever did a session, Elizabeth called me on the telephone. She asked if I could come over at 8:30PM for a new life style. I walked over to her place in the early evening up Franklin Avenue past the Magic Castle. She lived a mile away from me. I dressed discreetly with a coat over my costuming. I buzzed the door and she let me in to the high rise that was close to La Brea Avenue. There was a dirty aura that misted her occupancy as I entered. This man or client of ours was standing in her living room, tall and dangly. He looked about 40 and had on a messy business suit, all wrinkly. Elizabeth handed me a $100 bill. I took it and hid it where she told me. She then announced to the world and everyone who may hear me, "You look like your name should be MADELEINE". I then went into the bedroom with this man. Elizabeth closed the door behind me.

"Veronica" sat in the living room, watching over the session. Inasmuch as my going through a training course, we caroused, with me being at the bottom. As the cat let the mouse dangle on a chain, I was lost in those sensations that were of my own choosing. At the conclusion of which... I was now, totally out there, for who could ever measure the entire sacrifice of my soul? Then, most abruptly, (just like God knew it)....during that very first contending, within 20 minutes, mother nature hit with a real earthquake as the 9th floor swayed off, of....Hollywood Boulevard. While I, Rebecca Evans was being tied up in a bedroom for the very first time with a 6 foot tall stranger. After the rocking stopped, we looked around unknowingly, then laughed off the nervousness. The movement was a 5.9 on scale. We were lucky but the Heavens had spoken.

In the two weeks that followed, I worked with "Veronica" and another girl named "Holly". They were both a little silly, as one dated and supported a black man and his recording studio and the other one chased blond surfers that didn't like her and wanted no part of a hooker's life...neither did the black guy, because he made passes at me. In not wanting to get caught up in anything too heavy with men like that, again, ending up in the same situation and wondering about the wasted measure doing it.....I resented it. The time gone by had made me old, beyond my years. But in the next few months, I would endure, (I thought out of necessity) a couple of boyfriends on and off, relationships that lasted for about a month, that is, same pattern, only less of it. Because in the next two years, I would finally quit seeing men with certain predispositions as attractive and as appealing as I used to. I just couldn't fit in.... to...the bottom... anymore... it would have killed me...........eventually.

Holly and Veronica taught me a lot. Learning, that we "girls" go to mansions, hotel rooms and homes with a client's proper identification, telephone number and address listed in the telephone directory..... Being informed, that the city had Playmates, Pets, and "Professional Cheerleaders" working through escort services....using fake names... It was shocking to me but so-called Professional Cheerleaders only make $150 a game. Now how could they possibly live on such wages? Fake boobs and plastic surgery and clothes costs thousands! Thousands!

"Veronica" was frenzied and way, way out there. She kept a very dirty apartment with used cat litter all over her bathroom floor.... The place reeked of bad smells. This Elizabeth woman, or "Mistress Veronica", as we called her, used to pick up the phone 10 times an hour during a session. She would also start screaming at me on occasion, sometimes in public. Elizabeth thought that she had the right to dominate me fully in my everyday life. She thought that she had me as a personal slave. Now I didn't mind playing in sessions, when I was getting paid $100 bucks an hour while risking my life during training with strangers as they tied me up and gagged me in unexplored terrains. (Realizing I got lucky in trusting these interlopers with an exhilaratingly dangerous moment, of living on the edge.......where some people never make it back....alive.....)

Eventually, I would start doing appointments in my own apartment, sneaking.....(I must have been out of my mind, my world had been turned up-side down...everything I believed in was gone.) Staying low key on purpose, trying not to attract any attention. Never dressing too flashy when I'm meeting my clients (at home), and my high heels were never too clunky, on the sidewalk, (as Holly taught me). Never slamming doors that would be heard, I kept things discreet for a while. Until my neighbor Susan started snooping, and in return, told the landlord. He asked me what I was doing, and I just told him, flat out, that I.....was....

"Beating men, making money and having no sex."

(He seemed to have no problem with it, for awhile...until he thought...I was making more money than him.)

Trying to present myself as a conservative woman in baggy clothing, while walking around the neighborhood here. I never wanted to draw attention to myself because I liked my low-key operation and the way it kept running with out a lot of difficulty. If your one girl, the police hardly bother you because your not worth it to them.. They like to get several girls at a time on a "bust", it saves the taxpayer's money. And while the police do make calls, like once every four years during the elections.......they would ask.....(with their stern voices....) if they could do illegal things on the telephone...I responding, would scream on the other end of the receiver........

"Don't you know that's illegal!!!!
"You can go to jail for that!!!"

They would never bother me again. Although I did have a couple of clients who had been in law enforcement, who liked to cross dress....After I started doing the radio shows they would ask me for valuable information regarding psychology and domestic battery and sexual harassment cases..... I would freely give anyone information regarding these topics...... especially around 1994 and 1995...... I really wanted to help ..... In 1996, when domination became "cool".... I remember hearing a Mistress tell me that she thought it was cool the way some detectives faxed her over some information. They wanted to warn her and they wanted her to let the other women in our profession know that there was a very dangerous man out there who had made an appointment and had beaten up another woman. I said it's almost like they're hoping we'll attack the criminal.....

Five foot seven inch "Jim" came in as a "customer". We had a great time. Before leaving, he had given me his telephone number. I called him a few months down the road....

His telephone answering machine reply said,

"Hello, this is Officer So and So..."

Figuring he had caller ID.... I left a message,

Then he called me right back, my figure of speech was calm and light hearted....

"You never told me you were a police officer."

His comment being;

"You hypnotized me into submission."

(That was also a day I decided to put make-up on...

for the first time in years...)

Officer "Bill" called me back a few weeks later, saying;

"I wonder if you could help me?"

My response was; "Of course."

He informed me;

"Well, me and the boys have been having some problems trying
to get this woman to testify. She's a victim of sexual harassment.
Her boss has been sleeping around with several of his employees
and has a habit of threatening people with their jobs behind

closed doors. The gossip at work is terrible and her boss keeps
getting away with it because subordinates are afraid of being
ridiculed. I would really like you to make a phone call for me."

My reply was;

"What do you want me to say?"

His reply;

"Tell her she's not the only one."

"That we have proof and evidence."

I walk out my front door through the courtyard, down to the street and I see officers all over Hollywood, especially undercover. Sometimes they're parked right in front of my building, running up the street with pizzas in their hands, smiling at me.

In the process of learning about Power & Oppression, Dominance and Submission in the months that followed from people around me, I would now comprehend the law and learn how to keep me as safe as possible. In the year that followed I would slowly build a dungeon and try to learn as much as I could.

Dominants need dungeons!

Half the Dominants in town worked out of their homes because the clients were made up of a submissive nature, so much more so, then men into straight sex. The Women in this town had elaborate contraptions while mine were minimal for comfort. And because I still think that most of this stuff is really crazy, I only had a tie down table which was an antique Wood Carved Spanish Couch which looked like it came from the Middle Ages. Plus, there were the various ropes, blind-folds, hand cuffs, hoods, clamps, paddles, leather and latex costumes, all hidden, in hat boxes. I even had semi-suspension in my small hallway. There was a whole section of wigs, large, large size high heels and large silk dresses and bras and under garments and nylons for cross dressers. Although my place still looked like an apartment with a lot of nice antiques and garage store goods. There were a lot of artists in the area who had beautiful things they had to sell at times. I was there to fetch some items and had received two six-foot tall fake tusks that went well in my dungeon.

"SUB-DIVISION II"

"Madeleine's Personal Dungeon"

This is an esoteric society that I'm now part of. I'm writing a book that may set the world on fire with change and new ideas. Truth outweighs emotional impact. In the D&S Community, the Dominant is Queen, for she has earned the right. And with a culmination of events that led me to explore issues of a sexual nature, which seemed to have been set up for me (in this lifetime). In knowing that my one hour sessions are limited fantasy charades, with the knowledge of the limits of fragmented reality....

I love being a Dominatrix....most of the time. I love the part where men bring me money all day long, I like the power that money brings. Although, sometimes, it can be slow... and you have to direct a lot of energy into answering phones...being there all day... calmly watching every second, every hour seven days a week. Because you could leave for just ten minutes, and that's the moment your call comes in...and you missed it. So you don't have much of a social life. And I still haven't gotten a beeper yet, or cell phone...While playing, I personally feel that B+D is not normal behavior. It's just a condition I got myself into. I'm not addicted, my barriers have been broken down. There are a few other things you should know about my working conditions... I never work when I'm angry, I fear I might really hurt someone. ...I play a heavy game and I take responsibility for my life as an adult. In this business, we bend the law quite a bit and find loopholes in it, just like attorneys and politicians. And, in the state of California, it is legal to spank people for money, you just can not have sex with people for money.

It was a tricky situation, having someone call me from a gas station right across the street from my house, meeting strangers....WONDERING, is the guy a cop? Or is the guy a psychopath, or is he just a true submissive? I'm hoping he's the latter.... It's important to pay attention. There are some people I won't even make appointments with, like the ones who are too aggressive on the telephone, especially, when they try to control the conversation. You can not disagree with me and expect to make it in here, especially when the male species has more upper body strength than a female.

I remember a man calling me on the telephone one day, he sounded uneducated with a slur, but in reflection, he was quite smart......

He asked me, if he could do some particular something...
(I can't even remember what it was...)

And my response was, "Do you know that's illegal?"

Then he said, "Yea, but do you still do it?"

I smiled, hung up the phone and never made an appointment with him.

Therefore, if I scream and yell at you on the telephone and if you're a true submissive, you're definitely coming in here to see me.

In speaking with some of the other women in my field, I realize that some "Females of Significance" are very nice. A lot of women in my business were now getting married, while still "performing". Some still worked as Dominants and some had "Men of a higher class who supported them", as one of my favorite clients, "Sissy" said. Sissy was a multi millionaire who had gotten that way via the copy business in Hollywood. Eight by ten pictures are an abundant business in the city full of hopeful stars. All of Sissy's friends loved him as he would throw little parties at the Beverly Hills Hotel and invite several of his personal gentleman friends along with us working girls for entertainment. Sissy spent hundreds of dollars every week and I had him for a few of those occasions. For three whole months Sissy loved me. Once, Sissy had left his three thousand dollar wedding ring on my coffee table after leaving. I called him immediately while he was still on the freeway and he made a quick U-Turn back here and retrieved it. It got to the point to where I could tell Sissy wanted to jeopardize his own two year marriage when he started asking me to show up at his mansion while his wife was still working during the daytime…during the daytime. Sissy was too overwhelming for me and he did actually almost leave his wife for another woman, another working Dominatrix. The three of them, (the husband, the wife and the Dominatrix) had a big meeting and everything. But Sissy was so gracious with me and I should have been better to him. I should have taught him to keep things discreet and private. He could have stayed in his marriage with me as the Mistress. Some Dominants were discreet and kept their business behind closed doors, like myself, working on other "projects" It's important to keep a good cover because of people's prejudice. …. Some Dominants are afraid to talk to other women in our field because they have been set up in the past…by other jealous dominants ..or men…or even friends and neighbors.

Furthermore, it's misleading, there are risks and pressures in being a dominatrix. This is a very calculated thing I'm doing. As of late, my personal life has become my professional life. I've hardly taken any time off. I've worked a long time, alone, especially after working with crazy Elizabeth. I don't have a body guard, or a driver. Moreover, I'm a well-paid concubine in a city where the fornicators sleep till 3:00 P.M. I try not to get impulsive, I need to be well contented so I can keep my mind focused on business without any distractions to safety….

"Rarely on occasion (like once every three years) I get afraid of working, of even moving off the couch to see new people. I think about the people carrying knives and having a sink to work with…"

Discriminating more freely and being more conservative than most other girls, I made less money but made wise investments… Most people in the adult entertainment business moved around a lot and blew a lot of cash! I try to bottom line everything real quick in reality with a savings account, for something to fall back on. Some of the women in my business do save money, very, very few get rich. It's also a known fact that most of the women in the "sex" trade have been sexually abused. They keep trying to fill in "holes" that will never mend with expensive drugs, mates and alcohol. Most of these women could never acknowledge or admit the damage done to them, it's been normal living for way too long….

Women in this business get big, big dogs, or work in groups, or for men. Sometimes they have "boyfriends" or "friends" hiding in closets, other rooms or back yards. Safety is an issue, and one I think about all the time. I've been lucky. I haven't made anybody angry.... in watching sharp definitions. There are consensual B&D sessions.... And there are people out there forcing things on people who have no idea of what they are getting into.... Just like there is consensual sex, then there is rape.

Conveying a story about a Dominatrix in the scene awhile back. She had converted a Los Angeles warehouse in a bad part of the city into her work space. There were a lot of gates and heavy doors and it was hard to get into with out an appointment. She had a few girls working for her, all with advertisements in the local L.A. X Press. She was gay, young, beautiful, and very abusive to her clients. You had to be into "hardcore" (into extreme pain) to love her... Mistress Connie would do sessions while clients really screamed. (I hear...) and she didn't care. She also left marks all over a married man who once asked her not to... and she did it anyway. This client of Mistress Connie's, perhaps trying to explain his extreme beating in a last ditch effort, lost everything. He couldn't go home for a week, had to get a hotel and "hide out" while his bruises diminished, and while losing his job, he then lost his wife and his son in the process. I heard that a lot of people were mad at Mistress Connie and she had to leave town to avoid some things and I haven't seen her ad in years and years in Los Angeles.

I never wanted to own a club and manage other women. Once you become more than one person, the laws change. I could go to jail for someone else's blunder if they get imprudent or greedy while working under me.

THERE IS A CLUB SCENE IN TOWN. I'm acquainted with Jim, the First "Master". He owns a dungeon in the Valley. Lady Laura just passed away from cancer, but stayed in the field until the day she died.... (I wonder where she is now?) They both had their own places in Los Angeles and they both were able to manage other girls successfully for decades. A few years ago, another "club" owner put a hit out on Lady Laura. All of this is public knowledge and documented in court. The club owner who tried to have Laura killed, terrorized everybody. He would have men call ads of girls working alone, make appointments, then, have thugs go over and beat the girls up. A girl in our business ended up dead because this greedy man wanted everyone working for him. (To my knowledge, the man who put the hit out on Laura never messed around with Jim, the owner of the Chateau....I guess Lady Laura was too close to this guy's dungeon, who eventually was stopped by police for harassing people in our "field"... Thank God...)

To my knowledge.......Jim is still running the Chateau and Lady Laura's goes on through her girls. The club owner who hired the hit on Lady Laura went to jail and got beaten to death in prison.

AND THE IRONIC GESTURE TO THIS STORY IS...about six months before I got into this business....when I was still "pure"....the same man, the owner of the "Leash & Chain" who put the hit out on Lady Laura ended up helping me get away from Sonny. Although I never knew it, he did, through an old boyfriend named Tony, who was trying to help me escape the thugs. (All the boys were mean back then and to fight fire with fire, you had to get meaner than mean.)...to survive.

Still, with my suspicions on the telephone, I watch my back. LISTENING CLOSELY to VOICE INFLECTION AND TONE, wondering if the person on the other end is a true SUBMISSIVE? Most are. In paying attention to what is behind their words, their gestures. When they're too aggressive, I back off. I have to wonder if these men are serious, or if they are just calling to get off on the sound of my voice....because it's a crank....

I take all my sessions personally and will only see clients I feel safe with. THIS IS A JOURNEY FOR ME. If I do not like a client, I will not see him anymore and it could be for any number of reasons. There was a very cute client I had once from South America. I had a one-day crush on him and let him stay in my apartment. While I was in the shower with him, he told me I needed a bigger bust line, first warning. (I wasn't good enough for him). Then he told me that he could never go back to his country again. I asked him "Why?" He responded, "Because I beat up somebody pretty badly." Quickly, I asked "Was it a man or a woman?" He in return "Does it matter?" That was the end of that conversation and meeting forever.

Most clients you would never think about, but some are the exception. Can you imagine "The most beautiful man in the world" coming into see you in the middle of the night?

I will keep "Will's" description an anonymous blurb to protect his true identity.

"Will" had a deep voice and whether he was blond or dark haired, he was extremely handsome. He was always polite, about ten years younger than me. And for a while his image was plastered all over T.V. and on the sides of RTD Busses here in L.A. We never spoke of these things in person or in session in the middle of the night. He always remained fully in character as he would walk into my door and extend the money. I've seen "Will" every year, going on ten and he never calls me unless he's coming over. He's never wasted my time.

I am only into the lighter side of bondage and discipline play. There are some things I say, no, no, no to. Honestly, I can't stomach some of this stuff done in sessions, in particular, "strap ons", which are fake penises that women wear and insert in men. I don't personally think that any kind of intercourse is cool. It's too intimate for me and I personally think that only bi-sexual guys like that kind of stuff any way. Of course, rape fantasies are off limits to me. Although I think its fine to play little spanking games, like bad school girl or what ever...... I LOVE to dress men up as big babies. That is one of my favorite fantasies. I also thought about getting a big bird costume and running around the room in it.

I do foot fetishes which are quite easy. I enjoy them. I used to be a waitress for 10 years, so to get a foot rub, can you imagine? A foot fetish can get more complicated with "tickle torture" and rope play that holds a person still as your "tidbit" goes hysterically unstable, and ballistic, laughing as you run feathers over his soles. Foot humiliation can lead to kicking a man when he's down. And we may think that it's strange, the worship of armpits or faces or hands or feet. The media has glamorized Tits & Ass for so long, they have also displayed violence on T.V. We can see killing, but not sex. One of my good looking, young, and well off clients told me the other day,

> "It's hard, being the head of a multi-million dollar corporation
> and telling people you have a foot fetish."

I never see couples. I'm afraid it could lead to jealousy.

Getting back to my personal relationships for a moment, what hurts me at this time more than anything else is not having the connections with my family that I wanted to, in this life time. I would miss the love and the comfort of these women's and men's arms as they would blame me for everything. I could barely contain a whisper in my after thoughts... longing to connect to someone... something to love. These people really hated me and I would be all alone in this life, unless I could create something more compelling. I just wanted to have my grandmother see her favorite grandson grow up....which she did. We had so much drama in our existence, driven by extreme poverty. My grandmother lost two boys in her life span. First, her younger brother died while in her care in the 1918 epidemic. The second time, it was her oldest son, he was crushed to death at 12, playing on a stock pile of rail road equipment. And while my sister Edith was smoking $500 worth of drugs per week and living like she was living in white Ethiopia...with her new husband.... She and her kids were homeless. I saw this and rushed in, but at times it was worthless. Edith was my grandmother's favorite, and because of this, every lie Edith ever told was believed. My grandmother and Edith both had three children, with the two oldest being boys and the youngest a girl. They were both very poor and had no men to support them. They had a lot in common. And I was the one who had the abortion.

Remembering a time I went to visit my sister, Edith in the Las Vegas desert, after watching the way that she was living with three kids in a 78 Oldsmobile. She was with this big guy and they were both staying on this big guy named Tony's boss's junkyard. The kids were enduring in an open gutted out trailer with no water and no electricity. They were not brushing their teeth or taking baths. Edith and her boyfriend, I would soon find out, were staying up all night doing stimulants which made it impossible for them to wake up in the mornings. While giving her 250 dollars, (just that week...) before I knew any better. I came back to Los Angeles and lost my voice for the first time in my entire life. I was supposed to go on the "Peter Tilden Show" but had to call in and cancel in a wave of a barely heard whisper. I quietly said a prayer in the back of a taxi cab while coming home from a clients at 9:30 A.M.. after being up all night... Thinking, "Oh please lord, please lord, if I had a choice of doing these shows with Peter, or of my little sister and her children just having a home... LET THEM HAVE A HOME INSTEAD."

I lost the show for 6 months after that. They didn't call me for one single episode, until Peter went out on a limb again...My sister had sued somebody for taking advantage of her and won $5,000 in a lawsuit. She got her shit together for a year. My grandmother, who wasn't all quite all there to begin with, knew what I did for a living, but asked me to take my sister's two little ones in, which could have led to my arrest with my business. But still they put this pressure on me with their insecurities and bull shit and denial. I was their escape goat with money. And with my mother's tales... Well, I'm sure they thought I deserved it. They were ashamed of me and my work and they would never admit it. As my mother and her husband took vacations to the east coast from Texas while Edith and the kids went homeless...I'm sure they thought, we deserved it. But now the children have a roof over their heads and an education.

I sometimes yell at the wrong people...with my post traumatic stress disorder...In being so neurotic at times with men's traditions and how they bestowed these insecurities upon us women to begin with. I now know that men were not made as monogamous creatures to begin with. But they forced these dilemmas upon us women, in hypocrisy and in turn, at being held down, we wanted to tie men down in the good girl customary ways of man's structuring of the world. It was the formalities of social conditioning that men were mostly in charge of, giving them the power and control to do whatever they wanted to, in most cases, in turn leaving us women vulnerable, especially in perception. We thought that we needed men's power for survival.......as most people still wanted to have an "old fashioned relationship" that just didn't exist in most instances, anymore..... They wanted that modern twist to their old fashioned ties, with women working harder then men...as women had broken the tradition, just not to it's full extent....yet.

"SATURDAY NIGHT, AUGUST 17th, 1996"

IT'S A SMALL, SMALL WORLD..... The weather in Hollywood last night was clear and beautiful as I discreetly took my small frame out and walked two short blocks to Athena Gardens, the Greek Night Club on Cahuenga Avenue. The place had been there for at least 15 years just south of Franklin Avenue. It was 10:00 p.m. as I slipped into baggy clothing so that no one would try to come on to me in this place, still not wanting or even ready for relationships with men. Plus, I didn't want to get a reputation as a loose girl in this establishment that I liked to escape in. I kept my Domination business private and told everyone I was a writer.

I enjoyed the Greeks for some odd reason. The Mediterranean people understood battles that most Americans would never have.....

(And I had to fight with Sonny to keep what I had....)

The Athena Gardens reminds me of old Las Vegas. The night club is now on the "up & up". Although, along time ago, I heard that it wasn't. The owner's husband, the "real owner" can never come into the United States again because of the Federal Agents... given the fact that he shot and killed somebody in the United States and never went to prison for it. With myself, feeling like a modern day gangster, (treading ahead of the pack for awhile, using psychology and control, finding loop holes in the law like an attorney does. Feeling like I have one of the biggest scams going on right now...Because even though it's taboo and unacceptable, I love what I'm doing right now and can't believe I'm getting paid to do it.)

Perplexing.... I used to work in the Middle Eastern Taverns, so the Belly Dancers, band, bar people, singers, stars, owners, politics and different cultures.....with their philosophies ... were nothing new to me....

Rena was having a hard time holding onto her business because she wasn't corrupt. She seemed like a good woman, loosing money in the process of the laggard economy. And as I visit her club, about 6 times a year... because it's close... I must have picked up on some aura or mystique, thinking I may find answers here, somewhere in the crowd.

IT'S A SMALL, SMALL WORLD, as I walk into my past, and into the Gardens. I SAT AT THE BAR AND JACQUES LAZAR A BUSINESS MAN CALLS ME over to sit at his table with a friend. He introduces me to a blond I remember..... saying, "This is Maggie." I said, "As in Margaret?" While all the memories came flooding back. Musing, Maggie was a friend of Emma's, Sonny's new "girlfriend".

I STOOD BACK TO TAKE IN A BREATH, as she said, "Oh my God", her jaw dropped, (this seemed to be the normal reaction from anyone who really knew this man named Sonny, the way I had.) And you know, it was very convenient for me to go to Rena's club now that I had my own money. And most of the employees knew me, especially, the new one named Maggie. With her standing there, we both silently looked at each other. She and Jacques were getting ready to eat dinner together as the club always gave meals to it's employees, and Maggie was the new one as Jacques was friends with the owner and had gotten her this position. Jacques always sat at the same table in the power seat facing the front door right behind the cashier's register.....with lots of beautiful women as he called them. He was forty, but looked like he was in his sixties. He had been beaten to death and brought back to life, once. Jacque had been in the wrong place at the wrong time, at another club, I think it was the Private Vail on Sunset. Jacques had been through hell and back again, for some odd reason, I enjoyed talking to him. (I think it was for that very same reason, this unlucky event of his, in which he said death, was really quite pleasant.. It was the same thing that my sister told me about her experience with an accidental overdose she had......)

But there were other things I watched at his table with his entourage...Just a thought for a moment as I sit here...but sometimes in life, the battles we fight are so real.....that we "really have to be there", to get what we want. Most of the time, I never liked playing games. I'm glad I finally grew up, somewhat. Musing the presumption I might find love if I become a movie star. So I left Hollywood and it induced me back, and into 710 TALK RADIO, expressing the opinions about the life of a Dominatrix. And here I was, sitting at a table full of actresses and Jacques was paying the bill. So I concentrated on being really nice to him because the other women weren't really paying that much attention to things other than themselves.

Maggie waited tables and I sat with Jacques's gang. We swapped tales of glory, of living through the battle. As I realized how lucky I had been, for in suffering pain and sorrow, came knowledge. Because something really devastating makes you have to change. And as the blond and I had both known Sonny, it had been a horrifying rehabilitation. At least I wasn't so wrapped up in fear, like I used to be, wondering if Sonny was going to get me. Or set me up by way of a mutual acquaintance that he had befriended. Now, my knowledge has armed me with getting straight to the point of what I want, and staying focused on it. Because some people will cost you, and you need to improve those hints to get rid of them. I've also learned not to take the bait in the bite of other women....their comments, that is... as I remain cool and numb. Because my ego has completely left me.... for awhile. As I sit there and make fun of myself , they all laugh at me in my low key outfit.

Just a thought, but, what makes some women so vicious with one another here in Hollywood? I think it's because men pit women against women in the competition for men, especially in the Entertainment Business. It's like some of the men I know in "the biz" have "Rock Star Fantasies" in which they see themselves as the center of attention with lots and lots of women fighting for their affections. So as these men like mud wrestling and cat fights, they never made it to the big time to be worshiped by hundreds of thousands. In most cases, I'm also finding that narcissistic women make bad candidates as mothers, given the fact that their own obsessive needs to preserve their femininity are sometimes based upon the manipulation of sex being used as an aphrodisiac. And with all these man made insecurities, in which we misinterpret sex as love.....even at the cost of divorce with left over children.... these things seemed to be instilled upon us, from earlier days in the way some of us were raised....And if we let this behavior control us, we become jaded and feeble towards one other. (While functioning in nature I was never taught to be compassionate towards ALL human beings growing up, I had to learn this.)

And in not holding Emma responsible for going out with Sonny, we had both been deceived, we had both been sitting in oblivious bliss, following the voices of men. (And her, right into a straight jacket I heard.) Sonny put drugs into Emma's coffee after he married her. Then, someway, somehow Sonny locked Emma up in a mental institution, having her father agree to give Sonny power of attorney over Emma's $180,000..........until the insurance money ran out, and his spending sprees.......

As he pulled a...

Big, big scam...

on her

too.

Not knowing exactly what Emma did, I heard that she had been brought up in a dysfunctional household in which her father had sold her out. Emma's father was one of the biggest "pimps" in L.A. who married Emma's mother. So Emma was used to this type of behavior that always gave into assholes. But it seemed that Emma had a heart. I heard that two years after her ordeal, of losing everything... she was still hanging out with Sonny's mother. Emma still thinks her enemies are her friends because of her upbringing.... And I heard that Sonny's mom had conned Emma out of some money too, someway, somehow............. the tribe was pretty much in tact. .

I was the lucky one, the one who met Kim, Sonny's other victim, in time at Phil's studio, where Maggie was an office worker for Phil, and there the circle goes. Maggie was also a friend of Emma's..... they both were exotic dancers together at the Private Vail.

And to think that Maggie ties in so much to this, why was she always our connecting fiber? The last I heard about Sonny, he had a new girlfriend named Charity who was a successful actress. Story goes, they were doing the radio circuit here in California for the Battered Women's Foundation, right around the time of the O.J. Simpson Trial.

Through encounters, the last I heard...

Sonny had left Emma the exotic dancer for Charity the soap opera actress. All three had lived in the same building, one, just one story down from the other.

They were setting up victims through victims... the pattern runs on character traits. And men like Sonny can smell them on you, your friends, your mother, with like being alike, most times... He can also manipulate some men, with enticing women as bait for them among other devices. Most of his prey were so overworked, and too impaired by strain to logically look at evidence. And while you were sweating, Sonny would charm your "friends" with his so called knowledge and acted gentleness. With the quiet tyrant's way of reproducing systematic episodes, Sonny gathers information through other people sometimes in giving gifts for conclusions and erudition. He'll find out what matters to people enabling him to push buttons with energy and tremor. And in his fake concern, join their cause and open up to them. So if you didn't watch it, he could get just the right information out of a confidant to set you up with, like your hopes and dreams. Or where he may find you, or what your troubles are...Or how he leads your acquaintances into believing he wants to help you, while all the time, behind your back lying, using the notions of others to be played like puppets.

And to think that now......Sonny and Charity were working the Battered Women's Circuit. As let me guess, Charity, the "Cover", with her track record being in Network TV, she loved the spot light and it was easy for her to work the "Radio Waves". And Sonny, or now "Rick Colombo", as I hear they were calling him.... (His "Fake Mafia Name Connection" to promote fear in his "marks" were the way they were dishing it.) What a game sporting team those two were, victimizing victims. And of course, he was in the background as her secretary or her boyfriend, or even her husband? With him, never being photographed... as he listens and studies the vulnerability of others, looking for a hint of emotion, a response to a question.

Sonny could give excuses that would evoke emotion in his followers of duplicity, in charm that hid anger and madness at the world.

The last time I saw Sonny, he had a wedding ring on his hand and it was Emma's, that was back in 1991... IN FRAGMENTS OF MY MEMORY PROCESS...I'll remember the effects of Sonny, and keep it all clear.

But as the story goes, back in 1991, out of Sonny's lying mouth.. Because I remember the time he left me, I knew about Emma, really, I did. Sonny told me that "Emma was living with her boyfriend who beat her up all the time." "And stole her car.." "And he, (meaning Sonny) was going to help her." Well, I heard the real story a year down the road, that Sonny actually paid to have Emma raped by Eddie so that he, Sonny, could look like a hero. Obviously, to further manipulate, he told Emma, (who was aware of "Rebecca being the upset girlfriend at the time.") "That it was my friend Eddie who did this awful thing to her." (And I hope that Emma is still not dumb enough to believe, that it was my friend, Eddie. Because it was actually Sonny's friend Eddie.)

I told Maggie three years ago, "That everything Sonny ever said, was just a lie." And he was a lie, and I, had somewhat loved him, almost trusted him for a brief moment of time.

In their methodical plans in which Charity was now part of.. I wonder if stupidity just caught up with her or if she was just like him?

For some women...

Isolation can elicit salacious doctrines…

While always inducing and influencing.......

In the short time, Sonny was with Charity, she had lost her looks and gained 100 pounds. As always, in the abyss with Sonny, almost every woman goes to hell....

I was one of the only women to ever beat Sonny, with his own con. One of the only people to ever get anything back from him, was me...I worked so hard for it and I guess it was just my instant karma. The other women had much more than I. But they received their earnings in different ways... Kim was a very good, rich housewife with millions who thought of work as supervising servants around a household. Emma worked hard as a dancer, training for many years for a big income, but she was still lost within him, Sonny that is...

Months down the road, I heard that Sonny was so good at what he did, he pitted a pair of Professional Psychotherapists against one another with the opportunity of making money, one against the other and they were a married team. The couple got wise in the middle of the game and nipped it in the bud. But they still have knotted quandaries after Sonny, after many happy years of none...

Two and a half years after Sonny left me...he drove right past my house, the way he does all his victims, scoping them out. And as I just stood there, holding myself hysterically inside while my heart was racing so fast I got dizzy... and while shaking distress grabbed me, I fell in place, rocking back and forth, quietly. Remembering in Sonny's eyes the victim is to blame, as he likes to keep watch on all his squandered entities... He smiled at me as he drove by, which was easy for him to do. I hear that he only lives a mile away from me now, at the base of the Hollywood Hills.

Or, somewhere on Santa Monica Blvd.....

But at the time, my grandmother was staying with me, and I feared for her. Two years ago, back in 1994... Sonny drove by my house a short while after he raped me, because he was finished with me, and onto someone else's money. Then I met Kim who in turn knew Emma, (Sonny was also through with Emma in 1994). And as Emma had given me Sonny and Charity's phone number...because again, they had all lived in the same building....

Leaving a message was a bold move, but I never wanted to see Sonny come by my house again..... SO IN 1994, I left the following verse on Charity's answering machine... (fully aware that Sonny might also hear it... he always screened all of his victims calls as he baby sat.) And to think I called there...Oh, both places, that is.... Maybe it was dangerous, but I had to call their place, here in Hollywood...and the Battered Women's Foundation in Los Angeles with an anonymous tip. (And please note that I lied to Sonny and Charity to protect Emma, and to keep secret, the fact, that I had so much information and clear cut knowledge under my belt. But still, foreboding panic mobbed me), after being influenced on the entire story of his preceding quandaries.... his real jail record.... (which was 10 pages of Extortion, Grand Theft, Pimping & Pandering.. Etc, etc..) Thank God sweet little Emma gave me Sonny's Driver's License number.... it cleared up so much when I could see his personal track record of deeds done on to others.....

The message I left for Sonny and Charity was clear.......(A woman's voice was on the machine..) I hung up the first time, but called back and said...."Hi, my name is Rebecca Evans, and you don't know me, but yesterday, a guy named Sonny was followed going to your residence. The time was around 4:30 P.M. as he drove right by my house on Grace Street, and my new boyfriend who is a Private Detective followed him over to your place, or the place I'm now calling. This man brought great harm to me, always blaming an Art So & So in a good guy, bad guy routine of his, because these guys are partners. And I want to ask him to please stop driving by my home or else my boyfriend is going to have to do a lot more digging. I hope you're O.K. If you need anything, please call me at

....(gulp)....213........ "

(And that was the end of the communication.)

Two hours later I received my last known phone call from Sonny. (I also get cranks). It was about 6:30 P.M. on a weekday. I picked up the phone...

He said, "Rebecca."

(In following this story, you'll find that I did not recognize him, not even for a moment... but then that's deep rooted psychology, to forget about the trauma. I had forgotten his voice.).

I said, "Who is this?"

He said, "Rebecca, I didn't drive by your house yesterday." (There was urgency in his voice...)

And screaming at the top of my lungs in rage and anger,

I said, "You're a fucking liar!" (And now for the scare tactic that I had learned in acting and especially from watching him...in a very low, calm voice that held steady because I had taken in a deep breath...)

I said, "If you ever drive by my house again, you will be followed."

Click, and I hung up the phone....before we got in, any deeper....

"SUB-DIVISION III"

HOW DID I GET FROM FLEETWOOD MAC TO ALANIS MORISSETTE? From my past, of being taught that women always sacrificed for men, and resenting it. The men I was with, wanted me to play the perfect female. And when the going got rough, and I didn't hold up to their great expectations...because I was putting all of my energy into them to begin with. Well, nothing was ever good enough, partially because of my own emotional difficulties in not wanting to be accountable for notions......

THE REVERSE SIDE OF FEMALE DOMINATION IS THIS...Remember when you were young, and still a virgin? Well, when I was that age I had what is now known as a common rape fantasy.....You know, where Prince Charming comes in and takes you? (And remember, in your daydreams, he's always good looking.) But anyway, you just have this "power" over him, as he just has to take you.. Because as the deeper psychology goes.....You have ascendancy over this man's inclinations, which you think of, as "love". Your womanly beauty or sex appeal is way too much for anyone to handle.

Especially yourself...

So your prevailing as a woman comes in your female attraction. (And thinking that beauty hangs on....) to a man or anything else, forever. Your compulsion to love, which you may think, no one else has.....but you, is nothing but a lie. Everyone loves! While pondering that you still get to keep your virtue, because you were forced, and that makes you... not bad.... not guilty of sin, for wanting him. You're the "victim" in your own sexual preference and outcome. You gave into the powerful bad boy's condition. Prince Charming is responsible for everything, and you don't have the burden of guilt for your very own desires and illusions of wet, wet dreams. And do you know what? You cannot be a good girl, and like bad boys...because bad boys make you do bad things

WAKE UP, WE'RE NOT LIVING IN A FAIRY TALE!

If I could tell you the differences between then and now. I used to spend so much time with men who got off on keeping me down in unknown selfishness. In the past, most of the men I met really didn't have much power to begin with. I didn't understand that the men I kept choosing were no good for me, that they were holding me down in their own commonalities. They were people who did not deserve to rule me, or anyone else, for that matter. In the process of spending years with these types of individuals, going, nowhere.. I got caught up in their tales of glory, with their lack of intellect, along with my own for choosing them. And in noticing that I was still, somewhat, overwhelmed by the same type of men, I was just spending much less time with them, like a month instead of years. It was a lot of work for me to fight... being brought up in the south where a lady was a lady. My first few encounters into the world of D&S were huge contentions for me.

But it was more work, in the long run, letting people keep me down, than moving forward. I think I've been successful as a Dominatrix due to the fact, that I care and have regard for the people who come in here to see me. With these "slaves", I was meeting men who were a lot nicer to me than most of the men I had dated in the real world. I vowed to never get personally involved in any way, shape or form with any and all clients. I knew it could lead to problems by watching similar situations in the past. My girlfriend had once married a "trick" and everything was fine until the divorce. He used to call my girlfriend a slut and a whore in front of their young son. These men, no matter how your relationship or pattern changed with them, would always think of you as second-hand, a used prostitute; A used woman for sex was only good to these men as long as you, the woman, performed a function in their lives. I never asked for or expected any "slave" to rescue me- the way I had in my past relationships with men. I always budgeted my own money and never spent extraordinary amounts of funds, ever. I never called clients to solicit them. For a couple of years I did have an attorney who worked for the Russian Mob. He came into see me on occasion before I found out he worked for the Russian Mob. The first night he called, booked a session and came over to my gothic environment, I broke a rule with him. It was midnight and late and I let him sleep in my living room with me for a couple of hours under a large blanket on the floor. I never completely fell asleep but watched, I could never relax with anyone else in my space. I was too generous to him under my own selfish whim of not wanting to be alone that evening after years of complete solitude and having no real contact from anything human. I didn't know that he was ultra rich and a middle aged-trust fund brat who had never been married, nor ever shared his money with anyone on a charily basis and I should have made him pay for every single second that he was with me. But anyway, I slowly found out he had some dangerous idiosyncrasies in a two year time span. The first warning signal I received was that I had memorized his telephone number off of my Caller ID. He would call me and pretend to be someone else. I played along for a while, thinking he may have been embarrassed. He was always nice at first. Then, it got to the point, to where he expected so much for so little. He would always come in and pay me for two hours in the middle of the night…the middle of the night. But one evening, he blurted, "Don't put me on a time table!" He wanted to stay for hours for free. He never gave any free time for being an attorney and told me he charged clients double in the evening. The attorney had a boot fetish and would want to purchase hundreds and hundreds of dollars on expensive boots from Sax Fifth Avenue but then barley pay me. The money he wanted to spend was for his enjoyment only and not for the benefit of paying my bills to keep a safe roof over my head and a saving account for emergencies. He started calling me, making appointments hours ahead of time, only to stand me up. I had to quit seeing him for my own mental sanity. He was beginning to use money as a weapon and tried to use it to manipulate my vulnerabilities. He was beginning to brag about his 180 acre estate and talk of marriage kept going on forever. I couldn't let myself become weak to him and on one occasion even took money out of my own savings account to pay for some necessities for my household. I was never attracted to this man. I have to be in love with somebody to live with them. After my high school sweetheart, I don't think I truly ever loved a man again. The only reason (through the years) I was ever with a boyfriend was because of social conditioning. I now understand that 90 percent of all women will end up alone at some point in her lifetime. It took me many years to figure out that I didn't want to compromise for anything because I paid for everything. This man was confused about love and was abusing me because of it. So, one night, I verbally attacked this man, screaming and yelling at him about the way he was fulfilling his fantasies and I myself, manipulated a break-up. I could not become vulnerable or submissive with him in my new professionalism with men. I could have "played him" the way most of the women do in my business and made a fortune off of him. But if he ended up giving me a fortune, he would have resented me in the end. He could have even started problems. I had to break out of my old ways and quit being the submissive one. In my course and study of my personal relationships....... The ones from the past were eating me up. The same thing kept happening over and over again. I had to grow and learn an empowering experience, for me to progress on the secular plain of living. I looked 40 at age 29. I noticed two years into doing this, things begin to click about the power structure and the abuse of power. After my "change", I took ten years off my face with less stress. I now try to never deal with liars, because you don't find your answers in lies. But I can't kid myself.... There is always some type of "power game" that a lot of people play in real life, in work, with friends, and family.

Out there in the real world, you have people manipulating and controlling the lives of others in totally destructive ways. I try to contain honesty in my sessions...I don't like deception here. But there may be others, out there, who are not playing fair, with big guys jumping out of closets, or far, far worse. Just remember, that each particular experience is different in nature, no two people are alike. Considering, I have a unique experience and in this business, I personally choose to treat each individual specimen with kid gloves. It's always consenting adults here. I don't want to mislead you and tell you what I do is glamorous, it's not, and it can be perilous. What is a controlled environment anyway?

At the beginning of my sessions people know the rules and either person, slave or master, can conclude the game at any given moment. With my hands on training in "psychology", you have to consider all the needs of others, and your responsibilities to those obligations being fulfilled, along with your safety. I have to give to my clients. Clients have feelings, too. I take control by making people feel comfortable. You see, someone will come in to visit me after I have spoken to him on the telephone. So imagine how he must feel, to come into an unfamiliar place, with a stranger that he must learn to trust behind closed doors. These men take confidence in me with a foreign sexuality because spankings or dressing up like a woman gets them excited and turned on.

We must pay attention to the assemblage. Men into the "power structure" are usually overburdened with the pressure and stress of impeding responsibility. These sessions release tension from someone's everyday intrusions... Their power is taken away from them and they are forced to do kinky things, things they actually want to do.... this fantasy is an escape for them.....

Some clients are exhibitionists, especially cross dressers. They are proud of the scene, and go out dressed as women to specialty clubs like the "Queen Mary" on Ventura Boulevard...... Most of these "feminine gentlemen" want more gentleness and less B & D. They share their little dreams with me, and no one else, unless they are seeing another dominatrix.

90 percent of my clients want privacy because they are afraid of what their family and friends would think... I don't want any of my clients to feel resentments because of me.

Some slaves have actually turned and flipped out, which could be very dangerous. Some clients do not feel comfortable with their own sexuality ...they could be embarrassed by it, or feel threatened by it. They could even possibly turn violent...and you hold the key to their safety in keeping their secrets. No one wants to feel pathetic or ashamed in public. I've had clients tell me that after leaving other places they felt dirty, but after leaving my place, they felt good about themselves.

Just last week, I had a client tell me, "Don't forget how sensitive I am", as he was singing in the shower. This is, in no way absolution for anyone's sins. You can never pay penance here.

Some clients get addicted to you, for domination can be like a drug for them, as they get an urge for "therapy', you reign them. Few clients are rich and can come in as often as they like. Other clients are poor, and they have to save up. I never mislead my clients on with false promises, like I could be their girlfriend or wife. I am cheaper than a housewife and being a wife or a girlfriend is way too much work for me. Especially, concluding, I like being the mistress.

I contemplate the fact that before I finish my escapade that I will have been with 100 men a year times 10, which equals to over 1,000 men. I have been with more men than most Casanovas have been with women. A gentleman caller phoned the other day. He said, "I want to find out what this is all about?" I responded, "If you're not into spanking, or being dressed up as a female, then I'm not the woman for you."

In my studies, and in my experience of learning that the whole world operates on this psychology, I have noticed that my examinations have filtered into my everyday life, someway. In my business, men tell me what they want up front, and I supply it to them, at a cost, no lies, no deception. And there is another thing you should know about me, in my business, I ONLY PICK ON PEOPLE WHO ARE BIGGER THAN ME, who want it. And that makes me powerful to them, there is mutual reservation here. People trust me with their secrets,
As we must be discreet to protect their privacy....
Because they have other lives they lead....
FOREIGN TO THESE.......
HERE.
(IN MY DUNGEON.)

Someone once asked me why I didn't have my rich clients finance my projects...by getting loans....I told them that a loan might be misconstrued as blackmail. So while working on an hour by hour basis with each client, I give them a lot for their money. I DO THINGS WITH THEM OTHER PEOPLE DON'T ENJOY. And I am patient, slow and steady wins the race, and I have been in the business a long time. Perhaps in the past, dealing with some of the people I've dealt with, well, you wouldn't want to coerce any of them.

I turned down a "$50,000 deal" from "investors" to start "my own club" two blocks away from Master Jim's...I'm glad I didn't accept the "offer" because a friend and I figured out that it was probably a set up for me to take the fall in case anything went down...like the police or something. As the business men wanted my name on the ownership but the "investors" would control the money. So out of ego and greed, almost everyone wants a piece of the action now, and no one wants to be responsible. This business may not be what it used to be.

I never wanted to be a stripper....performing for men....but now a lot of strippers in Los Angeles want to be me....a Dominatrix... Most people tend to think that this is about beating and abuse. They tend to work in environments that pit women against women in the competition for men.... and that is not what female domination is all about. We have a lot of new people in this field right now, who don't know what they are doing. A man just died in the Hollywood hills of suffocation because someone didn't know what they were doing... Suffocation can go to the point of passing out, and I prefer not to go there in session.

The energy it takes to do this stuff is unreal. FEAR WILL MAKE YOU PAY ATTENTION to every single nuance, especially when you're meeting a new client. (People could still bring in weapons....)

One evening, I tied a man up. I really pushed him, accelerating his limits, watching him squirm, I laughed. This man loved his Dominant Mistress. He took me out to dinner the next night as we shared this event. And even though he looked like a movie star, I could barely glance at him. I was somewhat embarrassed and again, with my own personal reasoning, I thought this man was weird, having a deep sense, that something is wrong.... with all of this. My slave found our session to be exhilarating...advancing his "ThreshHold" that far, making him forget about his everyday obligations. But sometimes I wonder, how much, is too much?

Another time in session, while in mummification, a captive broke out of eight layers of industrial plastic wrap rolled around him. Eight layers. The guy was six foot two, two hundred and 20 pounds and looked like he was in good shape, just disorientated, like he was on alcohol. He was more than strong, (and I didn't know it....) And this was quite alarming to me...I turned my back for five seconds and didn't comprehend that he had just lifted his arms upward like a martial artist in a trance......

My character burned out one Sunday. Sunday, which was the day of the week I seemed to be making the most money, but also the day of the week you are "supposed to take off for spiritual reasons, like God". (During this one particular session, I had that one particular issue in the back of my mind the whole time....drifting. The client I was playing with made me nervous). And while this guy was in my apartment, I dropped into a semi nervous breakdown due to a culmination of many factors. Such as the experience I had, doing some pretty intense sessions with this same client for many a Sundays in a row... Sunday. I was doing heavy torture to a high intense pain subject to begin with. It involved burning... He was pleading for "Mercy", and (while musing the sacrilegious aspects to all of this...) I was afraid of slipping too far.....not wanting the smoke from a cigarette to go directly into my eye, his molecules burning through the air, his fragments landing inside of me through the air we were breathing...then suddenly, the nerves in the left side of my face went still in Bell's Palsy. The semi stroke stiffened the left side of my face, and I still had half of the session to go but didn't know what lay inside of me. (And while still giving hundreds of dollars to an unappreciative sister, who in her drug crazed rages would in turn twist events around and say I was greedy. The hundreds that I had given to my family around Christmas time should have gone into my teeth, instead, which probably started the infection to begin with.) I wouldn't see my own face for two hours until going to the store later on that same Sunday.. I looked into the mirror and noticed that half of my face was not moving. I wasn't afraid. (Now if my body wasn't moving, that would have been a different story....) But I liked the way the "stiffness" had flattened my lip line...for the side that had become afflicted was the side that had carried the most stress to begin with. It was amazing but having Bell's Palsy took five years off my face. I went to the doctor the very next day, I probably should have went on Sunday, but got lucky that it didn't turn into a stroke. Smoking and a lot of stuff had harmed me although I did have a quick recovery.

IN THE 1990S there would now be a lot of women in Los Angeles and New York wanting to become Dominant Mistresses. Girls would get apartments in high rent districts, like Beverly Hills and do sessions at "home". Another Established Dominant informed me that when she and I both started, there were only 24 Dominants in town, now there were almost 250...in just a few years ….Thus, a lot of girls couldn't make a living anymore…. unless they were really dedicated. Mistress Michelle told me that "People think, all they have to do is get a pair of thigh high leather boots and they can become a "Dominant Mistress"."

I turn down business because there are some things I will not do. I SELL SPANKINGS, not sex. (And in the state of California at this time, you can beat people for money, you just can not have sex with people for money. You can not kiss people for money and you can not touch people's private parts for money…and hand jobs are also considered prostitution).

I did try going into business with a client once. He ended up bringing his fantasies into our endeavor, which made it hell on me and commerce. He kept screwing up on purpose, so that he could be disciplined..... For not only was I financing a business, I had to baby sit a photographer...on the phone at night, talking and talking......(also giving him money for meals at times…)

I purchased $2,000 dollars worth of computer equipment for a business that we were going to start together. It was a "production deal". Well, when the photographer got all the equipment, he decided he didn't want to do the job anymore and that if he was going to, that "I better make it worth his while." He also wanted to keep the equipment in his apartment and slowly pay me back in cash for it over the next following 2 years. Thank God I had a written agreement with this man.... It cost me $500 dollars with an attorney to get my stuff back. I then, didn't talk to the photographer for a year… Then, out of the blue, (as maybe all should be forgiven).......he called to tell me that some publisher loved our stuff and was going to pay us $3,000 for the rights of the photographic work, titled "Colossal Dreams". We split the profits 50/50. Then I was informed that the photographer tried to pass me off as just the "dumb model".... and he owned everything.

One time I ended up getting a huge crush on a client, it was a mistake. The guy was blond, drove a Porsche and managed rock groups. Chris had an office at Raleigh Studios. Almost anyone could get a key there and rent out office space and call themselves a producer. The place was an old sound lot used in the Golden days of Hollywood that had now become decrepit.

He was a lot like Sonny, charming and cute and a daredevil on the road. Chris asked me if I would deposit a check for $17,000 into my bank account. He said that it was payment due to a band he managed, but that he, himself, wanted to keep it with little Rebecca's help. Chris wanted me to "Give him half the cash." "Draw it out of the bank, right on the spot." Hence, I found out what a big mother fucking lying creep Chris was….. Thank goodness I know a little bit about the law. Anytime someone deposits more than $10,000 at one time into a bank account, the IRS is alerted….(I knew that as soon as I, Rebecca, now "Mistress Madeleine", deposited the funds, I would go to jail as soon as the I.R.S. tracked me down.) Chris knew I would have gone to jail for stealing funds and he could have told people that he had never met me in that capacity…and had nothing to do with the "deal". My feelings for him diminished within weeks, unfortunately, it should have only taken seconds.

I NOW HAVE BECOME A PROPERTY OWNER WITH THE MONEY I have saved and have paid taxes on….Yes, you see, I file my taxes every year, I have to because I have too many things. Oh things, that I have bought for practically nothing…You see, during the beginning of the 90's, people were selling things for needed cash. And since I had saved almost every single penny that I had ever earned because I felt I had no one else to fall back on……by not going out on the weekends….and stuff…I denied myself certain privileges which I hoped would lead to an early retirement with lots of jubilee. (But I would have lived my life based in sin by most religious standards…) And sometimes that bothered me….but not as much as my other life did….for awhile…

And as this book is written...

I have witnessed things which I felt needed to be expressed, like the prejudice against prostitutes and the way people treat them for their sexual preference in victimless crimes…. most of the time. Yes I say most of the time because some prostitutes do hurt people. They set clients up with pimps, with blackmail or what ever…

"SUB-DIVISION IV"

I wanted all of my new neighbors to like living near me and under me...no complaints. I wanted them to think, "Oh, what a nice quiet lady we have around here, she never disturbs anyone." (Imagine, a herd of loud rockers with drums...) Perhaps in being alone, thinking I didn't deserve to have another relationship, especially, with what occurred in the process of meeting Sonny and how badly things turned out. The two babies I lost or threw away in not being dealt the right cards to begin with...... I never wanted that to happen again. I knew I had to learn to communicate with people on a different level.

While submerging myself, sometimes, my neighbors wouldn't see me for a couple of years. I hid a lot in my nice warm cozy apartment I've made this way through times of use. On one occurrence, I remember someone saying, "Oh, your bangs have grown out..." (Yea, all the way to my bra length...) And I liked not running into anyone. Musing, let me have peace and quiet... I have to protect my clients and their names from being discovered...

Some of my neighbors, (because of Susan) treated me like I was some sort of low level broad who didn't know anything.... I never could have friends here, in the landlords building, as the new tenants would hear the girls talk and lie about me...(These women who had so much time on their hands, had it because they were all living on welfare. None of them labored for a living but seemed completely capable.) None of them had children. All they wanted to do was antagonize me by blocking my three and a half foot walkway leading into my living room as they would sit there and call me their competition. They began blatantly flirting with all of my men friends and calling me names when no one else was listening. I never started a fight with these women but I would watch to see which men fell for their bait. I learned to keep complete tally of all my clients and if any one of them flirted back, he never came back in here to see me. Susan's acquaintances on two occasions demanded to borrow my things, like parking spaces, or telephones rudely, for their purposes....... I mostly got this sort of treatment from women who liked trying to challenge me. One woman told me that I dealt with perverts in a harsh tone. Then that very same female told me a year later (after the radio shows had become popular...) that she wanted to become a pervert too....... There have been a few times, in the last 15 years, that we would even get the police called to our "home location" and they were always called on the other people in this building. The landlord's crew always seemed to attract a lot of the wrong type of attention. Knock wood, the police have never come in for me.

It's hard writing this book, because I want to give you complete truth...the good and the bad of things. There are a few principals I've learned about others in the time and moments spent here, through 1988 and 1996.. The most important thing I've learned about abuse that helped me out, is this.... I remember calling Rose at 710 talk to tell her the very same thing that she exposed. It must have been in the air that week, because a big psychotherapist had come up with the very same conclusion, and that was this, "If the abuser blames the victim for his or her outrageous antics, it proves the abuser has animosities against the victim to begin with." "By calling the victim a whore or some other name…." In as much, as the abuser uses anything they can as an excuse to defend themselves in their fleeting endeavors at someone else's expense, and then undermine the abused person's good intentions with their innuendoes of insult, as they add injury to outrage.

In my last performance on radio I mentioned that I was writing a book for battered women using the psychology of dominance and submission, explaining my situation. Hearing that a lot of big Hollywood producers were currently in development. They were out to find the right perspective, fiction or truth, with "heart" that would make middle America cheer. Screenwriters were writing, and none of them could find the right secrets, the right twists and turns for years…….none of them. Comprehending that some people were trying to get knowledge.

Meeting male screenwriters who were trying to write about women in my field….. with their egos.. and my purpose …. also gave me bad positioning. It's just sad that I didn't get out to meet nicer people. They are out there. But due to the fact that I had to stay in certain areas to run my business….. (like low rent Hollywood, until the housing fees exploded with the World Famous Kodak Center on Hollywood and Highland)…….I still had other people around me, without much means of their own…so they had plenty of time for digging and pushing my buttons on a daily basis. With consequences leading me to become rude with the wrong people who didn't deserve it. While I was still performing on "The Peter Tilden Show with Tracy Miller" which was named in"Los Angeles Magazine" as one of the best things about L.A. I decided to contact the Producers Guild of America. I heard that there were a few production companies in development of a Dominatrix story. With in hours some female assistant at C.S.I. Productions called me, wanting to see "Rebecca Evans". After an exchange of several phone calls over several days….. I yelled at the same assistant in a panic and in a flurry of emotions, of memories that had come flooding back in the past few days with regards to Sonny. She had just called me at the wrong moment. The production Company then went on with some other Dominatrix in a good story on an interesting episode. There was nothing familiar with mine in their first aired episode on C.S.I. But as the years progressed, things had changed and I again attempted contact and had sent out a few pages of "Rebecca Evans" to the very same Production Company. Miss Ally Hawkins wrote me back on March 30, 2005 saying that they were not interested. Then, with in months of my letter, all of a sudden C.S.I. had now come up with a new story line for a second episode with the Dominatrix. The Dominatrix they used was attractive but not appealing. With all of the prime time exposure this female counterpart of mine got, she never became a star. They did a big P.R. campaign with their Dominatrix on morning television saying that they could not come up with a good story line for years and years. They couldn't find a synopsis that was anything new or special, but they did receive my few pages. And their second episode went into the contemplation of God and death and protecting children from evil men, just like my book does. I've tried to be quite guarded, especially with people stealing information for unjustful enrichment in Hollywood for screenplays…….. (taking the best scenes or plot twists, character emotions for motivation, and etc…then incorporating them into a story for film…….) writing the short version, of the long version book…

I sent off a script I wrote to the highest class porn company in the world, that did a centerfold of Betty Page who is, now, well known for B & D, (but not at the time of her "layout") This porno company had shot the famous pin-up model in pink... The work this company presented to the public for sale had no reference to anything pertaining to the Bondage &Discipline world or market place...prior to the 1990's.. A few years before, they had even referred to Bondage & Discipline as being "sick". Anyway, this company writes me back a letter, returning my script, (which they could have copied). They kept my radio show tapes which were included......and told me that their company was not doing anything like my presentation. Then, they went on to ask me if they could see more of my work. Over the next two years, this company changed it's entire programming package to include "comedy domination", especially, on their network programming... This entity, with a prehistoric view of women, (to begin with...) that pits women against women in the competition for men.... muses that they can do female domination, when this is not what female domination is all about. For how could you work for, or be shaped by a man, and still be a TRULY DOMINANT FEMALE? And you know what, after seeing this major corporations "art", I was glad that I didn't take credit for it. I heard their network lost a lot of money over the next couple of years.. The man who had founded this company, which other people had gotten big egos over and almost ruined it by the amount of lawsuits for copyright infringements....anyway, the owner and founder of the porn empire had to go back to work , he had to come out of retirement to save some public image and he had to fire some people.

Concluding, "Female Domination" is now "Politically Correct" in big cities like Los Angeles and New York. Most people tend to follow the trends.... The masses will follow what ever the media tells them to. People should watch that they are not deceived, because….

What has the world come to?
To misunderstand so much?
As the sheep of the world will follow....
what they must…

With my reflections from past chapters, I've learned that when you can finally learn to take control and accomplish tasks on your own, you'll feel better about yourself. You'll probably take control in a different way than I have. Remembering, not to fall backward, in not feeding into your own submissiveness, as energy directed over time is valuable....it slips into the crevices of your life. While not knowing everything......

Maybe I'll give away my soul in all of this...

or maybe I'll have a purpose.

"EXCERPTS FROM THE MEDIA"

In a double whammy of concentrated letters and after thoughts, I, (through the media) have made things acceptable in Los Angeles that were not acceptable before.

In adhering to Peter Tilden's perfect circumstances… I spent two, to three days a week working on the script for the Saturday Morning Show. I had now become a regular on an affiliate radio station owned by ABC and Disney. Using no prurient materials, we got to beat up on man kind for all of his wrong doings during the days of the O.J. Simpson Trial.

While taping "The Morning Kick Off Show", I met John Tesh, who had to be one of the kindest men that I had ever run into. It was a brief encounter and only in studio, he was a Christian man and very married. John "picked me up" because I had "tripped on a line" in a room full of Hollywood executives who didn't take kindly to someone messing up…it didn't look professional…. John Tesh stepped right in, threw just the right line in and I said something back that was smashing and brilliant. John helped save my job that day. It gave me the confidence to go on to other episodes… Along with Peter Tilden's prodding.

In creating a poetic display of openings that felt appropriate at the time ……things got interesting when I had constituted a new character named Guy De Bo…(with a long O)…into our performances….Asking Peter and Tracy, "Do you want to meet my little man?"…. As Peter was urging Tracy (on the air), to just say "yes"…I said, "Here he is."

Peter Tilden
"Not only do you have an imaginary friend, but you
have given him a last name."

Mistress Madeleine
"That's right"
"Do you want to hear him?"

Peter and Tracy
"Oh sure!"

Guy De Bo
(yelling in high pitch)
"HELP ME! HELP ME!"

Peter Tilden
"How did you shrink him down in size?"

Mistress Madeleine
"Do you know what Thigh Cream is?"

Peter Tilden
"Can you revive him with water?"

"If you quit using the thigh cream, would
he explode back to his normal height?"

Mistress Madeleine
"Well….."

Peter Tilden
"Wait a moment, I don't want to ask questions
and I don't want to see pictures…."

Three weeks down the road, we did another show featuring Guy de Bo, the two inch man.

Peter Tilden
"How are you today?"

Mistress Madeleine
"I am going to a funeral."

Peter Tilden
"Oh, I'm sorry."

Mistress Madeleine
"Remember Guy de Bo, our 2 inch man?"

Peter Tilden
"Yes"

Mistress Madeleine
"He got caught up in the paper shredder."

Tracy Miller
"Oh no!"

Mistress Madeleine
"Let me tell you what happened."
"He was misrepresenting business deals and forging documents…."

Peter Tilden
"Guy de Bo was a little liar!"

Peter persuaded me into doing a cable access show with an Assemblyman who believed in paddling. "There was such an upset, though, for which the Assemblyman's P.R. Man got fired for not getting the "reel" back. The Assemblyman's people said they didn't like the way we were cutting it, with the subject matter at hand, with Peter's "Demonstration of Paddling."

You see, I was playing a news correspondent interviewing a 60 year old politician. He was sitting, watching in shock and horror as "Mistress Madeleine" takes off a business jacket right in the middle of an interview revealing a Dominatrix outfit. A good looking slave then enters the stage in long black leather pants, with a black leather hood on.... then, hit, hit.... bang...bang.....all happening live. We got video footage at public access of Bondage & Discipline in which we can only use our imaginations. Our efforts did not go hard core but we did get cuts of the assemblyman laughing all through this. I never released the show after it was taped on January 5th, 1995.... I received a telephone call from Jim, the P.R. Man, and the following conversation occurred;

This one particular day I happened to have a new group of friends around me. This one day. I never have people in my apartment, I am more than a hermit when I'm not working with a client. But this one day, 3 men, one being Peter the Slave, a CAMERA-MAN and an ATTORNEY just happened to be over. Peter the slave and the camera man were both at the taping. We were all sitting around in my apartment right after an "episode". The phone rang. I went over to pick up the receiver with everyone listening in close proximity. JIM THE P.R. MAN of the 60 YEAR OLD POLITICIAN was on the other end.

Mistress Madeleine, "Hi. How are you doing?"

Jim, "I'm O.K." "But I really need to ask you a favor.."
(Jim was a very attractive man, 6 ft. 185 pounds, with dark hair...)

Mistress, "O.K."

Jim, "When the assemblyman's wife found out about this
incident, she burst out in tears, right in the office."

My attorney and friends were all laughing. I looked at them, astounded and horrified. I felt really bad for this lady and the Congressman... That was when I, Mistress Madeleine decided, it wasn't a good idea to release the tape.

Mistress Madeleine, "I feel bad about that. I told an assistant of the
Assemblyman's that we were going to use
comedy to draw in the audience. What do
you want me to do Jim?"

Jim , "We want you to shelve this project and pretend like
it does not exist. If you shelve the project, we can
get you more guests."

Mistress Madeleine's buddies and friends were laughing in the background, saying

Buddies and Friends
"Yea, like more conservatives!"

Jim , "As we know, you are trying to make a name for
yourself."

I thought ,"Oh, yea",

Jim, "The head of our office hit the roof when he heard
about this."

Mistress Madeleine, "I'll take all that into consideration, Jim. I
don't know what I'm going to do, but I'll call
you with an answer."

Jim , "I wanted to ask you something."

With Rebecca trying to evade his question because she thought he wanted his tapes
back

Mistress Madeleine, "Hey Jim, what do you think about........?"

When Rebecca/Madeleine couldn't hold out any longer, she could have just hung up with
an emergency. But, in compassion and curiosity......

Mistress Madeleine, "Now Jim, what did you want to ask me?"

Jim, "Well, in my personal life, I'm pretty liberal and I do
go down to L.A. bars a lot. I wondered if you
wanted to go to a swing party tomorrow night?

Mistress Madeleine, "What?"

Jim, "A swing party."

Mistress Madeleine, "You mean where people swap? How old are you?"

Jim, "28."

Mistress Madeleine, "Have you ever been to a swing party before Jim?"

Jim, "Yes."

Mistress Madeleine, "With whom?"

Jim, "I had a girlfriend about a year ago, but now she has
a new Republican boyfriend and I wouldn't think it
appropriate to ask her out again."

Mistress Madeleine, "Where did you find out about this party?"

Jim, "The Orange County Register."

Mistress Madeleine, "Boy, you Orange County People sure know how to party. (In pun.) Was it an ad? What did it say?"

Jim, "For Adventurous Adults.."

Mistress Madeleine, "Was there a phone number?'

Jim, "Yes."

Mistress Madeleine, "Well, I don't know Jim. (In pun) I sort of feel uncomfortable on a first date and all…

(Madeleine was laughing under her breath as all three of her friends stood close by, warning her not to go…)

"Don't you know any nice girls from Orange County?"

Jim, "They're all too shy and close up when I talk to them about this."

Mistress Madeleine, "I don't think that we should go out together before we get this matter resolved between our attorneys. But then, you probably wanted to keep this matter personal and not business, right Jim?" (under hysteria…making this man in politics whimper…)

Jim, "That's right."

Mistress Madeleine, "I don't feel comfortable with this. We have to get this matter resolved first. Besides, aren't you afraid of the sperm flying through the air and hitting you in the face from a bunch of swinging dicks?"

Rebecca's/Madeleine's friends were rolling on the ground at this point..

Jim, "I think they're secured." (It sounded like he was keeping a straight face during all his humility.)

Mistress Madeleine, "Where?'

Jim, "Some place on the ground."

Mistress Madeleine, "Now Jimmy, would the Assemblyman
approve of you calling me?"

The attorney, camera man and Peter the Slave are all motioning it was a set up and to hang up.

Jim. "No, the Assemblyman wouldn't approve of me
calling you."

Even in the face of controversy, with myself becoming a Dominatrix, knowing that people used to laugh and spit at me behind my back. But now, it's a different story. Ever since the radio shows started happening, everyone wants to be on the Bandwagon in L.A. I guess with this Media thing going on, Peter's given me a chance to turn my writing into something of interest, to the public of Los Angeles. In making B&D a cool thing for a while in our Big Polemic Adventure. (Peter told me that he tried to pull off a similar Dominatrix character for years but couldn't do it successfully until I filled in her shoes, that I was his script come to life.) But I worry, in not wanting to mislead the masses, in doing a "Gracie Allen doing a Dominatrix.." with no bad words..... OUR PRODUCT WAS MAKING EVERYONE AT KMPC A TON OF MONEY. THE RATINGS WERE HIGH, so high, that the top brass was afraid of our smaller station stealing their larger station's audience.....and I was a Media Sensation....

There was a short lived local talk show in Los Angeles for a period. "The Marilyn Kagan" people called me and asked me to be on their talk format and I showed....When I arrived one of their staff members called me a media sensation... I declined being on panel because of the set up...(it was prurient in nature...) But stood in the audience and after a big build up, was introduced.... With my comedic talent and quick wit thinking, I twisted Marilyn Kagan and set her up for a great punch line, the audience liked it and men started cheering... "Give me therapy!" Four producers lined up to meet me after the show's taping. As I have to admit that Marilyn was a good sport and it wasn't quite what she had expected....

Peter Tilden had created "The Dominatrix Mail Bag", with my very own theme music… Every Saturday Morning he would ask me questions that only I could answer.

(Although, we all understood that I am no one to ask questions about moral obligations)

Out of Peter's mail bag, a question popped up.

Peter Tilden
"Dear Mistress Madeleine, if a man and a woman come over for
dinner at my house, and we have a few drinks because I'm a
male….. and they start getting intimate with one another in front
of me, should I assume they want me to be part of the situation
because they are starting in front of me or should I just politely
excuse myself and watch from another room?"

Signed Curious Steve….

Mistress Madeleine
"Did the couple steel any silverware?"

Peter Tilden
"No, they didn't"

Then, on another show telling our audience…..

"I have a 15 minute coupon for anyone who wants it!"

Ending that particular show, telling Peter,

Mistress Madeleine
"Next week a big Senator will be writing in!" With Peter
exclaiming, "What?" I responded, "I should say, an
Ex-Senator! You're going to love this one, NEXT WEEK!"

On another episode, telling a stranger….

"I'm going to stick my fingers up your nose and hold your
mouth shut for 5 minutes…"

Exclaiming on the 4th of July Show…

Mistress Madeleine
"We don't go for the heat, we go for the big time heat here. And
if you set a fire, you need a spanking!!"

Telling Peter, on our last show that …

Mistress Madeleine
"We have pulled off something brilliant. We have pulled
off a Dominatrix for an Affiliate of ABC and Disney".

Peter Tilden
"Well, now that we've highlighted it, we probably won't be able
to pull it off much longer".

I had now become a regular on an affiliate radio station owned and operated by Disney and ABC....MAYBE IT WAS ALL PERFECT TIMING, BEFORE AND DURING O.J. with such a controversial character, they put me on a pedestal and enhanced my image... They embraced me and for the very first time a Dominatrix was getting respect. (In the past, people were always afraid of us calling us weirdos)...But my personality and voice on the air earned a different tune. For the first time in history, while doing my radio shows, domination became respectable. Betty Page's B & D photos became the "big boom", bigger, than what they ever were before. Men who only shot show girls and strippers were now shooting the "Dominatrix" Scene. And a lot of stations started to copy our format with the same type of character. Peter sensed my anguish... and with people's neediness...even mine....The station wasn't paying me for my work. And I don't know who the real boss in charge was, because the station was in the middle of changing owner's hands and I didn't want to rock the boat. (I was hoping that the writing credit would help propel me into a new career, with long term benefits….) I put so much energy into the "shows", I was drained and the work had been mostly unrewarding. I couldn't concentrate on my Domination business and also write. So, I kept moving, ahead... I sped.

Peter, Tracy and I were brilliant together at slapstick comedy, but that's what it was... It wasn't the real thing, there are risks.. . So in my mood or disposition that I carry through here, as a writer, my manifestation in conveying a story. This performance I set forth on paper as a subjective expression of my inner experiences with embellished polish.. It was a show, that was all….

I GAVE TWO WEEKS NOTICE IN 1996…………

But maybe someday,

I'll go back...

One Saturday evening, while out with a man of "great stature", (a man who had lost ten million dollars of daddy's hand out money in ten years, buying art and other useless objects)…

While walking into a restaurant named Morton's, a place that only the rich and famous go to. The restaurant is not even advertised, you have to be in the "know" to even know where to go. William and I were immediately escorted by the male host to an eight top in the center of the room. It was as if my escort owned this huge table while everyone else was crowded into 8 tops. Bill informed me (through gossip), that men only took out women that they wanted to be seen with... meaning…that women had to dress right and look good, or the men in Hollywood would only use them behind closed doors for blow jobs…

A week later, I found out, (via a call from Bill), that Morton's was packed with every "Big Movie Producer" in town and everyone wanted to know who the "Mystery Woman" with Bill was. The woman in the vintage honey brown leather poncho, and a hat to die for, crowned upon her head, was. Bill's girlfriend had left him because of this. And I didn't know it at the time, but Bill's business card had been found on one of the biggest Hollywood Madams in town, the one who had made the cover of Esquire and Bill couldn't be caught in another indiscretion. If he was really a smart man, he could have informed everyone that I was an actress because I had a Screen Actors Guild card. But just like so many immature people, he was caught up in fantasy land. Bill my escort informed me so boldly on the telephone that he would sue me if I ever told anyone that he was out with me, a Dominatrix….This was while I was still doing "The Peter Tilden show" on KMPC, writing and performing all the dialogue and having the right introductions could have possibly helped my career out….and put me on a different path…

Stunned,

(at this minor incident)

I learned, never go out with this man again.

WORDS FROM "ST MATTHEW" & "REVELATION"

(The Bible)

ST MATTHEW:

CHAPTER 26

1. AND it came to pass, when Jesus had finished all these sayings, he said unto his disciples,

2. "Ye know that after two days is the feast of the pass over, and the Son of man is betrayed to be crucified.

3. Then assembled together the chief priests, and the scribes, and the elders of the people, unto the palace of the high priest, who was called Cai-a-phas,

4. And consulted that they might take Jesus by subtilty, and kill him.

5. But they said, not on the feast day, lest there be an uproar among the people.

6. Now when Jesus was in Bethany, in the house of Simon the leper,

7. There came unto him a woman having an alabaster box of very precious ointment, and poured it on his head, as he sat at meat.

8. But when his disciples saw it, they had indignation, saying, to what purpose is this waste?

9. For this ointment might have been sold for much, and given to the poor. When Jesus understood it, he said unto them, "Why trouble ye the woman? for she hath wrought a good work upon me."

11. "For ye have the poor always with you; but me ye have not always.

12. "For in that she hath poured this ointment on my body, she did it for my burial."

13. "Verily I say unto you, Where so ever this gospel shall be preached in the whole world, there shall also this, that this woman hath done, be told for a memorial of her." "14"..."15"....

REVELATION:

CHAPTER 17

VISION OF THE GREAT WHORE

1. AND there came one of the seven angels which had the seven vials, and talked with me, saying unto me, Come hither; I will shew unto thee the judgment of the great whore that sit upon many waters:

2. With whom the kings of the earth have committed fornication, and the inhabitants of the earth have been made drunk with the wine of her fornication.

3. So he carried me away in the spirit into the wilderness: and I saw a woman sit upon a scarlet coloured beast, full of names of blasphemy, having seven heads and ten horns.

4. And upon her forehead was a name written, MYSTERY, BABYLON THE GREAT, THE MOTHER OF HARLOTS AND ABOMINATIONS OF THE EARTH.

5. And I saw the woman drunken with the blood of the martyrs of Jesus: and when I saw her, I wondered with great admiration.

6. And the angel said unto me, wherefore didst thou marvel? I will tell thee the mystery of the woman, and of the beast that carry her, which hath the seven heads and ten horns.

7. The beast that thou sawest was, and is not; and shall ascend out of the bottomless pit, and go into perdition: and they that dwell on the earth shall wonder, whose names were not written in the book of life from the foundation of the world, when they behold the beast that was, and is not, and yet is.

8. And here is the mind which hath wisdom. The seven heads are seven mountains, on which the woman sitteth.

9. And there are seven kings: five are fallen, and one is, and the other is not yet come; and when he cometh, he must continue a short space.

10. And the beast that was, and is not, even he is the eighth, and is of the seven, and go into perdition.

11. And the ten horns which thou sawest are ten kings, which have received no kingdom as yet; but receive power as kings one hour with the beast.

12. These have one mind, and shall give their power and strength unto the beast.

13.   These shall make war with the Lamb, and the Lamb shall overcome them: for he is Lord of lords, and King of kings: and they that are with him are called, and chosen, and faithful.

14.   And he saith unto me, The waters which thou sawest, where the shore sitteth, are peoples, and multitudes, and nations, and tongues.

15.   And the ten horns which thou sawest upon the beast, these shall hate the whore, and shall make her desolate and naked, and shall eat her flesh, and burn her with fire.

16.   For God hath put in their hearts to fulfill his will, and to agree, and give their kingdom unto the beast, until the words of God shall be fulfilled.

17.   And the woman which thou saw is that great city, which reigneth over the kings of the earth.

"Excerpts from a "Course in Miracles"

"You can not be saved from this world, but you can escape from it's cause…"

"And that is what salvation means, forgiveness."